Praise for

A SPARK OF WHITE FIRE

Named to LITA's Hal Clement List of Notable YA, 2019

"Sangu Mandanna's *A Spark of White Fire* is full of brilliant, complex characters against a compelling mythological canvas. It's full of love and gods, reversals and surprises. I loved it and can't wait for the next book."

—Kat Howard, Alex Award-winning author of
An Unkindness of Magicians

"A vivid labyrinth of lies and loyalties. Mandanna has built a dazzling worldyou'll see stardust every time you close your eyes."

—Olivia A. Cole, author of *A Conspiracy of Stars*

"A gorgeous marriage of science fiction and fantasy. Meddling gods, princesses in exile, and cities aboard spaceships. This is nothing like you've ever read before."

—Justina Ireland, *New York Times* bestselling author of
Dread Nation

[*] "Sangu Mandanna seamlessly weaves science fiction elements with Indian mythology, creating a world that feels truly alive. Mandanna's characters are fully fleshed, especially the engaging and sympathetic Esmae. A Spark of White Fire is the first in a trilogy, and readers will be eager for the next installment."

—Shelf Awareness, starred review

"If you're looking for a spectacular and immersive read that you'll want to finish in one sitting, *A Spark of White Fire* should absolutely be on your list. It's an incredible story, and it will be a difficult wait for its sequel."

—SyFy Wire

"This is a fast-paced, engaging tale sure to keep readers hooked with its twists and turns while they wholeheartedly cheer for Esmae . . . An incisive story nuanced by dilemmas about love, belonging, and conflicting loyalties."

—*Kirkus Reviews*

BOOK ONE OF THE CELESTIAL TRILOGY

A SPARK OF WHITE FIRE

SANGU MANDANNA

Sky Pony Press
New York

for Jem, who gave me this universe

A SPARK OF WHITE FIRE

CHAPTER ONE

Someone will win *Titania* today.

She is the greatest spaceship that has ever been built—the warship that cannot be beaten. And the star system has talked of little else for weeks. From the gods in their lofty celestial realms to the garuda that live on the sun to the mortals on our planets and ships, *Titania* has shaped our every word: what she can do; who's likely to win her; what the outcome of the contest will mean for our world. It's a vast galaxy, spread across space and stars, and yet it feels so small when war and its infinite reach tiptoe closer.

It's like a game of Warlords. Wychstar is the checkered board where the battle for the crown must be fought today, the competition is the battle, and *Titania* is the crown. And as the minutes tick down, the pieces move into place.

A usurper king.

A heroic exile.
A jealous prince.
An old warrior.
A cursed mother.
A war goddess.
And a girl.

You'd be forgiven for thinking the girl is irrelevant. The other players are powerful, important, the kinds of people around whom legends are spun. They are mighty pieces on the board. The girl, on the other hand, is a pawn, noticed by almost no one, the least important piece in the game. She has no wealth, no glory, no power, and no family.

But she's not irrelevant.

I'm not irrelevant.

I tell myself that, day in and day out, and I've fought for every bit of pride I now have. And even then, it's hard sometimes to believe the thought. Even today, as the competition promises to electrify the world and I teeter on the edge of every desperate, secret wish I've ever made, I'm more afraid than I am sure. I'm afraid of losing my nerve. I'm afraid of failing.

I'm afraid I won't be enough.

"I know what you're thinking," says a voice behind me.

My arms are buried to the elbows in hot soapy water, so I don't turn around. "I'm thinking I shouldn't have promised Madam Li I would wash the dishes before the competition," I say, "because now I'm going to be late if I don't hurry."

The speaker moves silently. One minute she's behind me, the next she's at my side. She's in the form of an unremarkable young woman today, but I recognize her stern, impossibly dark brown eyes. Gods take on all kinds of forms to hide among us, but their eyes always give them away if you only know what to look for.

Amba, the war goddess.

"Esmae, I know about the dream," she says. "That dream you dare to lose yourself in when you think even the gods aren't paying attention. I know you too well. You want home, you want family."

"Isn't that what everyone wants?"

"Not everyone will fight for it the way I know you want to. I know you picture Alexi with *Titania* at the head of his army. You picture yourself with him as he flies her into war. He shines like gold in the sun, and the world explodes in fire. When the dust settles, you see him with a crown on his head. The war is won and you've both come home."

She says this without mockery, but hearing the words aloud makes me suddenly feel as though this dream I've clung to is nothing but a foolish fantasy.

Alexi Rey, the heroic exile, the banished prince of Kali, the rightful heir to the throne. He, his brother, and his mother were exiled from their home, their kingdom, by his uncle, the usurper king. Now, four years later, everyone knows he's preparing for a war to take his throne back. And who wouldn't want an unbeatable warship on their side in such a war?

"Are home and family really such impossible things to hope for?" I ask her very softly. "You can see ahead, can't you? Is it really so impossible?"

"You know I can only see snatches of what is to come, and even then, it's often only what *may* come." Amba pauses, considering me. "It is not an impossible thing to hope for, Esmae. Just an unlikely one. Alexi will certainly win the competition today, and I have no doubt he will fly to war with

Titania at the head of his army, but that doesn't mean you'll be at his side. And frankly, you are better off here. You've lived your life in the dark while his has always been lived in the light, but you must remember you are safe in the dark."

"You used to tell me I belonged on Kali," I remind her. "You told me my mother sent me away because of a curse, and you told me I could go back to her when I was older and could defeat the curse. *You* were the one who planted the dream."

"That was before the coup. Before Elvar stole the throne. Now Kali isn't safe for you."

"It's not the kind of dream that goes away just because it's not safe."

If I close my eyes, I can see her. A silhouette in the distance, too far away to touch. The sun around which I orbit, fighting to get closer. *Mother.*

Amba sighs, a frustrated breath of air that's weighed down by what she won't say. She puts one hand over my wrist, stopping me from scrubbing the bowl in the sink. "I am a goddess and I shouldn't have to ask you twice." Her voice is gentle but firm. "Do not go to the competition today, Esmae. Do not seek out Alexi."

I tug my wrist away. "Tell me why not and maybe I'll listen."

"Can't you just trust that I wouldn't ask this of you if it wasn't for your own good?"

"Your definition of *my own good* seems to be synonymous with making me unhappy," I reply, and the words open a jagged wound of unhealed pain that I haven't been able to forget or forgive, "so you should understand why I'm not exactly keen to obey."

Amba tightens her lips. "What *you* don't understand could fill the cosmos."

"Then explain it to me!"

"I cannot," she says. "And I cannot stop you from going to the competition either. Go if you must."

I laugh without any real humor. "Your limitations must really chafe at you. What would you do if you weren't afraid it would kill you? Lock me up to keep me from going?"

"It is an easy matter for a mortal like you to joke about it, Esmae, but death is not a thought that sits well with a goddess. The age of the gods will end sooner or later, and I would quite like to remain in the celestial realms until then. You cannot possibly fathom how wretched and painful the idea of a mortal life is when you are part of the stars themselves."

It's true. I can't possibly understand that, but I do understand she's afraid of it. They say that in the early days of our world, when the galaxy was new and the war between gods and demons finally ended and humans started to carve out spaces for themselves, the gods were dangerous to us. Celestial, star-born, a race of creatures who can bend the fabric of the world because they *are* the fabric of the world; we revered them and prayed to them and they, in turn, helped us and blessed us as they saw fit. But back then, they could also hurt us. They could seize us in their hands and rip us apart if they chose. We didn't stand a chance against such power.

A handful of gods, unwilling to hold such power over mortals, made a decision to grant us protection. The stories say they bound the power of all gods so that their kind could not harm us without falling from the celestial realms. Gods may provide weapons and play tricks and grant boons or level curses if they please, but they can no longer hurt us with their own hands, and they cannot physically interfere in our human wars. If they do, they will lose their immortality, and old age will kill them sooner or later.

Which is why Amba can't physically stop me going today, but I know she wishes she could.

"Tell me," I ask her one last time. "If it's really so important to you that I stay behind and live the rest of my life on this ship, tell me why, and I'll do as you ask."

"The truth will do more harm than good," she replies.

"Then I have to go."

Amba takes me in for a moment, grave and sad, and then vanishes abruptly into thin air.

This is not unusual. There's nothing constant about the gods; Amba has always flashed in and out of my life like a particularly stern bolt of lightning.

This time, though, she's left doubt behind and I don't have room for more doubt. My hands scrub dishes while my brain rockets through a thousand different permutations of possibilities—all the ways this day could go wrong, all the ways I could fail—and I can almost feel the fragile tension of my courage stretched too thin across too much.

The dishes are done. I must go.

I'm already late; the house has been quiet for almost an hour now. I've lived here all my life, in Madam Li's home for orphans and foundlings, and I've never known it as quiet as it is at this moment. Everyone's out in the streets, clustered near whatever tech screen they can get closest to so that they can watch the competition when it starts in less than an hour.

I dry my hands and grimace at my reflection in the polished metal freezer door. Untidy brown curls, a pale bronze elfin face with a pointed chin, gray eyes, smallish, sturdy.

Years of training taught me to move gracefully and I've just about mastered the art of holding my head high, but there's no getting away from the fact that I don't look like much. Not in the world of palaces and royalty, where my faded navy shift dress marks me as poor, a servant rather than a guest. A nobody.

I turn away from the freezer door and go outside.

The competitors have been arriving all day, a parade of starships swooping in to dock below the palace. Every hour or so, an electronic voice over the speakers announces updates on the level of resources in the base ship our entire kingdom is built upon. Today Wychstar is almost at a hundred percent human capacity. I don't think it's ever been this close to capacity before.

The narrow, crooked streets are busy and noisy as the market stalls and peddlers make the most of the crowds. At the end of every few streets, tech screens gleam while floating sun lamps beat heat down on the masses. The dizzying smells of roasted meats, spiced wines, and honey have almost drowned out the sharp, lemony tang of the air purifier that always lingers just beneath.

The kingdom doesn't look like it's built on top of a space station. It looks no different from the kingdoms on planets, which was a deliberate choice to make the first citizens' transition to life on a ship that much easier. The streets are like crooked, pastel teeth, each side crammed with colored shops and stalls and elevators and machines. Life on Wychstar is never quiet—the base ship beneath us is always at work—so even when there are no crowds and no chatter and no music, there's always the steady chug of water in the pipes below the streets, the whir of the engines even farther down, or the periodic creak of metal as machines power the atmosphere, water, electricity, and technology.

The constant hum doesn't bother me. On a spaceship kingdom, noise means all is well. Silence is far more frightening.

As I round a bend, the palace appears, all white marble and white stone, its tallest tower twisted up toward the shields that keep us safe from deep space beyond. I approach the entrance to the servants' quarters where I've worked a few times for extra money, where I know the guards will recognize me and pay me little attention. The advantage of not looking like much is that no one expects you to be a problem on a day when security is tighter than it's ever been in my lifetime.

The rooms of the palace are full of guests and the halls look splendid for the occasion, white marble walls splashed with hothouse flower petals, stairways garnished with leafy vines and bells. Everyone is gradually moving toward the grand Reception Hall where the competition will take place. I move in the opposite direction, away from the crush, and take an elevator down to the dock below the palace.

The dock is an enormous structure, and right now there are close to a hundred ships of all kinds inside, a sea of silver and rust. The air has a faint tang of fuel. It's a smell that conjures Rickard's voice, metal wings under my feet, and the sting of the wind against my skin. Precious, painful memories.

At the other end of the dock yawns the short, wide tunnel through which ships enter and leave. I can see the open mouth, the tilt pointing upward over the top of Wychstar's skyline, a perfect oval of stars and moons stretching into infinity. It's always been one of my favorite sights, that oval window that opens out to the rest of the world.

I search the dock until I find the ship that arrived just a few minutes ago. *There.* It's a simple vessel with a bulbous beetle body, no different from any other unassuming interplanetary starship, except for the crest on its side, a golden bow and arrow inside a circle. No ordinary bow, either. The crest is unmistakable.

Alexi's ship. He's here.

By the end of this day, Alexi will have *Titania*. And with her, he'll win his war. Alexi's uncle, the usurper king Elvar, will finally fall. Alexi will take his rightful place as king of the great spaceship kingdom of Kali. And I'll be there, too, exactly where I'm meant to be.

Titania can't be defeated in battle. She can't be destroyed. Here on Wychstar, they say our ruler, King Darshan, the man who made her, took a vow of silence for ten years. The gods were so impressed with his discipline that they granted him a boon.

His voice was hoarse and rusty when he said the first words he had uttered in ten years: "I want to build the most extraordinary warship ever seen. I want a ship so fast and so strong that it will never be caught or compromised. I want a ship that will never be defeated."

"You will have that ship," the gods promised.

No one knows why the king wanted such a ship so badly that he kept his silence for ten years just so the gods would grant him a favor. But they were true to their word. *Titania* is real, and she's here.

She sits on a special dais at the north end of the dock. She's deceptively small, beautiful, and terrible, dark silver and shaped like an arrowhead.

She's a bone for the hounds to squabble over, the prize of the biggest competition since the old days, when the gods would offer immortality to the human winners of their games. It seems absurd to reduce the greatest warship in the galaxy to a bone, but I think I know why the king has done it. Wychstar is his realm and I've lived here for all but a few days of my life. I've watched him for years. He's a fair ruler but also a clever one.

He wants what I want. He wants—

"He wants Alexi to win," Rama says behind me.

I whip around. "I knew it!"

Rama huffs. "I wanted to tell you something you didn't know, Esmae! I wanted you to be impressed and grateful that I provided you with such insight! You were supposed to be so grateful, in fact, that you would have then promised to carry out all of my royal duties so that I could stay in my bed and sleep."

"It was an admirable, if unsuccessful, attempt to continue down your path of irredeemable inactivity," I say sympathetically. "Maybe next time?"

This cheers him up. "I live in hope."

I'm grateful and he knows it. Rama is the king's youngest son, and my only real friend, and he's always shared more with me than he should. I expect his father's advisers would be horrified if they ever found out how much he tells me.

"How did you know I was here?"

"One of the guards told me he saw you," he says. "How I mustered the energy to come all the way down here to find you is beyond me, but here I am."

"Why does your father want Prince Alexi to take *Titania* from him?"

"He says he wants something only Alexi can give him. And he thinks the only way to persuade Alexi to give it to him is to offer *Titania* first."

"But what's the something that he wants?"

Before Rama can answer, a servant steps out onto the balcony behind us. "Your sister says you're wanted in the family quarters, my prince."

"Is it important? I'm in the middle of—"

"No, it's fine," I say. I have to go, too.

The servant's cheek twitches. He's not the only one who hates that I speak to Rama like we're equals.

Rama grins and meanders off, dragging his feet. He's like an especially lazy cat, all yawns and groans and a constant refrain of "Esmae, leave me alone. I can barely cope with the strenuous demands of everyday existence without the added trauma of your involvement. Why do you always require so much *movement* from me?"

As soon as he's gone, the old servant scowls at me. "This is what comes of goddesses sending gutter brats to the royal schoolroom."

"So you elevate the prince above us," I say, "but you're happy to cast aspersions on the choices of a goddess? You do realize a god is more likely to smite you than a prince?"

In fact, the opposite is true because gods can't smite without consequences. That said, they can certainly curse us. The servant glances skittishly over his shoulder as though afraid Amba might have appeared behind him to do just that.

"She's not there," I say helpfully.

His scowl deepens. "It's not the goddess's choices I have a problem with. The way you speak to the prince is a scandal. You should behave in a manner that better suits your station."

"Rama doesn't think he's better than any of us, so what business is it of yours how I speak to him?"

The servant grunts dismissively and storms away. I turn back to Alexi's starship.

And just in time, too. The door hisses open and a handful of people spill out. Guards and advisers, I assume, if their clothes and posture are anything to go by. After the advisers comes a tall woman in a warrior's armored tunic and then Prince Alexi himself. The woman stops just outside the doors and waits for Alexi to catch up so she can have a private word with him.

I move closer, down the stairs, away from the balcony, and toward the pair, blending in with the bustle of servants, guards, and pilots tending to ships and organizing the arrivals.

The woman is in her late thirties, with toned limbs and light brown skin, black hair shaved almost to her scalp, and long, narrow eyes. She looks familiar, and I wonder if maybe I've seen her on one of Rickard's many video cubes of Kali. She stands utterly still as she speaks to the prince, but it's the stillness of the cobras coiled in the snake pits of Sting.

And Alexi—

After years of hopes and questions and wishes left with milk and honey at gods' altars, we're finally in the same place. Finally together.

I've heard so many stories about him. He's known across the star system for his sense of honor, his bravery, his stupendous skills as a warrior. When he was five years old, he was kidnapped by a vicious *raksha* demon; when his father's soldiers arrived to rescue him, they found the demon dead, Alexi's knife buried in its heart. Dozens of warriors have tried to defeat Alexi in combat since then, boys and girls, adults across the entire gender spectrum, demons and half-demons. They've all failed. And yet, each time Alexi wins, it's with such grace that even the defeated love him for it. He never forgets a favor or a kindness and he never fails to help those he calls his friends. He's a prince of princes. And he's just seventeen years old.

He's tall and lithe and restless. There are coppery streaks in his short brown hair and a golden bow made of light is slung across his back. He has a handsome face, with a strong jaw and easy smile that have won more than his fair share of hearts across the galaxy. His eyes are clear and gray and so familiar that my throat feels tight.

I have to speak with him. *This is your chance, Esmae. Use it.*

I edge closer. A couple of the guards glance my way but then dismiss me as just another servant, no threat. A mere pawn on the board.

"Leila, don't pin all our hopes on this," Alexi says to the woman.

Leila. So she must be Leila Saka, his general and right hand. I've definitely seen footage of her before. She's terrifying on the battlefield, fast and lethal.

"She's just a ship," Alexi goes on. "An extraordinary ship, but a ship, nevertheless. She has limitations, she can't be everywhere at once. We won't win this war on her back alone. We need help from inside Kali, but that's become almost impossible since my cousin banished or locked up all our allies."

"*Titania* is the weapon that can turn the tide, Alex," General Saka replies. "We may not need help from inside Kali if we have a warship that can terrify your uncle into surrendering. And if nothing else, we're here because she is a weapon we cannot and must not ever let into his hands. I think the fire made it clear that he will do whatever it takes to be rid of you. And he's sent your cousin here to compete against you today, so I'd advise keeping your eye on him at all times or you may find him stabbing you in the back again. Literally this time."

Alexi laughs. He has a friendly, warm smile and his laugh is infectious. The corners of my own mouth tug up before terror flattens them again.

Move, Esmae.

But I don't. I stand frozen, jostled by passing servants and pilots, and can't quite bring myself to approach. *What if he doesn't want to talk to me? What if he laughs at me?*

And then, from above us, a bell sounds.

General Saka uncoils from her stance, dangerous energy humming, and gestures upward. "That's the first bell. We must join the other competitors."

She and Alexi start walking away, and all I can do is watch him go, afraid, frozen, and furious with myself.

My nerve failed. I had my chance and I let it slip away.

CHAPTER TWO

I rush to the Reception Hall, kicking myself the whole way. I can't believe my own cowardice. I've planned that moment with Alexi for months but faltered when it was time to act.

And if I faltered here, what's to say I won't falter again? What's to say I won't fail when it matters most?

The route to the hall feels endless. Windows flash by as I race down corridors and up stairways, but I've seen the view a thousand times and don't stop to look. Sun lamps, rooftops, tiny starships patrolling just inside the barely perceptible inner and outer shields. And beyond, in the distance, the planet Sting, which is where Wychstar was first built before it rose into the stars.

Spaceship kingdoms first came to be in the 1200s, when a number of men and women took flight from their planets and built new kingdoms among the stars, but eventually the practicalities of keeping a base ship fueled and stocked grew too cumbersome for most. Six hundred years on, only two of these realms have stayed afloat: Wychstar and Kali.

Kali. It feels universes away, a realm of warriors and myths and usurpers, crooked and beautiful. That's where I belong.

Home.

Madam Li's sanctuary has been a safe, comfortable place for me, but it's never been home. I was a foundling taken in and raised with an endless parade of small children who came for a little while and left when they were adopted or restored to their birth families. I stayed, waiting for the day I would return to Kali. Amba told me that was where I came from and that I would go back there one day.

Then four years ago, Elvar, the usurper king, stole the crown from his dead brother's rightful heirs and sent Alexi, his brother Bear, and their mother Queen Kyra into exile. But everyone knew Alexi would fight for his throne. A civil war was inevitable. It was then that Amba ceased all talk of my going home.

I've never stopped wanting it, though. I swore to myself that I would make my way back to my family one way or another. I swore to myself that I wouldn't be a foundling left out in the cold forever. I had prayed and trained and worked for it for years by then, and I wasn't about to give up that dream. Late at night, in the room I shared with girls who would be gone again in a few days or weeks, I held that wish close.

Now it's finally time to make it come true.

I reach the Reception Hall and slip inside just as the doors close behind me. The hall is enormous, with a domed ceiling and big windows, and a space has been cordoned off for the competition in the very heart of the room. It's packed with guests; excited voices, the clink of wine glasses, and the sickly sweet smell of perfume fill the air.

I search the hall until I find Rama and slip past the crowds to reach him. He's thrown across a bench with his eyes closed. How he gets away with behavior like this in public, I'll never know.

"So you really don't know what the competition will involve?" I ask him.

Rama deigns to open one eye. "I told you, Ez, Father's been so determined not to let any information leak out that he wouldn't tell any of us the specifics of the competition. He didn't want to give any of the competitors a chance to prepare."

"You're a prince! Third in line to the throne! How can you not know?"

Rama chuckles. "Rodi is first in line, and even he doesn't know. My proximity to the throne makes not one jot of difference to Father. He knows I'm a blabbermouth who can't be trusted."

"That," I concede, "is a valid point."

"I know as much as you or anyone else in this room. The competition will involve a single task—one that will require a great deal of skill in swordsmanship, archery, or some other battle-ish nonsense." Rama shrugs. "Alexi will win because he's better than almost everyone in the world at the aforementioned battle-ish nonsense. The only person who might possibly beat him is Sebastian Rickard himself, and he isn't competing."

Rickard, another powerful piece in this game of Warlords. Rickard, the old warrior, one of the greatest to have ever lived.

My teacher.

And the closest thing I ever had to a father.

Until the day he left and never came back.

"Wait." Rama opens both eyes and sits up abruptly. "Rickard."

I school my face into polite curiosity, hiding away how much the sound of that name hurts. As far as Rama knows, Rickard is no more than a legend to me. "What about him?"

"I *do* know one other teeny tiny detail about the competition. Father specifically wanted to rig the contest in Alexi's favor, to guarantee his victory even if by some mischance his superior skills aren't enough, so he made sure the task is one that only a student of Rickard's is likely able to complete."

This is a much smaller number of people than you would think. Years ago, Rickard was a close friend and adviser to Queen Vanya of Kali, and then to her son and heir Cassel upon her death. Back then, people came from all over the star system for advice and lessons in the arts of war, but King Cassel eventually grew unhappy and begged Rickard to stop giving away his secrets.

"What if we go to war again with other realms?" Cassel had asked. "What if these students of yours use your lessons against us?"

So Rickard made the king a promise. "I will teach your heirs everything I know, and your heirs alone. I will teach no one else."

That was twenty years ago. Rickard kept his vow. He stopped teaching, but when Cassel's heirs were born a short while later, he trained them as promised. Alexi is one of them. And Bear, his brother, is another.

I've seen the list of competitors. None of Rickard's former students are on the list, apart from Alexi.

"How does King Darshan know what Rickard might have taught his students?" I ask Rama. "How did he know which task to set?"

"They once knew each other," Rama explains. "A long, long time ago. I think Father wanted to be one of his students, back when he was still taking new students, but I don't think Father made the cut."

"Why?" I wonder. "Why Alexi? What does he want so badly that he's willing to give Alexi an unbeatable warship just to get it?"

"I wish I knew. My unsatisfied curiosity is unbearable, I assure you."

I look across the hall to where King Darshan sits on his throne. His face is turned toward the enormous arched windows that look out onto the endless black skies broken only by floating rocks, stars, gas clouds, moons—

—and *Titania*.

She's suspended outside now, the prize waiting for her winner. I'm sure some people think King Darshan must be mad to give away the unbeatable god-graced ship, but they probably don't know the other part of her story.

It's said that when Darshan asked the gods to help him build his warship, he asked for one more thing: "I want a ship that can never be used against me. Let it turn to dust before it can harm my realm or myself."

That part of the story has always made me sad on *Titania*'s behalf, condemned by the one who made her because he would rather she were destroyed than risk her hurting him in some way.

"I wonder if he'll miss her," I say out loud.

Rama stares at his father's face. "He didn't speak for ten years just so he could have her. He built her with his own hands and the gods' help. Of course he'll miss her." Rama cracks a smile. "And he won't give her up easily. That's why he isn't just gifting her to Alexi. He wants him to *earn* her."

"What about the others? There's a champion from each kingdom here today, and technically two from Kali. That's forty competitors. That's a lot of people who are destined to be disappointed."

"I think they all know they're unlikely to win. I reckon most are just glad they've even been offered a chance to compete. Everyone will have a shot at the prize. That's all they want. A chance. And, in any case," he adds, "Alexi is so loved and admired that they won't be too put out when he wins. They've trusted Father not to use *Titania* to bully and ruin them since she was built. They'll trust Alexi, too."

So loved. So admired. The golden boy. He's achieved so much in such a short life.

And lost so much.

The second bell chimes.

It's time.

CHAPTER THREE

The excitement in the Hall has reached a fever pitch. Rama joins his sisters and brother at their father's side. I move farther into the crowd, trying to blend in.

Three servants carry a number of different items into the hall. I hear the crowd murmur, puzzled and interested. The servants set up the items, one at a time, and my heart beats faster as I begin to recognize the picture.

A large golden bowl of water set on the floor.

A mechanical fish, no bigger than a banana, suspended from the domed ceiling about thirty feet above the golden bowl.

A heavy, exquisite bow laid beside the golden bowl.

A quiver of dozens of identical, ordinary arrows. One arrow for each competitor, I imagine, and some spares in case of accidents.

My breath catches. I know the task.

A near-impossible task.

Alexi will probably find it easy.

The vast room goes quiet as King Darshan rises. "Welcome, dear friends," he says. "Welcome to the competition." He points at the window. "The prize: *Titania*."

There are cheers. The crowds part at the other end of the hall and the doors open. The forty competitors enter, most with an escort of a few guards and advisers and even family members for support. Many are quite old, rulers and champions who have been established for decades, but a handful of competitors are around my age. They all look nervous and excited.

All, that is, except for Alexi. And his direct rival, the other prince of Kali. The jealous prince, the final piece on the board.

The cousins regard each other in stony silence. Max Rey, the thief prince of Kali, jealous and greedy, who helped his blind father Elvar steal the throne of the realm, who sent Alexi into exile. He's about as tall as Alexi and a scant few years older. Pale, black-haired and dark-eyed, spare and very still. If he's aware that the crowd hates him, that those assembled can't wait to see him lose, it doesn't show. He's only interested in Alexi. He certainly doesn't notice me, another figure in a crowd. He has no idea how much I wish the stone floor would open up and swallow him forever.

Alexi takes half a step forward. "Max."

"Alex," the older prince replies.

"I hope my aunt and uncle are well," Alexi says.

Max's teeth flash in something that isn't a smile. "I doubt that."

"I didn't expect to see you here. Have you come as Elvar's champion?"

"I'm here as the ruler of Kali. I rule with Father these days. Why are *you* here?"

"I'm also here as the ruler of Kali," Alexi says through gritted teeth. "I assume King Darshan has decided not to take sides."

They're each here to fight for their cause. And so am I. I'm fixated on them, the cousins circling each other like wolves, and I wish I was there. Beside them. *Involved*. I'm tired of this lonely, dark space on the sidelines where I've been all my life. Where I stand right now. I'm tired of the invisibility and loneliness of the shadows.

All my dreams, all my hopes, they're all here. Holding a breath. Waiting.

Not yet, Esmae. Just a little longer.

King Darshan clears his throat. The princes turn away from each other and face him. "If we are all ready," says the king, "I will explain the rules of the competition."

He approaches the golden bowl on the floor. At the far side of the hall, I can see a tech screen showing what everyone outside this room is seeing right now. Multiple videotechs record the competition from different angles; one of them follows the king.

"The task is not an easy one, but that seems only fair for a prize such as this. You will each receive a single arrow. You will lift this bow and string it, then you will fire the arrow directly above you at the mechanical fish." A small smile flickers over his face. A videotech zooms closer to the fish's eye and everyone can see the eye is about the size of a cherry. "I would like it if the winner skewers the fish through the eye, but I'll settle for whoever gets closest."

There's some relieved laughter in the crowd and among the competitors, but the king isn't finished.

"The fish will not be still," he warns. He claps his hands and the fish whirs to life, spinning faster and faster until it is almost a blur.

The king waits a moment to let this new fact sink in before continuing. "You will not be allowed to look at the fish when you fire the arrow." He points to the water in the golden bowl at his feet. "You may only look *down*, at its reflection in the water."

The room is silent, and then a ripple of hushed whispers and anxious voices moves across the competitors.

I watch Alexi. I see his hand grip the strap of his own bow. I see the grace and assurance with which he moves, like he's never doubted his place in the world for even an instant. I see his eyes grow wide as he realizes how easy this competition will be for him.

He looks left. I follow his gaze to a big, strong, stocky boy. My breath catches as I recognize him: Alexi's brother. He's sixteen years old, his hair short, flopping over his forehead, his nose crooked from having been broken twice. His real name is Abra, but he's known to everyone as Bear because of the sheer force with which he fights.

A wordless glance passes between the brothers, and I see hope glimmer in their faces. Kali is so close that they can almost reach out and touch it. When they win *Titania*, they will surely, surely, win the war. And when they win the war, they can go home.

"Princess Shay." King Darshan's voice pulls my attention back. "As the youngest competitor, you may go first."

The ruler of Skylark, just sixteen years old, looks like she would rather be in just about any other position, but she's no coward, and she walks bravely to the heart of the room. She struggles to lift and string the bow, then readies the arrow, angles the bow up while craning her neck to look into the water, and fires.

The arrow misses the fish by just a few inches. The crowd cheers. Princess Shay returns to her place with a cheerful shrug and grin.

It's a long competition and the guests divide their attention between the sport and the succulent refreshments laid out on a banquet table in the corner. Some of my favorite Wych specialties are on the table—skewers of roast lamb and plum pie and spiced wine—but my eyes never leave the competition.

Second to compete is proud King Ralf of Winter, who is missing an arm and refused long ago to be fitted with a prosthesis. He uses his teeth to pluck the bowstring, and he, too, misses the fish. Then comes a sharp-eyed woman who serves as champion to old Queen Miyo of Tamini. Her arrow hits the fish with a satisfying *thunk*, but a close-up from the video-tech shows it only caught the very edge of the tail.

On and on it goes. Two of the competitors can't string the bow, let alone fire the arrow, but King Darshan makes sure to applaud their efforts anyway. The most talented archers only just about hit the fish. No one comes close to the eye, never mind piercing it.

As the competition nears its close, only the two princes of Kali have yet to take their turns. This order was obviously not an accident.

Prince Max is asked to go first.

I watch him. His face is set, pale, utterly stony. There's no emotion to be read there. I look harder, though, and see it in the set of his shoulders and the tiny twitch in his jaw.

Terror.

Dread.

He can see the end coming, and can do nothing to stop it.

He strings the bow with ease and lifts it without any trouble. He nocks the arrow.

"So you came," a voice says quietly beside me.

I startle, then glance to my left. An ordinary old woman stands next to me. I'm sure she wasn't there two minutes ago. Her eyes give her away—Amba, disguised in another form.

"You knew I'd come."

"Yes," she says, and then moves away. She slips across the crowd until she's close to the front, watching intently.

That's when I notice. Lots of them are here. Dotted around the crowd, hiding in plain sight, watching the competition with their giveaway eyes. Gods. Goddesses.

Prince Max sees them, too. I see his gaze flicker right, see him take in their different faces and recognize them for what they are. He has met gods, then, if he knows what to look for. I wonder if some of them are on his side.

He turns his gaze back to the water in the golden bowl, points the arrow up, and fires.

His arrow hits the tail of the fish.

I knew his odds of winning were slim, but there was always a chance he had unseen skill, and my heart lifts with relief to see that he doesn't. He's good, but you have to be more than good to win this competition.

Finally, it's Alexi's turn. He walks forward confidently and lifts and strings the bow without effort. His movements are quick, deft, almost beautiful. His skills at warfare have always been glorious to watch.

He looks into the water and aims the arrow. Considers his position. Readjusts. And fires.

The arrow hits the fish with a *thunk*.

Alexi frowns. A *thunk* means the arrow didn't skewer the fish. I hold my breath.

As the mechanism slows and the fish goes still, the video-tech zooms in to show that the arrow hit the fish right beside the eye, missing by a hair.

Alexi's face lights up. The crowd bursts into cheers. Alexi gives them a quick, shy grin. He bows to King Darshan, who manages to restrain his obvious glee, and returns to his place with the other competitors. His brother whoops. General Saka's eyes gleam with triumph.

There's noise and joy all around me. A servant unstrings the bow and puts it back down beside the bowl of water. She starts to collect the arrows. The fish returns to its default setting and begins to spin again. King Darshan rises to his feet to officially end the competition and announce the clear winner.

This is it. This is my chance to do what I came here for.

I faltered once today. I cannot falter again.

The time has come to step out of the shadows.

Watch, I silently tell them all. *Watch, and I'll show you what I really am.*

I cross the hall. Blood pounds in my ears, drowning out every other sound. No one notices me. No one tries to stop me. No one cares about the girl in the servant's dress.

A pawn.

Unimportant.

Irrelevant.

The bow is difficult to lift, but I force it onto its point and string it. I pick up a spare arrow.

Now they care. I can't hear it, but I see it. The faces shift as they turn back, filling with confusion, surprise. There's a ripple of laughter. I must look ridiculous.

I nock the arrow.

Out of the corner of my eye, I see King Darshan staring at me in confusion. He raises a hand to summon a servant, but I see Rama place his own hand on his father's arm. Rama looks as stunned as anyone else, but he stops his father, making him give me a chance.

I see Alexi, caught in the middle of a celebration, his smile fading as he watches me. Our eyes meet for the first time in our lives. My throat closes up and I look away before I break down.

Years ago, Rickard flew to Wychstar on a short trip. On his third day here, a cold and bitter one, he went to the markets to look for a gift for his grandson. That was where I found him. I was nine years old. I asked if he would take me on as a student.

He told me once that he saw a small, shy, lonely child and deeply regretted that he had to disappoint her. "I'm sorry," he said gently, "I can't teach you."

"*Please*. I need this. It's the only way my family will ever take me back."

"I once made a vow—"

"I know," I said.

He frowned. I looked back at him. Hard, unflinching, determined to show him what I really was. And slowly, like the sun lamps brightening at dawn, understanding crept into his face.

"Your vow is the reason you can teach me," I said.

And so he did.

Today, I look into the golden bowl and see the reflection of the spinning fish above me. Every movement is familiar, like an old friend. This was a favorite exercise of his, one we did together a hundred times. He demanded excellence and I delivered.

I look past the ripples, past the tiny movements that are reflection only, cutting all the way to the whirl of the fish itself. Searching for its eye.

I glance one last time into the crowd. At Amba. Her ancient eyes are full of untold catastrophes. *Don't do it*, they say.

"Then stop me," I whisper.

She doesn't.

I leave the lonely dark of the shadows. I am in the light. Bow in hand. A pawn in a Warlords game.

Do you know what happens when a pawn gets all the way across the board?

She becomes a queen.

I point the arrow.

I fire.

And I skewer the fish right through the eye.

CHAPTER FOUR

When I was six years old, Amba visited me for the very first time. I was on the steps outside the children's sanctuary that day, nose in a book as always, scarcely even aware of the heat of the artificial sun beating down on me. Madam Li came out to find me, surprise and confusion all over her face. She was with a stern, beautiful woman.

"Esmae, this is the goddess Amba," she said, looking like she couldn't quite believe those words had come out of her own mouth. "She has asked to speak with you."

Madam Li is not a tender woman. She has a good heart, but she's also worn out and has no time for affection. In spite of this, I found myself grabbing hold of her skirts because I didn't want to be left alone with the strange visitor.

Madam Li extracted herself and went back inside, assuring me that I had nothing to be afraid of. I'm not sure she believed that, but she hadn't the nerve to question a goddess.

Amba eyed my book. It was a folktale, I remember that. A story about a queen who was cruelly betrayed and swore she would not wash her hair again until she could bathe it in her enemies' blood. "A little grim for a child, don't you think?" Amba had said.

I clutched the book closer. "This was the only book on Madam Li's desk this week."

"Do you like to read?"

"Yes."

"Why?"

This seemed a very foolish question. "Why not?"

Her mouth twitched ever so slightly. Then she said, "Your father is dead."

"I don't understand. I don't have a father."

"You did. He died today. It was quite unexpected and his death will have repercussions. I want to prepare you for your inevitable reunion with the rest of your family."

"I have a family?" I said, amazed.

"Yes." And she told me the story of how I ended up on Wychstar. The story of a cursed mother and a tragic sacrifice and how she, a goddess, brought me here herself to keep me safe.

After she finished her story, she held out her hand and opened it. On her palm lay a deep blue petal, as luminous and perfect as a star. It was so beautiful I could only stare.

"The petal of a blueflower," Amba told me. "Your mother gave this to you when she handed you to me. I took it so that no one else would, but it's time you had it back."

She closed her hand and whispered a blessing under her breath, and when she opened it again, the petal was gone. In its place was a jewel, just as blue and luminous, shaped like the petal had been. The stern cast of her face softened into a small smile. She pinned the jewel in my hair.

"Keep it close," she said. "As long as you do, no one can hurt you."

"What does that mean?"

"As long as you possess the blueflower jewel, you will be invulnerable to harm. Any wound you receive will heal immediately. Consider it my gift to you, a small consolation for the sorrow you will know."

I didn't quite believe her until the day I slipped and fell flat on my face. By the time I got back to my feet, the pain had stopped. I noticed blood on the floor, but no trace of where it had come from. There wasn't a scratch on me.

It was a wondrous gift, but Amba's words made it as bitter as it was sweet. *Small consolation for the sorrow you will know*, she'd said, and she had spoken only the truth. It was consolation and it was small; her gift couldn't keep me safe from the deeper wounds of sadness, fear, or loneliness. I kept the blueflower jewel close almost every moment of my life, but its power couldn't make me feel invincible. I have never felt invincible.

Never.

Until now.

When the fish slows to a stop and the videotech focuses on the arrow skewering its eye, I feel like I cannot be touched, I cannot be torn down. I feel like nothing and no one in the whole wide galaxy will ever hurt me again.

In the uproar that follows, I seek out certain faces. Like statues, they seem frozen in the chaos: Rama, gobsmacked; Amba with her eyes made of calamity; the thief-prince, wide-eyed with wonder; King Darshan, utterly aghast, but trying valiantly to hide it.

And Alexi. Everything else fades into nothing as I look into his face and he looks into mine. He's white as a sheet.

Then they all unfreeze, Amba and the other gods vanish into thin air, and the king opens his mouth to speak. "Let us have some order and decorum in the Hall," he says, but his voice is almost lost in the mayhem. "I must ask for your patience while I look into this unexpected development."

"Who is she?" someone shouts.

"She's a servant!" someone else says. The word, itself, doesn't bother me, but the sneering tone cuts deep.

"How dare a servant presume to compete against the likes of royals?"

"Silence!" roars the king, and the crowd goes quiet at last. "We will resolve this matter." His eyes settle on me again, his gaze stern and impassive. "Esmae, follow Prince Rama."

I quietly do as I'm told. Rama keeps making what-the-actual-hell-is-going-on-Esmae? faces at me, but two of the royal bodyguards have come with us and that makes him uncharacteristically circumspect. I reach out a hand to touch his, but one of the bodyguards shakes his head and I drop it back to my side. It's their job to be careful, but it still hurts. Despite having been Rama's friend, alone with him countless times over the past eleven years, they now think I could be a threat.

The lush, airy suite Rama takes me to is in the king's public quarters, the place where he holds private meetings with staff and guests. There's a long table and several chairs by the window.

"Feel free to sit," Rama says to all three of us, the first words he's said out loud since the competition ended.

The bodyguards decline, taking up positions in opposite corners. I sit reluctantly in a chair halfway down one side of the table. Rama sits next to me. He reaches under the table and squeezes my hand. I squeeze back as hard as I can.

"How?" he asks quietly.

Before I can answer, the door opens again. Rama and I rise as King Darshan enters accompanied by his daughter Radha. I assume he left Crown Prince Rodi to soothe the crowds while he deals with me. Alexi, Bear, General Saka, and Max Rey come in after him.

"Why is he here?" Rama asks in his usual lazy drawl, pointing at Prince Max. There's an undercurrent of scorn in his voice. No one likes the thief prince.

"Prince Max is here because he insisted," King Darshan says curtly.

Of course he insisted. He knows his kingdom is at stake. I'm glad he's here. I had hoped he would be.

The king takes his place at the head of the table and gestures for the rest of us to be seated. Princess Radha is on my other side; she gives me a sweet, reassuring smile. We were both very shy children and never had a chance to become real friends, but we've known each other most of our lives and I'm glad to have a friendly face beside me.

Alexi and Bear take seats opposite us. Bear doesn't even try to conceal his shock and resentment, but Alexi won't look at me at all. I give Bear a small smile, earning a scowl in return. I can't really blame him.

I dare a look at General Saka. She sits straight and dangerously still beside them. She meets my eyes, her own hard and cold as glass.

Prince Max considers each side of the table before wisely realizing he isn't welcome on either, and settles at the foot, opposite the king. I can feel him watching me, but he's much less obvious about it than the others. I can't tell what's behind the quiet surface of his dark eyes.

"There is no need to stand on ceremony in this room," says King Darshan. "In the interest of keeping this quick, you may all speak freely."

"Thank you—" Alexi starts.

"What this girl has done means nothing," General Saka cuts in, swift as a blade. She gives Alexi an apologetic glance for interrupting him, but continues. "Prince Alexi won the competition and won *Titania*. She was not on the list of competitors, she is neither royal nor a champion, and the competition had ended by the time she stepped onto the stage. Her attempt at the fish must, therefore, be automatically disqualified."

"Her successful attempt at the fish," says Prince Max with the faintest glimmer of a smile. I'm sure he's petty enough to be delighted that the world witnessed Alexi Rey lose. It's infuriating, but Max's delight is also exactly what I want.

General Saka glares at him but doesn't respond. She turns instead to King Darshan. "Who *is* she?" she demands. It's a bold tone to take with a king, but by all accounts, Leila Saka fears nothing and nobody. "You called her by a name in the hall. Do you know her? Is she one of your servants?"

"She's right here," says Rama. "If you want to know who she is, why don't you ask her yourself?"

General Saka raises an eyebrow at me. "Well?"

I consider my words, weighing how much to say. "My name is Esmae. I grew up in a children's sanctuary here on Wychstar. I work as a servant in the palace sometimes."

"And she's my friend," says Rama firmly.

"Your friend?" General Saka repeats. "And how did she come to be friends with a royal prince?"

"The goddess Amba asked a favor of me when Esmae was a child," says King Darshan. "She asked me to educate her in my royal schoolroom. She has shared lessons with Prince Rama since she was six years old."

Alexi's gaze finally snaps to meet mine. I watch his fists, clenching and unclenching on top of the table. I'm not sure he knows he's doing it. "Why you?" he asks.

"What?"

"Why you? You're no one. I'm sorry, I know that's rude, but it's the truth. Why did a goddess want you educated alongside royals?"

Max is incredulous. "You can't just say someone is *no one.*"

"Stay out of it, Max," Bear growls at him. "Why are you even here? Is it not enough that you stole everything from us? You're lucky I haven't cut your throat!"

"On a foreign king's territory?" Max replies. "That would be foolish, even by your standards."

Bear lunges, but Alexi grabs hold of his brother's arm and yanks him back into his seat. The bodyguards in the corners reach for their weapons.

Max doesn't even flinch.

"That's enough," says King Darshan. His voice is sharper than before. "You can all behave yourselves or leave the room immediately."

Bear's broad shoulders hunch like a chastised schoolboy, and I feel for him. I'd want to cut the throat of the person who stole everything from me, too.

After a tense, silent moment, Bear recovers himself and says, "Royal schoolroom or not, I know you don't have instructors here on Wychstar who can teach what she just accomplished. How can she possibly have such skill with a bow and arrow?"

"She can't," says General Saka as though the answer has suddenly become obvious. She springs to her feet. "She must have cheated!"

"That is a ridiculous accusation," says Rama.

"I did not cheat," I tell the general coldly. I expected the accusation sooner or later. The truth—that I've spent years working and studying—is more implausible than the convenience of a trick. "How would I have even done so?"

"You could have called on the gods to guide the arrow. You could have slipped a magnet onto the arrow's tip while no one was looking. You could even be an illusion yourself, a con engineered by the thief prince, while the real orphan girl Esmae is dead or locked up in a cell."

All possible, I suppose. Max frowns but doesn't defend himself or answer for me.

I stand to face her, looking straight in her eye, my chin raised. "None of those things are true. I skewered that fish because I'm the finest archer in this room."

Alexi cocks his head at me curiously. "Better than me?" It would sound arrogant coming from anyone else, but we all know the stories. I've seen the videos. He has good reason to believe his skill is almost unmatched.

"Better than you."

Leila Saka lets out a sharp burst of laughter. "She really thinks she's a better archer than Alexi Rey!"

"Why not?" Max asks. "You just saw her prove as much."

"I saw her fire one shot." General Saka sneers at him. "One shot proves nothing. I've given you three different ways she could have pulled that shot off."

"That one shot is proof enough for me," Max replies.

"You would say that. You'd say anything if it meant that Alexi doesn't win *Titania*."

"I'm sure he's already won *Titania*," Max snaps back. "It doesn't seem likely Esmae is going to get her, does it? You're all so bloody determined to disqualify her on the grounds that she's a servant."

I dig my fingernails into my palms, unclench them, tighten them again. Why is he, of all the people, the one treating me with respect and courtesy? I can't trust it. I know what he's capable of. I can't trust a word out of his mouth.

Max's expression shifts. He's looking at my hands. At my fists—clenching and unclenching. He glances at Alexi and I know what he's seeing. That fist on the table. Clenching, unclenching.

Behind me, I hear General Saka arguing with Rama and King Darshan about the competition. Rama is uncharacteristically energetic, refusing to back down from defending my victory. King Darshan wants desperately to agree with General Saka's opposition—he's set this whole thing up so that Alexi can have *Titania*, after all—but he also wants to be seen as fair.

As they argue, Max stands. I tense, but don't move, allowing him to approach. I let him not just because I want him to see the truth, but because I've never, ever been seen as clearly as I know he's seeing me now. He's cutting past it all, the servant's dress and lemony tang of cheap soap and the messy, tousled hair. I watch his eyes flicker from my hair to my nose to my eyes. Putting together all the little things he hadn't noticed before.

"Oh," he says quietly.

"So you see," I reply.

"I think I do."

I turn back to the table. "General Saka, you keep saying I don't have any right to *Titania* because I'm a nobody. King Darshan, you have always been courteous to me, and I will always be grateful to you for everything you've done for me, but I'm sure you agree with the general. Would you let me have the prize I won if I wasn't just nobody? If I was someone who mattered in your eyes?"

"I don't understand what you mean, Esmae," says the king.

Here it is. The beginning of the end of this Warlords game. One last play. The moment I've waited so many years for.

"I can lay to rest any question of my skill. I could, of course, spend a week showing you every sword trick I know, every battle strategy, every skill I have with a bow, but there's a quicker way. I don't think there's anyone in this room who doesn't trust the word of Sebastian Rickard. Ask *him* what kind of warrior I am."

A fragment of a moment, their faces frozen in shock. Even Rama, who knows me better than anyone, is caught off guard. Even he didn't look at Alexi and me in the same room and see the obvious.

"Rickard?" Bear repeats in bewilderment. "What does Rickard have to do with it? He can't be your teacher. He swore a long time ago that he would only teach my father's heirs."

"Yes, he did," I say.

Alexi and I have been in the same room for several minutes now, but no one has seen what should have been obvious. They see a prince and a servant. They don't see that both have copper in their brown hair. Or that they have the same eyes. From the moment they walked in here, they saw only what they expected and missed the truth.

They saw the pawn.

And missed the queen.

"I *am* one of your father's heirs," I say at last. "My name is Esmae, but I was born Alexa Rey. I'm your sister." I look at Alexi, into his ashen face and wide eyes. "Your twin."

CHAPTER FIVE

"You can't be," Alexi says, his voice little more than a croak. "We don't have a sister."

I've wanted this moment for eleven years, to finally look my family in the eye and have them see me for who I really am. My mother isn't here, but my brothers are. Alexi is. Alexi, who has been the bright half of my dark ghost for so long.

But I didn't want this moment to be like *this*. I wanted joy. I wanted love. I wanted the pieces to click together perfectly.

Elvar took that from me four years ago. He turned our home into a battleground and snatched away the joy we could have had.

And now we're here because of him. I'm doing this because of him. I exchanged joy for *this*.

"Rickard was my teacher," I say. "If he agreed to teach me and I'm not your sister, he must have broken the vow he made your father."

Bear doesn't even hesitate. "He would never have done that!"

"Then it must be true, mustn't it?"

"B-but," he stammers, "but our mother, she'd have told us if we had a sister! Why would she hide it from us?"

General Saka's expression has transformed to horror; now that she knows I didn't cheat, she has to face the unthinkable possibility that Alexi Rey might have an equal. "You have the same eyes, Alex," she says.

It's not just the eyes. Alexi, Bear, and I are a patchwork of the generations that came before us. Bear has more brown in his skin like our mother, while Alexi and I are a light bronze that's closer to the paler skin tone our father once had. We all have copper in our brown hair, but Alexi and I have our mother's gray eyes and Bear has our father's blue. And then there's Bear's eyebrows and Alexi's nose and my small, sturdy frame and all of the other little details I've traced back across years of our family.

"How long have you known?" Rama asks. He's using that lazy drawl again, but I know him too well. I've hurt him.

"A long time. Amba told me when I was six."

"So that's why she sent you to the schoolroom," King Darshan says, a puzzle at last solved. "She wanted you educated like a royal because you are one. Extraordinary."

Alexi shakes his head. "It makes no sense. No one's ever heard of Alexa Rey. There are countless records of my birth and not one of them mentions a second baby."

"No, but the records also make it clear that our mother refused all medical treatment while she was pregnant and only our father was with her when she gave birth. Didn't you ever think that odd behavior for a queen? She did it because she knew she was pregnant with twins and she didn't want anyone else to find out."

Alexi is silent. Bear stutters a protest, but then gives in and says, "But why? Why keep you a secret? Why would Mother send you away?"

"There was a curse. I don't know who cursed us or why, but I know it said that my birth would destroy us all. Amba says that our mother cried bitterly, but she gave me up in the hope that the curse would never come to pass. She begged Amba to take away her memories of me, and our father's memories of me, so that they would never be tempted to seek me out."

"She cried bitterly?" Max says slowly. It's the first time he's spoken in several minutes. "She asked for her memory of you to be removed so that she would never be tempted to seek you out? None of that sounds like Kyra."

Bear scowls but doesn't contradict him. No one seems to know what else to say. I watch Alexi. He's so pale and quiet. This isn't how I planned this; I wanted to speak to him before the competition, prepare my brothers so that we could act this scene out together, but I failed and now I'm performing this part alone. *The show must go on.*

"So what now?" Alexi asks me quietly. "You're my sister, but you competed against me. I can only assume that means you're not on my side."

This is the hardest part, the final move in the game. "I'm sorry," I say. "Don't take it personally. I just want to go home."

Alexi's smile is slightly grim. "You want to take *Titania* to Kali. You want the kingdom they took from me. You've chosen their side."

My heart aches. I hate that he thinks this of me. I wanted him to leave Wychstar after all this knowing he had a sister who would fight for him, even if she had to do it in secret, but it's too late for that now. I have to let him believe the worst. I have to let them all believe it.

It was like they said in the dock. *Titania* is an unbeatable warship, but she is ultimately a ship. She can't be beaten, but she can't be everywhere at once either. With or without her, Alexi needs help from inside Kali. He needs help cutting our uncle down from the inside.

And there was only one way I was ever going to convince my uncle that I was on his side: I had to compete against Alexi. I had to show them all just how valuable I am. I had to make Elvar and Max and every other traitor on Kali *want* me.

And now that they do, I have my way home. I have my teeth firmly in their throats. And when it's time, I'll rip them out.

And win this war.

"I want to go home," I say again, "And I'll do what it takes to get there, even if that means joining our uncle. I've been a ghost for seventeen years. I want my home back."

There's a ringing silence when I finish. I let it hang in the air, then turn on my heels and walk quietly out of the room before I burst into tears.

CHAPTER SIX

Rama catches up to me halfway down one of the servants' stairways. There's no sign of his bodyguards.

"Esmae." He sighs. "You know I loathe running at the best of times. Don't think for one second that I appreciate all the activity that's been demanded of me today."

"You didn't have to come after me."

"You may have failed to notice this, but I don't often do things because I have to." He pauses. "Am I allowed to call you Esmae or do you prefer Princess Alexa? Should I bow? Do you outrank me now? I think you might. You are, after all, heir to the throne of Kali, while I am only third in line to Wychstar's."

I glare at him, which only makes him grin all the more brightly back. "I am not the heir!" I snap. "My uncle is on the throne."

"And if your brother were to take back that throne, who do you think would be his heir?"

"It wouldn't be me after what I just did."

"I concede he might not want you to be after that display," Rama says, "and yet by right of birth, it's you."

I stop on the stairs and turn to face him. "Are you angry?"

"Anger is exhausting," he replies, "and if there's one thing I hate, it's an enterprise that's exhausting. Truth be told, Ez, it's your right to keep your secrets. I'm not upset you kept them from me, but I am a *little* cross you spent years letting me share *my* family's secrets with you and never bothered to mention you were keeping your own."

"I should have told you," I say. "I lied to you for years. And I'm sorry. It's not that I didn't trust you. I wanted to tell you. I almost did so many times. I guess I missed my chance."

He scowls at me. "You missed your chance? Really? You haven't stumbled across a single opportunity since you were six? How long would it have taken? *Rama, I am King Cassel and Queen Kyra's lost daughter.* There! What was that, two seconds? Three? You couldn't find three seconds in over a decade?"

"It didn't feel that easy," I say and start walking again.

"No," he says, gentler now, "I suppose it didn't."

We get to the bottom of the stairs and start down the corridor, past the palace laundry rooms, toward one of the servants' exits. Several people stop to gape at us. Not because of Rama; they're used to him wandering in and out of places royals don't usually go. They're staring because of me. Because they all watched the competition.

"You were very good, by the way," Rama goes on, lazy and admiring. "All that in there about doing whatever it takes to get what you want. Even I believed it for a moment. Then the moment passed. I know you too well. I know you're not the sort of person who joins the usurping uncle and jealous cousin who have made your brothers' lives a misery. So what are you up to?"

"I want nothing more than to be with my mother and brothers," I say softly, "but I can't protect them if I'm with them. No war I've ever read about was won on the backs of just ships and soldiers and weapons. We need more. We need someone on the inside to find out exactly where the traps will the sprung. To spring traps of our own."

"And do your brothers know of this plan?"

"Not yet. I was hoping to tell them before the competition, but it didn't quite work out that way." I swallow. "It's probably better this way anyway. If the rift between us looks real, Elvar is that much more likely to trust me."

Rama's face is more worried than I've ever seen it. "What happens if your uncle realizes what you're up to? It'll be *your* head on a spike."

"No one uses spikes anymore."

"A figurative spike doesn't change the fact that executions are real."

I manage a smile. "Then I'd better not get caught."

We duck into the cellars; the most discreet exit out of the palace is tucked away at the back. The cellars are dim and chilly, a labyrinth of rooms where the palace wines and preserved stores of emergency food are kept.

"You beat every single person in that competition," Rama says after a moment. "Just to trick your uncle into letting you get close."

It's not a question, but he's not convinced. I won't lie to him again. "No," I admit. "I wanted to win. Not just because it was *Titania*, not just because of the war. For me. I wanted to be in the sun just once." I smile ruefully. "Not that it matters. I'll be disqualified and Alexi will get *Titania*. Our mother chose him. The world will choose him."

I love my brother, but I've always wished that someone, just once, would choose me.

We turn a corner, and Amba materializes in front of us.

Rama lets out an undignified yelp and takes a hasty step back. I don't think he's ever met a god before. He's one of the few people I know who doesn't hold any devotion to them whatsoever. He's no more disrespectful to them than he is to anyone else, which is to say he's fairly disrespectful but somehow gets away with it, but he doesn't pray or make offerings at altars or care much about them one way or another. Still, it's hard to be irreverent when you're looking into the eyes of a god.

Amba raises her eyebrows at me. "I underestimated you."

"Most people do." She knows that. A part of me is disappointed that she did, too. I wanted her to know me better, to see me better than that. She was so sure she knew what I wanted. When she described that dream of me, of Alexi flying into war and me there by his side, she was so sure she understood. And she was right, of course, but she just didn't see it *all*.

"You have no idea what you've set in motion today," says Amba. Her voice echoes in the cavernous cellar space, bouncing off stone walls and glass bottles. "There will be consequences, and those consequences will breed further consequences, and it will go on and on until whole cities crumble to dust."

"All I did was shoot an arrow," I protest. "A single arrow can't do all that."

"Your arrow was a spark," she replies, "A spark of fire so hot and white that no one will be able to put it out. And even a spark of fire can consume an entire forest if it can jump from tree to tree. Watch, Esmae. Watch as one act leads to another and then to another after that. Watch the trees pass white flames on. Watch the forest burn."

And then she's gone.

CHAPTER SEVEN

Amba's wrong if she thinks I don't know there will be consequences. I've spent so long trying to anticipate every outcome of this competition that even when I wasn't sure I could beat Alexi, I considered what would happen if I did. I know what's going on across the stars.

I know there will be hasty scrambling for tech screens and the angry summoning of spies so that thirty-nine rulers and their advisers can find out as much as possible about the strange servant girl who beat Alexi Rey. I'm a wild card, an unknown, and they will all be terrified.

I know Queen Miyo of Tamini will join forces with Alexi, if she hasn't already, and I know Prime Minister Gomez of Shloka will call a meeting of the Forty Territories on neutral ground so that they can discuss how to deal with me. I know armies will be readied, ships poised to fly, shields activated around palaces, all of it put into place just in case they have to face *Titania*.

The rumors will spread until eventually the truth will spill out. King Darshan may already have been forced to announce it. *Princess Alexa, daughter of King Cassel and Queen Kyra of Kali*. It doesn't sound right, and yet it's who I am. It's what I've wanted all my life.

And my uncle, the usurper king of Kali, will be both furious and gleeful. He will hate me because I am yet another child of the brother who had everything, but he'll want me on his side. He'll want to use me against Alexi, the perfect foil to the golden warrior prince, the twin who can equal and crush his enemy. He'll want *Titania*. I'm counting on that.

Rama and I slip out of the cellar exit. "Are you really planning to go back to the children's home?" he asks as we walk away from the white palace walls. "You do know you're not just another face on the streets anymore?"

"I can't leave without a word to them. And there's something there I need before I go."

It's an awkward trip back to the home; royal princes and winners of warships tend to cause a stir wherever they go. Rama may be used to it, but I find the dumbfounded stares and whispers as we pass profoundly unsettling.

As soon as I set foot in the familiar patchwork of pods and rooms, the children mob me. They tumble over one another in their excitement and I can hardly keep up with their questions. *How did you do it, Esmae?* I hear several times. *I spent a long time learning* isn't a very exciting reply.

Rama eventually distracts them, and I escape to the room I share with three smaller girls. I pack what little I have into an old rucksack. It isn't much beyond some clothes and a couple of books, but I didn't come back for them. I shift the floor-board beneath my bed and draw out the bow Rickard gave me after I passed his first test.

The Black Bow. It feels warm, alive in my hands, a small but powerful bow carved from the black ashoka wood that grows on Amba's planet. It's not just a fine tool for archery; when an incantation transforms it into its celestial self, it becomes an explosion of radiance that can instantly destroy any and every weapon at which it's directed. *Titania* is pos-sibly the only exception. Other warships would crumble. Swords would turn to ash. Arrows would dissolve in the air. Lasers would vanish on the spot. Whole armies could be picked off and disarmed, and whole fleets of soldiers would die as their warships crumbled around them. Rickard taught me the incantation when he gave it to me, but warned me never to use it unless I had a desperate need. I haven't needed it yet.

I might in battle. That's the obvious place, isn't it? Technology allows us to make weapons that can level cities with the press of a button, but the laws of righteous warfare limit soldiers to the use of swords, bows, and other pre-in-dustrial weapons like spears, the *gada* mace, and hammers. Spaceships can be used in battle, but there are laws about distance and the type of laserfire and so on. There are many people who resent these limits, but the gods' laws are strict and the Forty Territories agreed together not to violate their code.

There's a sound at the doorway. I look up to see Madam Li.

"They're saying you're a Rey." She jabs her thumb back toward the tech screens out on the streets. "Is it true?"

"Yes."

She shakes her head. "You never put on any airs, never fussed about all the jobs you took on around here, never acted like you were better than any of us. I never would have guessed there was a princess hiding behind all that." Her long black eyes shift to the packed rucksack and she frowns. "You don't have to leave because of this."

"You know I do. Neither of us will ever get any peace if I stay here."

She notices the Black Bow. She takes in the celestial symbols notched into its grain. Her eyes widen. "Is that one of *their* bows?"

"A god's bow?" I can feel its energy, a faint thrum in my hands. "Yes. Amba forged it."

Madame Li touches her heart, then touches the bow for luck. She smiles at me. "Good luck, Esmae. Bend the world to your will."

I smile back. "I'll do my best."

I thank her for all she's done for me and then I leave.

Rama's outside. He looks like he's talking to himself, but I assume he's speaking to whoever's on the other end of the earpiece he's put in his left ear. When I approach him, he jerks his head at the tech screen at the other end of the street. "You're going to want to see this, Ez."

King Darshan is on the screen. "This was an impossible decision. Princess Alexa won the competition, but she was not on the list of competitors. Her entry should not count, and yet it would be unjust to pretend she does not have the kind of talent that is worthy of a prize like *Titania*. I decided it was not up to me to have the final say."

A murmur rolls through the crowd around us. I'm just as confused. Rama's eyes are twinkling.

"I put the question to someone who has more right to this decision than I," the king continues. "I asked *Titania* herself. And—"

He pauses. I hold my breath.

"—and she has chosen Princess Alexa."

I'm hardly aware of the noise and the heads in the crowd turning my way. Something expands inside me, painful and sharp. *Titania* chose me. She chose *me*.

I look past the tech screen, past the sun lamps, into the deep black of space. At my path home, lit by stars.

CHAPTER EIGHT

When we return to the palace, a servant tells Rama that Prince Max has sent word asking to see me. I agree to meet him in the royal family's library, where I wait surrounded by Rama's maps and Radha's books. It's a room I know very well, because it's also the schoolroom we studied in growing up, but it feels odd to be here as a princess and not as the orphan that the royal tutors didn't really want to teach.

Once again, Max Rey comes alone without any of his attendants or advisers. This time, there isn't even a guard in the room for protection. He probably thinks he doesn't need one; Kali is a realm of warriors and almost every person over twelve and under seventy can fight better than they can bake a loaf of bread. There's a reason Kali imports its bread from Winter.

"Do you prefer Esmae or Alexa?" he asks.

"Esmae's fine."

He takes one of the other chairs and leans forward, elbows on his knees, but hesitates as though he's not sure what to say. I consider my options. I certainly can't let him see the depth of my hatred for him, but I can't come across as eager to please either. No one trusts an overly friendly stranger. I have to make him believe my lie by offering up a little of the truth.

"You came alone," I say. "Brave."

"Why is it brave?"

"Because this would be the ideal opportunity for me to kill you if I were so inclined. I'm sure you'd put up a good fight, but I would win."

"You don't seem like a murderer."

"How can you know that?"

"You were taught by Rickard," he says. "Honor defines everything he does."

"Rickard isn't my teacher anymore."

Max frowns slightly. "Why not?"

"It doesn't matter." Rickard's face flashes in and out of my mind, with that sudden smile that would transform him. I'm surprised by how much it hurts to think of him. By how much I still miss him.

The very last memory I have of him is the way he stepped onto the wing of his ship and then looked back one more time. I was trying not to cry—he could see that, and his face softened. *You will always have a place in my heart.* Those were the very last words he ever spoke to me. They're the words I try to remember, the ones I cling to, because the ones that came before fill me with shame and despair every time I think of them.

Max is considering the stack of games on a shelf. "Do you play Warlords?"

I shape my mouth into a sheepish smile. "Not very well."

"I'm not very good, either," he says. "Shall we?"

He sets up the board. I fidget with my queen until it's time to put her down in her starting position.

"You're not a killer," Max says, his eyes on the pieces. His fingers move quickly, deftly. "You're someone who has spent her life overlooked and dismissed, treated like she's nobody. You're someone who just wants to belong somewhere."

I hate that he sees that. I hate that he, of all people, understands that about me. I don't reply. I make the first move, nudging a pawn up two spaces. Standard, safe.

"You don't have to believe me," he goes on, "but I know what it is to feel like you're never going to be enough."

I let out a sharp, brittle laugh. "Do you really? Crown Prince of Kali, ruling alongside your father? The thief prince with an entire kingdom in the palm of your hands?"

His eyes are on the line of king, queen, elephants, chariots, and horses behind his pawns. He moves a horse forward. "I'm a crown prince with no blood right to the throne my father holds," he says.

He's really Queen Guinne's nephew, the only child of her sister Maeve, orphaned as a baby and adopted and raised by Elvar and Guinne as their own. It's true that he isn't related by blood to Alexi or Bear or me, but what difference does that make? The world says many things about Max Rey—*thief* and *treacherous snake* feature most prominently—but I have never heard *not even a real Rey* used against him.

"You're adopted," I say and place one of my pawns where he can take it. A mistake a novice might make. "What difference does that make to anything?"

"So that's not the reason you don't like me?"

"I used to hate you," I say. *Reel him in with a little of the truth.* "My father died and for seven years my mother ruled as Alexi's regent. And that was when *your* father's patience ran out. They were children and you betrayed them. Your father took the throne. And then you didn't even stop there. You could have let them live in their home in peace, princes but never kings, but you didn't. You exiled them instead. *You* did that. Everyone knows it was your idea. You insisted they had to go. You took *everything* from them."

I take one of Max's pawns. He takes my chariot back in turn. "Alexi was thirteen, not three," he says. "He was never going to live in peace on Kali. He had too many allies in the palace. The moment he had a chance, he would have struck. I was not about to let your brothers stay on our kingdom when I knew they were waiting for an opportunity to skewer my father in the heart."

"You could have talked to them!"

"They didn't want to talk. I was seventeen when they were exiled. Your age. I was their childhood companion, their friend and cousin, and I betrayed them. Why would they talk to me? And my father had no interest in negotiating terms that would put Alexi back on the throne anyway." Max takes another pawn. "So they had to go."

He says it quietly but firmly. And I understand the logic, I do. Still, logic doesn't make it any less cruel.

"Don't pretend you weren't waiting for an opportunity to get rid of them," I say. "Everyone knows the stories. You were jealous of them. You hated them."

Max makes a sound that might be a laugh. "We're not so different, Esmae. I think you of all people know how it feels to spend your life watching someone else get everything while you get nothing."

I don't reply. How can I? What can I possibly say to refute that?

"The coup wasn't as simple as everyone likes to think it was," Max goes on after a moment. "My father doesn't believe he stole the throne, you know. The world is angry that my father took it from Alexi, but no one seemed to care when *your* father took the throne from mine."

"That's not fair. That wasn't my father's fault. That was the line of succession, not a coup."

"The point still stands. My father was the eldest, but our grandmother and her war council decided my father's lack of sight made him less capable of ruling and named Cassel the heir instead. No one cared that my father lost what should have rightfully been his."

"It's not the decision I would have made if I'd been queen and I don't think it's fair that Elvar was punished for his disability, but it doesn't excuse what he's done. At the end of the day, it was Queen Vanya's right as ruler to name whoever she wished as her heir. Once she made her decision, my father was her heir, and Alexi his heir in turn. What Elvar did doesn't put right the injustice that was done to him. All he's done is create a brand new injustice."

"Maybe, but Father doesn't see it that way."

"Why couldn't he contest Alexi's claim to the throne the proper way, then? He obviously respected Queen Vanya's choice while she and my father were alive. He didn't try to take the throne until after my father died. He could have spoken to the war council first. He could have asked them to choose between him and Alexi. Why did he have to *take* the crown?"

"I suppose he was still afraid," says Max.

"Of what?"

"Maybe he was afraid he'd be rejected all over again. Maybe he felt he had to take back some degree of control over his own fate."

The pieces flash across the board. Pawn, chariot, elephant, horse, queen. Protect the king, get rid of the others. I lose several pieces and take a few of Max's, moving in precisely the right places to engineer his win.

"If you're so angry with my father and me for what we did to your family," he says after a few minutes of silence, "why did you compete against your brother? Why did you agree to meet with me here?"

"I *was* angry with you," I say. "I was angry until I realized that I have no stake in either side. My mother didn't want me, my uncle didn't know about me. I just want to go home. If Alexi was on the throne, I'd join him. He's not. It's your father, and you. I don't agree with what you've done, and I don't trust you, but this isn't my war. I agreed to talk to you because you're the one who gets to decide whether to let me set foot on Kali or not."

He maneuvers his queen into place. I could escape the trap, but I don't. I shift my horse elsewhere instead. Max moves his chariot closer, ready to lock my king down and win the game.

"Kali is your home, Esmae," he says. "My father agrees. You are welcome to come back with me. Not to fight in our army. Not to be useful to us. You're not required to be useful to anyone. Live whatever life you wish when you get there. It's your home."

I stare at him, shocked. Not by the invitation, because I expected it, but by the terms of it. *You're not required to be useful to anyone.*

"Does your father agree with all of that?" I ask. "Are you sure he doesn't want me there just so I don't fight against him?"

"You're far too good to lose to the other side, it's true, but I don't believe that's my parents' only reason for inviting you to Kali."

"Far too good to lose to the other side? Flattery won't help."

"Telling you how skilled you are is hardly flattery. You just announced it to the entire world." He smiles suddenly, lopsided. "Flattery would be me telling you we don't need your knowledge or skill because your smile alone would turn attacking armies to dust."

I feel the smallest twitch at the corner of my mouth and squash it. I refuse to let him make me laugh.

Max moves his queen. "Warlord lock," he says.

The final move.

He's won.

"I'll come back with you," I say. *Finally. Home, and the means to crush them all.* I glance at the board. "And well played."

He stands up. "Maybe next time you might try to win."

I tense. "What?"

"You planned every single move of that game." His eyes are too shrewd, and a little amused. "It's not easy to manipulate the game so that the other person thinks they're winning all by themselves. I almost didn't notice. You're a brilliant Warlords player, but you want me to think you're not. You want me to underestimate you. I wonder why that is."

My heart beats faster. How does he see so much of what I am?

And how can I get past his defenses if he knows I'm coming?

CHAPTER NINE

It's decided that Max and I will travel to Kali on *Titania* while the rest of his attendants return on their own ship. I don't want my first meeting with *Titania* to be in Max's company, so Rama and I go down to the dock before the others.

She waits on her dais. She's smaller than most other warships, yet there's nothing small about her when you stand below her looking up. She's silver and beautiful and deadly, a beast with a dragon's ferocity and an arrowhead's elegance. The celestial symbols of the gods gleam along her wings. She has a quiet, otherworldly presence, like the calm before the storm.

Rama stays below while I climb nimbly onto her left wing and drop into her control room. Glass walls rise on two of the three sides, and inside are sturdy leather seats and a control panel with screens and switches. The air is cold, almost

as if *Titania*, sentient and suspicious, wants to show trespass-
ers that they're unwelcome. I shiver, but an instant later the
air grows warmer, softer. She's adjusted her atmosphere just
for me.

"Hello?" I say.

"Esmae." *Titania*'s voice is musical, pitched like a high,
clear bell. It comes from everywhere and nowhere all at once.
"You won me."

"You chose me."

"Yes. It's good to meet you at last."

"It's nice to meet you, too."

"Of course it is," she says. "I am unique, you know. It's
only natural to be fascinated."

I smile. "I am."

"Would you like a tour?"

I nod. Her voice guides me, and lamps spark on in rooms
as I enter them. I explore the controls. She shows me a
stocked supply room, a galley, four small bedrooms, weapons, emergency protocols, the maintenance logbook. Most
ships have scores of repairs and upgrades listed in their logbook, but *Titania* has just a handful.

After the tour, I return to the control room. She shows me
her communications and analysis systems, the code-cracking
software that can presumably get past almost any shield in
the universe, and a multitude of other advanced mechanisms
that I can barely understand.

"What do I do to fly you?" I ask her. She's the only sentient ship in existence, so I know very little about how she
works. "Do I just ask you to go somewhere?"

"There are manual controls if you want to use them,"
she tells me, "but I work best when I'm given an instruction

and allowed to follow it without clumsy human fingers interfering."

I laugh.

At the very end of the tour, she pulls up scans of her offensive weapons.

"You don't want to miss this part," she says, her tone edged with bitterness. "Wasn't this why I was made?"

Most ships have one launcher for rockets, laser fire, and arrowheads. *Titania* has an unprecedented five. And they have names: Righteousness, Strength, Courage, Beauty, and Patience. The gods helped King Darshan build the launchers into the ship and glorified them with pretty names.

I rub the goosebumps on my arms and flick the scans off the screen. "Is there anything in this world you couldn't destroy?"

"I doubt it," she says.

And look where I'm taking you. To a realm of warriors, led by usurpers and traitors, a king and queen who took my brother's throne for themselves. One way or another, I will keep her out of their hands.

I look out the front of the ship. The dock's oval mouth is up ahead and I can see beyond it—stars, wisps of gas, the faint shimmer of the shields. And an invisible path across the galaxy.

As I touch the controls, *Titania* whirs to life under my fingers, her engine humming beneath me like she can read my mind. She wants us to go out there together.

"Why did you choose me?" I ask her softly.

"Because our hearts are the same."

"I don't understand."

"I'm not a very bloodthirsty warship."

I give a startled laugh. "Really?"

"I was made for war, but I don't have war in my heart. It makes me joyful to fly, just as I'm sure it makes you happy when your bow feels warm in your hands, but taking pleasure in being good at what we do isn't the same as finding pleasure in using our talents against the rest of the world. I will fight if I must, but I won't enjoy it. I would rather be reading stories. Is all of that not true for you, too?"

"Is Alexi different?" It's a difficult question to ask. I've worked so hard to try and be a perfect warrior of Kali—honorable, fierce, and glorious, just like Alexi. It doesn't feel right to dig deeper into how different we truly are.

But we are different. I'm not my brother. I'm the shadow, and he's the sun.

"Yes," says Titania, "he's different. He has a good heart, but war is very much a part of him. He was born for the warrior's life. He was born for glory and bloodshed." She pauses, then adds simply, "I chose the one I hoped would end a war, not the one I knew would start one."

The competitors leave Wychstar one by one, each returning to their own realm with less good cheer than when they arrived. I watch Alexi and Bear go with an ache in my heart.

When it's time for me to say goodbye to Rama, I'm almost tempted to just stay, because I can't bear the idea of not seeing him every day. He hugs me tight, and I don't want to let go. How can I leave him behind after all the years we've stuck together?

We join Max, who is in the middle of a painstakingly polite conversation with the king. Rama steps off to the side to speak to Max, and King Darshan uses the opportunity to look me in the eye for the first time since I threw all his plans to the winds. "Good-bye, Esmae," he says, kinder than I expected. "You will always be welcome on Wychstar. I hope you know that."

"Thank you." I bite down on my lip, but the question slips out anyway. "Why did you want my brother to win?"

He turns away. "Does it matter now?"

Rama comes up behind me. "It's an old story," he says as his father leaves. "I asked Rodi. It seems a god once told Father he would get what he wanted if he built *Titania*. That's why he took that vow of silence. That's why he did all this. Because a god whispered in his ear."

"Which god? What was it your father wanted in the first place?"

And what does Alexi have to do with it?

"Rodi didn't have those answers," says Rama. "I'll have another go at pestering Father when this has all cooled down."

I suppose we'll both have to be content with this much for now. I give Rama one last hug and climb aboard *Titania*. Max is already inside the control room.

"Can you feel it?" she's asking him. "The echoes of them?"

He nods. "Yes."

I assume she means the echoes of the gods and goddesses who helped build her. I can feel them, too, in the otherworldly vibration in the air, the life force inside the ship.

Titania hums to life. I suddenly wonder if this is all a mistake. If I should stay here where the world is known and safe.

"Hold tight!" *Titania* calls.

And then she's moving and I, who have always felt steadier on ships than I ever could be on land, grab hold of the back of one of the seats and clutch it for dear life, fighting a surge of panic. We leave the dock behind and soar past the sun lamps, over the city, across the sky. We're in and out of both shields in seconds.

I whip my head back to see Wychstar grow smaller and smaller behind us until it vanishes into darkness and stars. My heart scrunches up with loss.

"She's so fast," I say, almost to myself. "It happened so fast."

Max turns to look at me. "This was an invitation, not a contract. You can go back whenever you want. Even if that means we turn back now."

"I'll do it if I must," says *Titania* in the voice of someone who is constantly forced to endure great hardships, "but I want it noted that I don't like turning 'round and 'round in circles like headless poultry."

"No." I shake my head, then turn to Max and repeat it. "No."

I walk past the seats to one of the walls of unbreakable glass. Aside from a few short trips with Rama, Radha, and their tutor, I haven't left Wychstar since I arrived as a newborn. The familiar shapes of the deep space around the spaceship kingdom—the only home I've really known—give way to new things, stars and rocks and gas clouds and moons, places I've only ever seen on video cubes or not at all.

"When will we get there?" Kali would normally be half a day's journey from Wychstar, but *Titania* is faster than most ships.

"Estimated journey time is five hours and six minutes," *Titania* says.

That *is* fast. I press my hands to the cool glass. Then I remember: I *have* seen these places before. I traveled these miles in the care of a goddess.

Time passes. I stay by the glass, transfixed by wonder and memories. Max doesn't disturb me. When I turn back a while later, he's still there, asleep, a book open across his chest. It's called *Lavya and the Thumb*, so I assume it's about Ek Lavya. He was an archer before my time who possessed such skill that he was on track to outstrip his teacher's favorite pupil. His teacher, who had promised his favorite pupil that he would make *her* the greatest archer of their time, stepped in. He asked Lavya for a gift and Lavya said he'd give anything. So his teacher asked for the thumb from his right hand. It's said he cut his thumb off without hesitation and smiled as he handed it over.

I consider Max for a moment, thinking of the way he looked at me after the Warlords game. I hate that this cruel, ruthless thief is the one who seems to see me better than almost anyone else. If only I could cut his throat now and be done with it.

"You think very loudly," he says, eyes now open.

"And what are my thoughts saying?"

"That you're not sure how to feel about me." He shrugs. "Understandable."

I open my mouth to reply, but *Titania* interrupts. "There's a distress call pulsing from coordinates not far from us. I think it's one of Kali's supply ships."

Max scrambles to the control panel. "Let me speak to them."

"—need help!" comes a crackly voice over the communications system. "They've cornered us and there's no way out. They've already destroyed one of the engines. Can anyone hear me—"

"This is Prince Max, aboard *Titania*," Max cuts in, and there's a gasp of relief on the other end of the line. "I can hear you. Tell me where you are and what's happened."

The voice gives us a location not far from our own, on a different route to Kali. "We were on the usual Tamini trade route," the voice explains, "and a fleet came out of nowhere. There must be only three ships out there, but they're warships"—there's a crack of launcher fire in the background to punctuate his point, and I flinch at the sound—"and we're just a supply ship. You know our defenses don't compare."

"What do the ships look like? What realm's coat of arms do they bear?"

The voice sounds afraid. "None, Prince Max, but we know whose ships they are."

Max sets his jaw. "I'll ask Kali to send help."

"Why?" *Titania* asks. "Kali's reinforcements won't get there in time. We will. We can help them."

"It's not up to me," says Max.

There's a pause. Oh. They're waiting for me. It hadn't hit me until now, not properly, that I'm the one who gets to decide where *Titania* goes.

"Yes," I say, "Yes, of course. Help them."

Titania immediately shifts course.

"You told me you don't want to be involved in a war," I say to her.

"I also told you I would fight if I had to."

She veers to the side, dodging an asteroid field and picking up speed. I look at Max and try not to sound as worried as I feel. "Who was that? What's happened to them?"

"Kali gets most of its daily supplies from Winter because it's by far the closest realm to us," he tells me. "You know that already, but what you may not know is that we also do a weekly run to Tamini for a few supplies that aren't easy to find on Winter. It's a relatively recent trade route. It sounds like one of the ships was attacked on their way home."

"Who would do that?"

Max just stares at me.

Alexi.

"This is what a war looks like when it isn't yet a war," Max eventually says. "Alex doesn't yet have the army he would need to take Kali back."

"And when you can't attack head on," I say, "you attack sideways. Cut supply routes, ruin infrastructure, destroy weapons so they can't be used against you later."

"Exactly." He gestures ahead of us. "What do you intend to do when we get there? *Titania* follows your orders, not mine."

I hesitate for a split second. This is my first test and it's an unexpected, ugly one. This is a fight, an actual conflict in which my uncle and my brother are facing off against each other, and if I do what Max wants, I'll be knocking Alexi back. It's the exact opposite of what I've come here to do, but they'll never trust me if I give away that I'm still on my brother's side.

"Do what you have to," I tell Max. "You're far more experienced at this than I am."

He nods, and there's a grim look on his face that makes me feel suddenly sorry for his enemies.

You're one of those enemies, Esmae.

I consider my next question carefully, then ask it as indifferently as I can: "Will my brothers be on those ships? I know they only left Wychstar a few hours ago, but—"

"No." The look on Max's face is impassive, but I wonder if he knows how relieved I am by that answer. "Your brother doesn't favor the sideways style of warfare. Honor is too important to him. So when I said the ships are Alexi's, I meant they're on his side, but I very much doubt he sent them himself. One of his generals would have done so. General Saka, if I had to guess. She's good at what she does. She knows how to win wars before they've even started."

"Two minutes to the location," *Titania* says.

My heart quickens. I move closer to the glass and look out but can only see more darkness.

"So Tamini has joined forces with Alexi," I say. Just as I expected.

Max's reply comes from behind me. "I expect they've been on his side for years, but we weren't sure until now. General Saka is one of Queen Miyo's favorite nieces, so she was always likely to back her." He pauses. "And only someone involved with supplies on Tamini could have made this attack possible."

I frown. "I don't follow."

"The warships couldn't have attacked our supply ship by accident," he explains. "We take precautions to protect the ships. All supply ships are cloaked. You can't just stumble across them even if you know the route they use. The only way to attack them is by disabling the cloak."

"Can't that only be done from inside the ship?"

"Yes, but not necessarily by a pilot. A device planted on the ship can jam the cloaking signal."

"And you think someone on Tamini had to have planted that device while they were loading the supplies."

"Yes."

I cross my arms and scrape my thumb across the opposite sleeve, back and forth, back and forth. I've spent years in training with Rickard, plotting wars in simulations, but the reality of this feels bigger and more dangerous than I'm ready for. I painstakingly planned every single move I would make to get myself to Kali to start dismantling my uncle's reign from the inside, and I pictured every facet of how Alexi would win. But now that I'm here, I'm afraid.

"There," says *Titania*.

I spin around and catch the flash of a launcher's fire from the corner of my eye. By the time Max and I both reach the glass, the flash is gone. Then there's another and another as launcher fire bursts out of the warships and strikes the failing shields of the supply ship.

It's battered and weak, a wounded dove suspended wretchedly in the air while three wolves try to tear it apart. The warships are brutish and gray. Part of the supply ship's shield is gone and at least half the ship is beyond repair; it's a miracle the control room hasn't shattered open and the pilots inside haven't been destroyed by fire or the vacuum of open space.

The harsh flash of the fire makes me want to cover my eyes, but I force myself to look. The assault on the supply ship is relentless, and I watch as the invisible shield crackles and flickers into sight each time it's struck. Most warships' shields can cope with an assault for hours, but a supply ship isn't built for such abuse. Bit by bit, the shield will break away until there's no buffer between the launcher fire and the pilots.

The attack pauses as *Titania* comes into view. The flashes fade away and the warships fix their attention on us.

Their launcher bursts to life again, only this time it comes at us. I take a step back. The world is a sunburst of brilliance and terror—

The floor trembles, but the world doesn't end. We're fine. We're completely unharmed.

Max's eyes flash. "Do whatever you need to, *Titania*."

And *Titania* obeys.

It takes just three seconds. The first is stillness, the lull before the explosion of the storm.

The second is the *boom* in the air, a vibration that rattles my teeth and makes all the hairs on the back of my neck stand on end.

The third is the blinding light that engulfs each of the three warships. I turn my head away and squeeze my eyes shut. There's no way not to recoil from that kind of light, and when I taste blood inside my mouth, I realize I must have bitten the inside of my cheek.

All goes quiet. The stark white behind my eyelids fades to darkness. It must be over.

I open my eyes. There's only a broken dove in the sky and the wolves are gone.

Gone, like they never existed.

That is the sheer power of the ship that can never be defeated.

Titania approaches the supply ship. She creates a seal between the ship's doors and our own so that the remaining supplies and the shaken survivors can board. She shifts back on course and the stars spin by again.

Max tends to the pilots in the galley. When he returns, he's alone. He hands me a cup of hot tea. I accept it because that's what you do, but my movements are as wooden as a puppet's.

"There one minute, gone the next," Max says. "I didn't know it was possible to cease to exist so fast."

Neither did I.

"I'm sorry," says *Titania*.

"Don't be," he tells her. "You were only an arrow. Someone has to draw back the bow and let the arrow loose."

He means himself, but it's exactly what I did, too. Drew back a bow and let an arrow loose. And now here we are.

I am small, I think, *an insect in a world of giants.* What can an insect possibly hope to achieve in a world like that?

But then, as Rickard would remind me if he were here, an insect can kill a giant with a bite.

The rest of the journey is uneventful, but I can't stop thinking about the destruction of the three warships. Then something miraculous wrenches me back to reality.

"Look," Max says.

I turn back to the glass. The star system flashes past us and then I see it in the distance, a shift in color that makes my pulse quicken. The dark of the galaxy bleeds away, replaced with newborn stars and gas clouds the color of fire. It's the Scarlet Nebula. And somewhere below it is the orb of the planet Winter, pale and white with seas and snow, and that means—

There it is. A speck suspended in the starry blackness beneath the nebula, growing larger and clearer as we approach. Something vast and tall and ferocious, with gleaming stone and wild forests, and sharp, spiky towers.

My breath catches. *Kali.*

CHAPTER TEN

Kali waits for me, a spaceship suspended in a sky of fire and black and stars. I press against the glass, as if I could will my body out of *Titania* and hurl myself even faster at my home.

As we get closer, what was a speck is now so big. I can't help thinking of Wychstar. Like my former kingdom, Kali is an entire civilization built on the disc-shaped surface of the base ship that keeps it powered and suspended in space. Like Wychstar, Kali has two almost invisible bubble-shaped shields around it: the outer shield, which extends about a mile away from the edge of the ship and maintains the atmosphere inside, and the inner shield, which has only half the radius and acts as a physical wall to prevent anyone from entering without permission. And like Wychstar, Kali is not as exposed to the distant sun as realms on planets are and instead uses powerful sun and moon lamps studded like stars over the cities to help re-create the days, seasons, and chemistry of their natural counterparts.

The resemblances end there. From this distance, I would have been able to see almost all of Wychstar, which plateaus across the surface of the ship. Kali is steeper and much, much bigger, sweeping upward from the wide surface of the base ship to the points of the towers of the palace, which seem to brush the stars.

We cross the outer shield. *Titania* slows, hovering, as Max broadcasts a call to the sentries. They send him a code. *Titania* keys it into her system and we're past the inner shield.

Erys, the capital city, spreads out before us. For all that Kali is a realm built on discipline, technology, and the steel of warfare, with little interest in frivolities, its creators must have had some whimsy, some fondness for enchantment. It's a fairytale realm from afar, a slice of another time, the streets paved in false cobbles and the shops raw and unpolished like cities of old. Weapons and modern conveniences and practicalities are hidden underneath all this. Air vents and temperature systems lurk under gnarled roots; thorny gardens are nurtured by chemicals to grow real fruit; tech screens and fingerprint scanners are tucked under wood and pebbles. It looks like a place where witches steal woodcutters' children from their beds, where gargoyles come to life when the nights grow dark, where headless ballerinas dance in the forests.

I drink it all in: the white dome of the University of Erys, the small starships circling above the city, the boats on streams of recycled water and the chariots on false cobbles, the fields littered with soldiers in armor like drops of moonlight.

Looming above the rest of the city are the honey-colored arches and spiky towers of the palace. Tall, austere, its balconies carved with statues of knights and chariots. *That's where my father grew up*, I think. *Where my brothers played as children. Where my mother lived and loved and grew so afraid that she sent me away.*

"Home," says Max.

I don't answer. There's a lump in my throat. *Kali*. It's perfect, and it's home, but it doesn't feel right. It won't feel right until my mother and brothers are here with me.

I think of my mother, though I've tried not to all day. While my brothers are weak points in my armor, my mother is the open wound anyone could use to destroy me. I dare think of her only in the quiet, late at night when I can cry alone and have pretend conversations with her, when I can secretly fall apart.

Now that my identity is out in the world, has she regained her memory of me? Does she remember her love for her newborn baby from seventeen years in the past? Or her grief when she had to let me go?

Or does she hate me for joining my uncle, just as my brothers probably hate me?

Now is not the time to think about her. I can't fall apart here.

As *Titania* swoops low, into a tunnel below the palace, the darkness swallows us. Max comes to stand beside me. With only the midnight tunnel outside, the glass is like a mirror and the sharp, clear lighting on the ship makes us look pale. Like silent ghosts, our reflections stare back at us.

Max is a good head taller than I am. He's full of contradictions: a steely jaw and hopeful eyes; a boyish grin and tired shoulders; kind to me, yet so cruel to my brothers.

It's time to get ready for the next step. I shut myself up in one of the bedrooms and do what I can to make myself fit for a king's court: wrinkles smoothed out of my unfortunately rather old and faded dress, loose curls schooled into order, scuff marks and dried dirt wiped off my old boots. It's the best I can do. It may be perfectly acceptable for Max to walk into the palace with his short hair messy and his shirt creased, but even his greatest critics won't dare look down their noses at him in his own court. I don't share that immunity.

The low buzz beneath my feet has stopped. I reach for the panel that will open the door, but don't press it.

"We're here," Max says just outside.

I hesitate. I expect him to tell me to hurry, to remind me that it's rude to make the king wait, but he waits patiently.

You can survive this, Esmae. You can beat them. I may be an insect in this world, but I bite.

I open the door. "I'm ready now."

"Your boots," he says, too observant. "You've wiped them. Why?"

"Why do you think?"

He's silent for a minute. "It wasn't necessary."

I look away. Max's scrutiny is too intense—inconvenient and dangerous. After a lifetime of loneliness, of invisibility, it's so tempting to allow myself to be seen, but that's exactly what I can't do.

When I don't reply, he turns and moves to the hatch. The supply ship pilots have already disembarked; I see them outside. I follow Max.

Kali's dock is larger than Wychstar's, laid out with precision, each ship in its own space and every space tagged with a number. It's beautiful to see the different shapes and sizes, the different tones of silver and chrome and gray. The clink of tools and chatter of engineers and pilots has a familiar rhythm.

As we step out of the hatch, everyone nearby looks up. Trying to pretend they're not there, I cross *Titania*'s wing and jump off the end.

A girl strides up to Max and me. She's made up of slender lines and sharp edges, a little older than I am and a couple of inches taller, with reddish hair skewered ruthlessly into a knot and a spray of freckles across her nose. She wears a sword on her back and a dagger sheathed at her waist. Her gray tunic has the Rey crest of a silver crown made of stars embroidered over the breast pocket.

"Sybilla," Max says, relieved, "I hoped it'd be you."

"Of course it's me," she replies with a snort. "I promised you I'd keep the hordes at bay. They're all pouting in the Throne Hall because I deprived them of the pleasure of seeing *Titania* as soon as she arrived."

Max grins at her, then looks at me. "Sybilla's a friend. She's in charge of palace security and is also the second commander of the Hundred and One."

The what? But this isn't the time to ask for details.

Sybilla has already cut in anyway, her eyes fixed on me. "Are you sure this is the same person who won the competition?"

He sighs. "Sybilla—"

"Not one scar," she says, studying every inch of skin not covered by my clothes. "Unmarked knees. No calluses on her hands."

"Sybilla—"

"She could be a decoy. Some kind of trap. Are we really supposed to believe a student of Rickard's escaped his training without a single scar?"

"*Sybilla,*" Max finally snaps, and she immediately falls silent.

My hand twitches towards my hair and the blueflower jewel. Amba's gift is not a part of me I'm ready to share with anyone here just yet.

"It's very nice to meet you, Sybilla." I look her straight in the eye. "I won *Titania*. Give me an arrow and I'll prove it if you like."

She considers me for a moment and then, almost reluctantly, nods. "I'll take your word for it. For now." She points behind us. "Those pilots are from our Tamini supply ship, aren't they? Why are they here and where is the ship?"

"I'll explain later," says Max. "Let's go inside."

Sybilla strides ahead of us, hard boots striking the floor. The cracked stone of the dock gives way to polished floors as we ascend into the heart of the palace. The stairways are narrow and steep, the hallways wider and without decorations. I notice the furniture everywhere is elegant, lush, and bolted in place. Wychstar is in a relatively quiet part of the star system, but Kali is much more prone to bumps and strikes from small asteroids and space debris.

As we cross stairways and bridges that arch over courtyards and gardens, we pass servants, who do comical double takes as they recognize me from the broadcast, and children, who giggle and scamper around us as though they're used to treating these parts of the palace like their very own playground. Max pauses to speak to most of them, and the smiles on their faces are unmistakably sincere.

I try not to let my surprise show. The prince so loathed across the galaxy seems to be much more popular on Kali.

"Who are the children?" I ask. I know the Rey family tree and I have plenty of distant cousins, but they're all older than the little ones I saw racing about.

"Their parents live all over Kali," Max explains. "My mother set up a school in the south wing a few years ago."

"He makes it sound so *nice*," says Sybilla, with a smile like jagged paper. "The fact of the matter is that there are families who want to be rid of their children, and they've sent them here because they know the queen won't turn them away."

"Their families don't want them? Why not?"

"Any number of reasons," says Sybilla, "Too poor to feed another mouth, difficult behavior, disabilities they don't want to deal with, you name it." She glances back at me. "You probably know as much about it as anyone. Max told us how you ended up on Wychstar. So you know what it is to be unwanted."

I blink. Amba's blueflower is no protection from that sort of attack, and it's amazing how much it hurts. I squash the urge to defend my mother, to refute it, to say *I am wanted*.

Sybilla walks a bit farther, then stops and turns around when the silence behind her becomes too oppressive to ignore. Her puzzled gaze shifts from my face to Max's furious one and back again. She blushes so red her freckles vanish. "I'm sorry."

"It's only the truth. Anyway," I add, more calmly than I feel, "it's very kind of the queen to look after them."

"She calls them her children." Sybilla says. "She calls *us* her children. I used to be one of them. All the Hundred and One were at one point."

I open my mouth, then shut it again. I didn't come here to stick my nose into her private life.

Sybilla turns a corner and stops in a pale, polished anteroom with a set of arched double doors that open at the far side. Her posture and attitude shift dramatically, becoming formal and polite. She nods at the guards posted on either side of the doors.

"Ready?" Max asks me.

I nod.

The doors open.

I clasp my hands together in front of me and count prime numbers in my head to keep myself calm.

The Throne Hall is a large room trimmed in honey and white, with a pale polished wood floor, arched roof, and white pillars that frame a wide path all the way from the double doors to a dais at the other end. Arched windows run down one side of the room and look out over the stars and snowy Winter. The room is packed with courtiers and soldiers, richly dressed, their faces in shades of cream, brown, black, and pink—a sly, curious sea pressed uncomfortably close.

The elders and prominent advisers who make up the war council have thrones of their own here, simple and austere ones set next to the dais. I see them out of the corner of my eye but don't dare look closer for fear of whom I may see sitting there. I focus, instead, on the four thrones directly in front of me. There are two carved gold ones in the middle of the dais with a simpler, smaller one on either side. My heart throbs with pain as I realize they were once intended for a king and queen and two child princes. Now only ghosts and usurpers sit there.

Both the king and queen wear blindfolds and crowns. His is the crown of the ruler, silver, cut like a wreath of knotted vines; hers is the consort's crown, silver, smaller and simpler. Elvar is a big man with a barrel chest. He adopted Max when he was about forty, and must now be at least sixty, his hair gone white and his hands slightly unsteady, but still he holds himself well, and I have to remind myself that he was once one of Rickard's students, too. Guinne is almost as tall as her husband. She's willowy and graceful, her hair still deep brown, and her face somehow simultaneously incredibly warm and incredibly cold. She looks exactly like a woman who could compassionately open her home to hundreds of unwanted children while banishing her husband's nephews from that same home.

"Max!" Elvar booms, rising. "I can't tell you how relieved we are that you've come home safely."

The queen nods in agreement, smiling gently in her son's direction. Max assures them that we were safe the whole time and gives the court a brief description of the assault on the supply ship. There's a great deal of tutting and anger and, at the end, a cheer when Max tells them how *Titania* dealt with the enemy ships. They want details about what she did and how, but Max remains stoic, almost curt, and doesn't join in the air of celebration.

When the story is done, the room's attention turns to me. There's a silence, so heavy with tension and anticipation that I feel sick. I wonder what's expected of me.

When he addresses me, Elvar's big and booming voice becomes quiet, almost tentative, like he's unsure. "Alexa?"

His tone makes my hatred falter. "I'm here, King Elvar."

"No," he says at once. "No, you mustn't call me that, my dearest, dearest niece."

I want to feel angry at what must surely be a false show of affection, but he sounds so sincere. His voice cracks in a way that I'm sure can't be faked. He takes two steps forward and stops quite close to me.

He raises a hand. "May I?"

I'm confused, then realize he wants to touch my face. His hand is quick, tracing my features with a gentleness that surprises me. I almost expected him to try to snap my neck.

"Cassel's nose," he says. Astonished, I watch a tear fall from under the blindfold, hitting the floor between us. "I never dreamed I'd come upon that nose again."

"Uncle," I hear myself say, "you have the same nose."

He chuckles. So do most of the other people in the room. "So I do, so I do. Forgive me, I'm in a sentimental mood." He steps back. "I'm very happy you're here."

"I'm happy to be here, Uncle."

He beams benevolently at me. "Ah, but you must be impatient to greet your beloved teacher. Don't let me keep you!"

My heart stutters, but I finally dare to look around the room. At the other set of thrones. And there, with the elders and the war council of Kali, sits a tall, weary man.

He looks so ordinary, always a shock given his reputation. He's old. No one knows how old; some say the gods once granted him a boon that froze him in time, but he always chuckled when I mentioned that little piece of gossip to him. He has broad shoulders that taper down into a body that's like an oak, ancient and unbowed, and his cropped beard and hair are gray. His skin is a deep rich black, scars knot his throat and hands from an old battle with a *raksha* demon, and his eyes are warm and full of kindness.

You will always have a place in my heart, he had said.

Rickard stands, then approaches me, and for an instant I'm so terrified of what he'll say that I can't breathe. He will never forgive what I did.

But his face splits into a smile filled with so much plea-sure there's no question that he means it, and I understand that a lack of forgiveness doesn't mean he loves me any less.

He holds out his hands. "Esmae," he says, his voice deep and low, and wrapped in my name are all the tender endearments that he doesn't say out loud. "Welcome to Kali. Welcome home."

I burst into tears and throw myself into his arms.

CHAPTER ELEVEN

The queen insists on seeing me to my suite of rooms herself. A guard escorts us across an arched honey-colored bridge and into a tower but keeps a discreet few steps behind. I'm curious to see if the queen will use this opportunity to put me in my place and remind me which side of the family tree rules Kali these days.

Instead, she talks animatedly to me the whole way about the palace, and how I should make myself at home, and what I might do to keep myself occupied if I so wish. She points out rooms she can't see, paintings of Rey ancestors and beautiful balconies that overlook the spiky rooftops of Erys. She tells me the family eats in a private banquet room and of course I must join them because I'm family. She asks me with genuine interest about my childhood in Wychstar. She has a calm, pleasant voice and is expressive with her hands.

I watch her covertly. She hasn't used her sight in almost thirty years and has obviously grown so accustomed to it that she has found other ways to get by; she knows the palace so well that she doesn't use a cane or falter as she walks, and she frequently cocks her head to one side as if she relies on her ears to do some of her eyes' work.

They tell the story of Guinne Rey and her blindfold on Wychstar. Apparently, when she fell in love with Elvar, she swore she would wear a blindfold for the rest of his life. "If he can't see beauty or ugliness in the world," she said, "I choose not to, either." He tried to talk her out of it, but she had no intention of allowing anyone to sway her. The story then says that when she had duly worn the blindfold for fifteen years, the gods were so impressed by her strong will that they granted her a boon. No one knows what she asked for or if she has even used it yet.

Rama and I talked about her once. "I wouldn't have done it if I were her," he had said. "I'm sure it was supposed to be a very romantic gesture and all that, but I'm not impressed."

"Which is not in any way a shock to me," I replied, "You're about as romantic as an onion."

"A valid point, but that's not what I meant. Choosing to live with a blindfold seems like a kick in the teeth to the blind people who would probably prefer to be able to see. And wouldn't it have made political sense for at least one of them to be able to keep an eye out for their enemies?"

"I agree," I said, "but don't you think she had every right to do what she wanted with her own body? Her eyes, her choice."

"She may regret it now," he replied. "They don't feel safe, you know, she and King Elvar. Father uses the word *jumpy* when he talks about them."

I push the memory aside as the queen comes to a stop before a set of doors. She turns the knob and the scent of lavender escapes from inside the suite.

"These will be your rooms," says Guinne. "I'm sure you must feel overwhelmed, so I'll leave you to rest. Please do let us know if there's anything we can do to make you more comfortable." She takes my hands in hers and gives me an unmistakably genuine smile. "We're truly glad you're here, my dear."

I kept silent in the Throne Hall when Elvar said as much, but this time I can't help myself. "Are you glad because you were afraid I would join my brother?"

The guard behind us makes a choked sound. Guinne's calm, on the other hand, remains unimpaired. "Of course I was afraid of that," she says. "It would be absurd not to be. I am, however, also glad you've come to us for less selfish reasons. I think you'll be happy here."

I open my mouth to reply, but she hasn't finished. "They didn't want you, Alexa. We do."

She releases my hands and walks away. Such kindness, such warmth, and yet I know what she's capable of. What they're *all* capable of.

I enter my suite of rooms and press the panel to shut and lock the door. I let out a breath, incredibly relieved to be free of curious, suspicious eyes.

"There you are!"

I shriek.

"What a sweet, melodious sound," Rama remarks.

The outer room is a simple but rich space occupied by cream sofas with emerald cushions, a pale green rug, and a white desk. There's a tech screen perched neatly on top of the desk and that's where I find Rama, his face grinning out at me.

He waves. "Max gave me the code to your suite." So now he calls him *Max*. An abrupt shift from just earlier today when it was *thief prince*. "Where have you been? I've been waiting at least twenty minutes."

I smile so wide, my cheeks hurt. "Has it only been a few hours since I last saw you? I've never been so happy to see anyone in my life."

"That's only to be expected. This face is, after all, a masterpiece of aesthetics."

I laugh, but it comes out sounding more like a sob. "Just come visit me soon."

He pauses. Frowns. "Are you safe? Have they threatened you? You can come back—"

"No, it's the opposite. No one's given me any reason to be afraid, not even Elvar. They've all been kind to me."

"Is that bad?"

My dearest, dearest niece.

They didn't want you, Alexa. We do.

"No," I say doubtfully, "Not bad. Just odd."

It's the sincerity that bothers me. I expected kindness, the slimy kindness and flattery that people resort to when they expect something in return, but I can't shake the uncomfortable feeling that Elvar and Guinne are sincere.

"I expected them to act like enemies. I didn't expect to be literally welcomed with open arms."

Rama pokes the screen the same way he would poke my nose if he were actually with me. "Give it more than a few hours, Ez. It may turn out exactly as you expected."

CHAPTER TWELVE

A bell sounds for dinner. When I open my door, Sybilla is there, her hand up as though she'd been about to knock.

"Good, you're ready," she says.

I'm not put off by her brusqueness. "Sorry," I reply, aware that someone who handles palace security can't possibly have much spare time. "I didn't know they'd ask you to escort me—"

"It's not a problem. I'm coming to dinner, too. Even if I weren't, part of my job is to keep you safe, and that will probably be easiest if I stay close. I suppose that sounds absurd to you. After all, you're you. You could probably protect *me* if we found ourselves in a pickle."

"Do I need protection?" I ask. It's not exactly a surprise. "Does someone not want me here?"

Sybilla gives a shrug. "No one is universally popular," she says before pointing to the left. "The family banquet room is this way, Princess."

"Esmae."

"Princess."

"I'll break you eventually," I mutter.

She doesn't reply, but I spot the briefest hint of a smile.

Family mealtimes appear to be lavish affairs. The table is strewn with dishes, roasted roots and steamed fish with lime and chilies, peppered crab and lamb skewers in the Wych-smoked style, buttered beans and spicy lamb stew and fluffy white rice topped with feathers of steam. A gorgeous dessert selection of berries in chocolate and rich plum cakes and gooseberry tarts has been drenched in honey and wine.

My eyes pop. I think of the little ones at the Wych children's sanctuary, and my chest tightens with guilt; I'm here while they'll never have a feast like this.

The king, queen and Rickard are already in the room, along with a sleek, wiry man probably in his forties.

"Who is he?" I whisper to Sybilla.

"The queen's brother, Lord Selwyn." There's thinly veiled dislike in her tone. "He's on the war council. He's very close to the king and queen."

When we're introduced, Lord Selwyn's voice is like warmed honey, but I don't trust it. It takes me a minute to work out why. It's not just the hostility in his eyes or the fact that his is exactly the kind of slimy friendliness I had been prepared for; it's the way he shifts when the king shifts, moves when he moves, folds himself into the spaces closest to him like a shadow. It's not protective, it's *possessive*.

I move away from him and count the number of places set at the table. Max isn't here yet, but there's also one other person missing. Someone offers me spiced wine and I grip my glass tight, too uneasy to relax, and I notice that Sybilla keeps shifting from foot to foot like she wishes she were anywhere but here. It's this shared discomfort, perhaps, that sees us edge closer and closer together until we're tucked in a corner next to one of the guards.

He's scarcely more than a boy, this guard. He has bright brown eyes, and beigey gold skin, and he starts to chatter as soon as we get close to him. Sybilla allows it. His name is Jemsy. He's eighteen and he's under Sybilla's command, as are his younger brother, Henry, and their even younger sister, Juniper.

Jemsy elbows Sybilla in the ribs, and she glances around the room to make sure no one's watching before jabbing him back. "I'm surprised you're here, Sybs," he says. I'm amazed that anyone is allowed to get away with calling her *Sybs*, and the ferocious look on her face suggests she'd quite like to punch him, but she refrains. Jemsy turns to me. "Sybilla has been invited to family dinners for years, but I can count on one hand the number she's actually come to."

"Why not?" I ask.

"She's not one for social niceties," says Jemsy, earning another jab in the ribs.

A plate of lamb skewers appears before us. I reach for one, and the scent—the combination of succulent lamb and smoky, peppery ovens—takes me abruptly back to Wychstar. The sensation is bittersweet. It's not just about the loss of specific things, like Rama's lazy grin and the feel of the coarse dish soap at the children's sanctuary and the rumble of the elevators skating up and down their shafts; it's the loss of the *known*. Wychstar was predictable, the days carved into a pattern I could foresee. It was order and symmetry. Kali—disciplined, steely Kali—may as well be chaos, the numbers all askew, every variable an unknown.

Sybilla and Jemsy are still talking. When they mention the Hundred and One, I take the opportunity to ask about it.

"Who are the Hundred and One?"

"Max's force." Jemsy beams with so much pride, it's hard not to smile back. "Handpicked warriors, the best and brightest of the younger generation."

"Stop boasting," Sybilla snaps. "We have a long way to go. The faction is quite new; we've only been training for five years."

"We'll be at the heart of the fleet if Kali goes to war," Jemsy adds. "In the meantime, we train, we double up as guards and protectors, and we assist the sentries out by the shields." His eyes widen with sudden excitement. "You could join us, Princess! We could become the Hundred and Two."

I try not to look appalled at the idea of fighting for Elvar. "Thank you, but I don't think I'd be of any use to you."

"What?" He's incredulous. "How could you not be? You were one of Rickard's students! None of us have ever had even a single lesson with him, not even the prince—"

Sybilla's annoyed now. "Stop it. She didn't come here to be pestered."

Jemsy's words niggle at me. They make me think unexpectedly of a small boy in a palace, a thief prince years before he did anything wrong, and how he must have felt watching Alexi and Bear go off to learn from Rickard while he was excluded. What had Max said to me? *I know what it is to feel like you're never going to be enough.* And then later, *you of all people know how it feels to spend your life watching someone else get everything while you get nothing.*

A heartbeat, and then it's gone, the unhappy vision blinked away, the unwelcome feeling of kinship erased.

The guard at the other end of the room clears his throat. Jemsy gives us a quick, sheepish grin and returns to his spot in the corner.

"I'm not one of Rickard's students anymore," I tell Sybilla. "I know he must still go see Alexi and Bear to continue their lessons, but he hasn't come to see me in nearly two years."

"He does still visit them. Twice a week. Why doesn't he do the same for you?"

"I wasn't a suitable student," is all I feel able to say. She stares at me but doesn't push. I almost laugh. I envisioned Max as an envious child, but I'm just as full of envy. I'd give almost anything to be one of Rickard's students again.

When the silence between us stretches uncomfortably long, I ask, "Do the Hundred and One really have to be at the heart of a war? Aren't there more experienced factions already prepared for battle?"

"Yes, but their numbers aren't what the king would like them to be. The queen first suggested the fleets needed new blood. A lot of the older soldiers have either retired, or are too old to be of any use in the field should we go to war, or—"

She stops abruptly, looking uncomfortable.

I frown. "Or?"

"Or," Max says from behind me, "they left to join Alexi."

"Oh."

"Leila Saka, for example. She was once one of our best, but she's your mother's oldest friend and she chose their side over ours." He smiles slightly, ruefully. "Rickard was your brothers' teacher, but who do you think was mine?"

"You were taught by General Saka?"

"Yes."

They barely even looked at each other on Wychstar; I never would have thought they'd once been close. I can't imagine how much hurt and anger and betrayal must have lurked under their silence. A teacher and her student, each betrayed by the other, standing on opposite sides.

A movement to Max's left catches my eye, and I look over to see that an elderly lady had entered the room with him. Elvar goes to greet her. She's older than almost anyone I've ever seen, small and bent like a hook, leaning heavily on her stick. Her eyes flash blue, sharp, and clever.

Max notices where my attention has gone. "I promised Grandmother I'd escort her to dinner."

"I didn't know you had any surviving grandparents."

"I don't. She's my *great*-grandmother. And yours, as it happens. Everyone here calls her Grandmother."

I look at the old lady with renewed interest. We have only one great-grandparent left, Elvar's grandmother Cassela. My father was named after her. She was Queen Consort to the King of Kali until he died. Her eldest child was my grandmother, Queen Vanya.

The old woman turns then and her eyes settle on my face. Something in her expression sends a shiver down my spine. I take a step back and my back collides with Max's chest.

He steadies me. "What's the matter?"

Instinct tells me to flee, but it's too late. I find myself trying to back away even more, but there's only so far I can go with Max right behind me.

"So this is the girl. The one Kyra tried to get rid of." The old queen's voice is loud and pointy, like the end of a sword, and it makes everyone turn in our direction.

"Let's not talk about that tonight, Cassela," Rickard says. It sounds more like a command than a request.

She flaps one of her gnarled hands to silence him, then takes one of mine between both of her own. "I'm sorry," she says curtly. "You were an innocent and did not deserve to be punished by the curse. I didn't expect Kyra to try to rid herself of you, but I should have. It's always the way, isn't it? They say the god Ness was told his child would one day kill him, so he tried to swallow all his children to prevent the prophecy from coming true, and consequently forced his daughter to fight back. His desperate quest to sidestep the prophecy made it come to pass, just as your mother tried to sidestep her curse and has only ended up setting you against her. I'm not sorry for any pain she has known, but *you* did not deserve to bear the brunt of it."

"Grandmother." Elvar finally finds a space to interrupt. "What are you talking about?"

She tuts, like the answer should be obvious. "It was I who cursed Kyra, of course. I am the reason she sent this child away."

"You? Why would you do such a thing?"

"Why wouldn't I?" she says. "She killed my daughter."

CHAPTER THIRTEEN

I wrench my hands out of the old queen's, but she's nowhere near finished. "Let me tell you what the goddess Amba told me." In spite of the horrified looks on the faces around her, she continues. "There was once an adventurous, ambitious young girl named Kyra. She swam deep into the seas of the Empty Moon to find the blueflower, a bloom so perfect that even gods are entranced by its beauty."

These are Amba's words, the same ones she used when she first told *me* this story.

"The girl offered the flower to the goddess Amba, and Amba, who appreciated the beauty of the flower and was impressed by Kyra's courage, gave her something in return. 'Three times, I will come to your aid,' she said. 'Three times, I will grant you a wish. Choose wisely.'"

No one seems to know what to say.

The old queen looks hard at me. "Well, great-granddaughter? What comes next?"

And I find myself answering. "To seal her promise, the goddess gave the girl a single petal from the blueflower."

No one in this room can possibly understand the significance of that detail, of course. None of them know that petal became the jewel pinned in my hair as we speak.

"Some years later," I continue, "Kyra made her first wish. It had consequences she didn't intend, and she was cursed for those consequences."

The old queen gives a sharp bark of mirth. "That was it, was it?" she crows. "Amba didn't tell you the truth."

"She didn't tell me it was you who cursed us, no."

"She didn't tell you why I did it, either, I suppose." Her eyes needle into mine, shrewd yet unexpectedly full of pity. "What did she say about your mother?"

I repeat what I explained to Alexi and Bear earlier. "Amba said that the curse said I would destroy my family. My mother sent me away so we would all be safe. It broke her heart, but she believed it would only be until I was old enough to understand the curse and then I could subvert it. Amba erased my parents' memories so they wouldn't be tempted to look for me too early."

The old queen looks around the silent room, then nods her head. "Not very Kyra, is it?"

"I suppose she could have done that," Guinne says, though her voice is threaded with doubt.

"She didn't," says the old queen, "because that's not how it happened. It would seem Amba went out of her way to spare your feelings, child. Let me tell you what she told *me*. Kyra fell in love with a boy named Cassel. He was heir to the throne of Kali, and his mother, the queen, wanted him to marry a princess from another realm. Dismayed, Kyra impulsively wished she could marry the prince instead."

Guinne frowns. "She wished that? Exactly that? She didn't try to word it more carefully?"

"She didn't think to," says the old queen grimly, "and so Amba granted her wish. Queen Vanya died that very day."

I pale. "But gods can't hurt mortals without becoming mortal themselves! Amba couldn't have killed her."

"She didn't have to. All she had to do was give Kyra an idea, and let Kyra act on it if she chose to. And Kyra did. In all the time she'd spent on her youthful adventures, she'd picked up a few unusual skills and she knew just how to meddle with elevator mechanics to ensure that the elevator in question would malfunction. And it did. With Vanya inside."

I open my mouth but no words come out.

"To be fair to Kyra," the old queen continues, "Vanya wasn't supposed to die. When the elevator mechanics went awry, Kyra had intended to arrive on the scene as if by pure coincidence, activate the emergency brake, and save her. Amba had told Kyra that if she saved Vanya, the queen would be so grateful, she would grant Kyra any favor." Cassela sighs, an old, sad sound. It must be so painful for her to talk about the death of her own child like this. "What neither Amba nor Kyra knew was that the emergency brake on that particular elevator was unreliable. She pressed the button, but it stuck. She had to press it again, and by then it was too late. The brake didn't catch in time."

"An accident," says Elvar softly. "That's what the engineers called it. No one realized."

"Cassel became king and Kyra became his wife," the old queen says. "Kyra's conscience would not let her rest easy, much as it will surprise some of you to hear she has one. She came to me and confessed the truth. She hoped I would grant her absolution." Cassela snorts. "I did not. You know how they say that the gods' favorites can wreak havoc with just a few words? I am one such favorite. And I wreaked havoc. 'Your selfish desires brought destruction to my daughter's door,' I said, 'and so I curse you to a future in which your daughter will bring the same to yours.'"

"Cassela, how could you?" Rickard demands. "You didn't just curse Kyra. You cursed a child who had done nothing to deserve it!"

"As I said," the old queen replies, with a hint of what could be shame, "I'm sorry. I, too, was careless with my words." She turns to me. "When she gave birth two years later, Kyra bore twins. First came a boy, perfect and loved, and then a girl, who filled Kyra with terror. Amba let you believe she was heartbroken to part with you, but the truth is, she wanted only to protect her son. As soon as Cassel left the room, she snatched you up and put you in a sealed boat and jettisoned you out into the darkness of space."

"She didn't do that!" I protest. "She gave me to Amba, and asked her to take me somewhere safe."

"She put you in a sealed boat," the old queen says again, gently this time. There's too much pity on her face.

"Kyra shipped her away in a pod?" Elvar demands. "A newborn baby? How did she expect the child to survive?"

The silence hurts my ears.

"She didn't," I say, my tone numb. "My mother didn't expect me to survive."

Splinters cut into my heart. I don't want to believe the old queen's words, but I do. Because her story fills in the gaps. It answers questions I never dared to ask, afraid of how much the truth would hurt. Why would you send your daughter away only to reunite with her later? It never made sense that she wanted me to find a way around the curse when I was older. Why not, instead, keep me close and teach me about the curse early on so that we could be careful yet still stay together?

So many questions I didn't want to ask, but now I have the answers all the same.

I've loved her all my life, and she wanted me dead.

"She was not quite so cold as that in the end," the old queen tells me. "There was little chance that the child in the boat would survive, but Kyra regretted her rash act, and she called upon Amba a second time. 'Let her live,' Kyra prayed. As before, she did not choose her words well. What she should have said was: *Let her live, but let her live a life that will never allow her to enact the curse upon me.*" Cassela shrugs one shoulder. "She did not say that. And, as before, Amba granted Kyra her wish."

Let her live, my mother had said. And as far as my mother knows, I'm now the exact enemy she feared. *Let her live*. And so Amba took her at her word and did just that. She let me live so that I could grow up and take a warship away from my brother. She gave me a blueflower jewel that would let me live no matter who tried to cut me down. *Let her live*. My mother couldn't have had the faintest idea what would result from that wish. If she had, perhaps she wouldn't have made it. Perhaps she wouldn't have shown what little mercy she did.

The silence in the dining room is absolute, broken only when Cassela, herself, hobbles across to the table and drops unceremoniously into a chair.

"Well?" she asks. "Are we going to eat or not?"

So my mother cast me adrift. And before that, she killed a queen. And the person who cursed her for it was my own great-grandmother.

I spent my entire childhood wanting a family, and *this* is the one I got. The gods have a twisted sense of humor.

I want to flee, but I stand my ground. Why should I feel embarrassed or ashamed? I didn't make any poorly worded wishes. I didn't curse anyone. Like *Titania* earlier today, I was just the tool someone used to try and destroy someone else. I was the arrow, the old queen the archer.

No, that's not quite true. Grandmother may have turned me into an arrow, but I took back control the day I asked Rickard to train me. I took back control when I competed for *Titania. I* did that. No one made that choice for me.

And that choice is why I'm here. I refuse to flee.

Dinner is a stilted, awkward affair. My appetite is gone. And Lord Selwyn, the queen's brother and the king's shadow, uses the opportunity to ask me a series of questions obviously intended to catch me out in a lie. I expected to be treated with suspicion, and had prepared for it, but I'm too tired to guard myself well.

In the end, what makes me snap is not the questions, themselves, but Lord Selwyn's use of my name–*Alexa*. The name I wanted to claim so badly, the name so like my brother's, the name my mother gave me, the name that now hurts.

"Lord Selwyn, would it be too much to ask that you call me Esmae? I find my given name quite unbearable after Grandmother's story."

Lord Selwyn raises his eyebrows. "How I envy your blissful certainty that one can so easily discard a name, dear princess."

"And why can't she discard it if she wishes to?" Sybilla asks. "Why should Esmae Rey be any less suitable than Alexa Rey?"

"Ez-may." The old queen overemphasizes the syllables with the expression of someone picking up a dirty handkerchief. "I'm not sure it's a name for a Rey. Mind you, nothing can be worse than Abra. Kyra's family name! She gave birth to a second son and named him after her own family! We can only be thankful he goes by Bear, which does not exactly scream royalty but at least is not *her* name."

"Bear's name is irrelevant, Cassela," says Rickard, "And I see no reason why Esmae can't be a good name for a Rey."

"What does it *mean*?" she presses. "For Alexa, you know, means *protector*. As does Alexi, for that matter. Both are excellent names."

I've always assumed Madam Li picked my name at random when I was taken to her as a baby. I never bothered to find out what it means. It was supposed to be temporary, a placeholder until the day I could proudly claim the name Alexa Rey.

Max is the one who answers. "It means *beloved*."

"That is hardly suitable," Cassela complains. "*Beloved* is not a good name for someone who will one day be queen of Kali."

The entire table pauses, a theater tableau of half-raised forks and glasses poised at lips and widened eyes. Lord Selwyn's teeth snap together like this has only confirmed his belief that I am a viper in their nest. Rickard gives me a look of profound pity.

Very stiffly, I say, "I'm afraid I fail to see how my ascension to the throne is inevitable, Grandmother. Surely Max's children will inherit after him?"

"And who will inherit if Max dies before he has any children?" Lord Selwyn asks. "You will, dear princess, as the only

Rey left on Kali. It would be only natural to consider that an attractive possibility."

"Esmae doesn't share your sense of ambition, Selwyn," Rickard says, his voice dry as dust. "What *you* consider an attractive possibility is unlikely to be so to her."

Rickard's statement eases some of the tension, but it's already too late: I see the fleeting doubt on some of their faces, the suspicion, there and gone again. Elvar and Guinne twitch their heads in my direction. *Jumpy.* That's what Rama said his father used to call them. I don't think they're seriously wondering if I intend to assassinate Max, but Selwyn has let the idea creep across the table like poisonous smoke, and it's only a matter of time before someone breathes it in.

I glance at Max to see how he's taking the idea that I would murder him for his crown. He looks somewhat amused.

"No one's talking about Max *dying*," Cassela says irritably, jabbing a piece of lamb with her fork. "I was referring to the fact that the line of succession is by no means decided as yet. We don't yet know for certain that Max will inherit the throne when Elvar dies. Elvar could name Alexa his heir instead."

My mouth falls open. Is that even possible?

Lord Selwyn is even more aghast. "Absurd!" he snaps. "The king would never disinherit his own son."

Cassela scoffs. "Why not? It wouldn't be the first time a ruler made that choice."

"And I am not the king's own son, anyway," Max points out. He doesn't look amused anymore.

That statement just seems ridiculous to me, but neither Elvar nor Guinne argues.

"I'm curious," Lord Selwyn says coldly, "was the princess invited to Kali just so she could replace my nephew?"

Max opens his mouth, but I reply first, just as coldly. "Why should it matter who is named heir? Alexi was my father's heir, yet you may have noticed he is not king. Clearly, the line of succession is utterly irrelevant on Kali these days."

Lord Selwyn's smile shows teeth. "Those are rash and poorly considered words, princess, and you may wish to take them back."

"I see no reason to take back words that are merely facts. Alexi was my father's heir. Alexi is not king. What part of either of those statements is untrue?"

I regret the words as soon as I see the way Lord Selwyn's knuckles go white around the stem of his glass. "I will not be spoken to with such insolence," he snaps. "This is not Wychstar."

Out of the corner of my eye, I see Max fix his father with a look so intent that I'd swear Elvar can feel it. The king's voice cuts across the table. "That will do, Selwyn. As king, I think *I* am better suited to decide what behavior will or will not be tolerated. Let us leave it at that."

Guinne tries to steer the conversation away, but then there's a rumble in the distance, and it grows like thunder until the glasses clink and the silverware rattles noisily on the table. Sauce sloshes over the side of a bowl and splashes the snowy tablecloth, a spreading stain that looks like blood.

Anxious, I glance at Rickard for reassurance. He gives me a small smile. "It's just a rock assault. Nothing to worry about."

I had no idea they were this intense. I whip my head around to the window, but the skies look calm. No space debris, no asteroids. The rock must have struck us on the other side of the ship.

The room trembles and my muscles tense. It's a brief disturbance, hardly even a minute long, but in that minute, it feels like the asteroid may just tear the base ship apart.

I almost wish it would.

CHAPTER FOURTEEN

I wake just after the sun lamps spill dawn into my suite and dress quickly. If Lord Selwyn is even half as determined to send me back to Wychstar as I suspect he is, today may be the only chance I ever get to see Kali.

It's early, but the palace is already thrumming with activity. The base ship vibrates far below us and the austere, honey-colored hallways are filled with footsteps, the clink of dishes, a multitude of different voices. Servants curtsy to me as I pass them, an odd experience I don't think I'll ever get used to, and every guard I encounter asks me if I need an escort.

I stop at a balcony to look out at the city. The Scarlet Nebula is a stain far beyond the shields. Small ships dart to and fro, on patrol or on a trade mission. The streets below twist and turn, busy with shopkeepers and armorers and traders. Crooked, copper-colored chimneys spit coils of smoke that curl up and are sucked away into the base ship's flues. The sweet, spicy scent of Kali's traditional berry wine drifts across the crisp, recycled air. Every now and then, an electronic voice crackles mildly over ever-present speakers, summing up the population's use of resources: *Kali is currently at 85 percent human capacity. Water pressure will be reduced by 1 percent for the next two hours.*

I watch silver specks working at battle formations on a distant training field: the Golden Lotus; the Dove's Kiss; the Embrace—all oddly beautiful names for such sharp, disciplined movements, all so familiar from my own lessons with Rickard. Two small warships face off above the field's soldiers, their armed warriors leaping clumsily from one wing to the next as they learn how to battle in the air. Wing war is as popular on Kali as it is on Wychstar for obvious reasons; Rickard spent much of our time training me in it.

I watch the ships wistfully. I don't miss the swordplay much, but there was beauty and exhilaration in racing across a flying ship. I miss the precarious dance from wing to wing.

Time to move on.

The palace, itself, is immense, but I explore as much as I can without attracting too much attention: the kitchens, the dock, the dice rooms, the banquet halls, the weapons room. I breathe in the leather and metal and fire of the weapons room. I watch the dice players win and lose money, property, even loyalty. I lose myself for over an hour in the library, in the pages of books on mythology and politics and glorious adventures.

I try very hard to not think about my mother.

Eventually, I find myself in front of the gods' altar in the conservatory. A simple, ancient column, made of the smoothest and darkest marble, the altar is inscribed with the two hundred and nine names of the major gods. The room is domed, glass-roofed, and exposed to the stars, and there's the usual wooden bowl in front of the altar for offerings. It's a beautiful place.

I didn't think to come with milk and honey, but I could make a different offering. I check myself: tights, tunic dress, leather vambraces, and just the one pocket in all of that with only a scrap of creased paper inside it. I smooth the slip open and turn it over. I must have scribbled the first half of a geometric equation on it at some point, because all that's left is a few inky numbers faded from a wash. It'll do.

Each of the gods' symbols has been carved into the floor across the conservatory. My eyes fall on the wolf symbol of Valin, mostly because it looks like a careless child has scratched over it with a knife, but he's a god of wisdom and choices and that seems fitting for the circumstances. I don't think I've ever met him, but he's always portrayed in paintings and books as a knight with a sword on his back and one of the deadly hounds of the Empty Moon crouched loyally at his side.

I smooth the creases out of the paper and fold it into the shape of a hound before placing it in the offering bowl.

"Valin?" My voice is hardly more than a whisper, but it's audible; you have to say their names out loud to get their attention. "I don't know what to do. I may not have much time here. And my mother—"

"He can't answer you."

I spin around. Max stands in the conservatory doorway. His eyes are fixed on the offering in the bowl and there's a funny look on his face.

My own fills with heat. "I didn't know you were there. How much did you hear?"

"Most of it," he admits. "Why do you feel like you may not have much time here?"

"I expect your uncle to try to send me back to Wychstar. You may have noticed he doesn't like me much."

"He can *try* sending you anywhere he likes. And he'll fail. It's not his decision to make."

I wonder if Max means it, but I don't press the issue. Pointing to the wooden bowl, I ask, "Why are you so sure Valin won't answer me? Only the gods decide who they answer."

Max shakes his head. "I didn't say he won't answer you. I said he *can't*. He's gone."

"He's dead?"

"About a hundred years ago. Didn't you know?"

"No." I give the altar a rather bitter look. "Well, that's typical. I ask a god for help and it turns out he doesn't even exist anymore."

Max fixes his gaze on the clumsy, creased paper hound in the bowl. "What did you hope he could do for you?"

I shrug. It's not a matter I intend to talk to him about. Instead, I ask a question that's bothered me since yesterday: "Did you try to kill Alexi?"

He frowns. "What?"

"I overheard General Saka and Alexi talking yesterday. They mentioned a fire."

Max pauses and then says, "When we exiled Kyra and your brothers, we sent them to a house in one of Winter's cities. We had it built for them. It was supposed to be a safe place, somewhere they could make new lives for themselves." He scrubs a hand over his jaw. "There was a fire about a year after they arrived. They got out just in time."

"But?"

"But Leila Saka is obviously convinced the house was a trap and the fire was my attempt to murder Alex and Bear."

"Was it?"

Max gives me a long, silent look that makes me feel like I've made a mistake. "You ask an awful lot of questions for someone who only wanted to come home," he says before walking away.

I've only just left the conservatory when Rickard finds me.

I want to turn and run when I see him, partly because I don't know if someone's sent him to chase me down, and partly because this is the first time we've been completely alone since that terrible day on Wychstar and I don't know how to address it.

He smiles, and I return it cautiously. It's not the same between us, and I don't think it ever will be, but I'm glad for even this much.

"There you are," he says.

"Am I wanted?"

"Elvar and Guinne have organized a procession for later this afternoon. They want the people of Erys to see you." Rickard's eyes twinkle. "I have, however, been asked to inform you that you may refuse to participate, and no one will hold it against you."

"Do you think I should do it?"

"I don't think you should be paraded about, but part of royal life is getting to know the people your family rules. If you want to claim the space you would have occupied if Kyra had never sent you away, you'll need to attend events like these." He glances around us to make sure no one is nearby, then adds, "And between you and me, Elvar is desperate for the stability your presence could give him."

"Me?"

"He has supporters, but he's afraid Alexi has more. You are Alexi's sister and Cassel's second child. Elvar and the war council hope that your public acceptance of his rule will help legitimize him."

I study Rickard's face, but it's impassive. I asked him once how he could serve my uncle after what he'd done. "Maybe if you had threatened to leave with Alexi and Bear," I had said, "Elvar would have let them stay, rather than risk losing you."

"My loyalty is to Kali," he told me back then, "not to the man or woman who rules it. My family is in Kali. My heart is in Kali. And you must remember, Esmae, that Elvar was once one of my students, too. I knew him when he was just a hurt, hopeful boy who wanted nothing more than to prove he was worthy of his family name. You of all people should understand how that feels. Loyalty is not as black and white as you think."

I want so badly to know how Rickard feels about the current situation. What he really thinks of me. Is he glad I'm here? Or is he disappointed in me for stealing *Titania* away from my own brother?

His tone softens. "I know you've dreamed of Kali, Esmae. I remember the girl I met in a market years ago. You were a brave, lonely child with a hungry heart and enormous dreams. You have one of those dreams in your hands now. You're here. And if you want to stay, you'd do well to win yourself Elvar's trust and goodwill."

I wish I could tell him Elvar's trust and goodwill are exactly what I want and that I intend to use them against him. Instead, I say, "I'll join the procession."

"Good." He offers me his arm. "It's not until after midday, so come, let me show you around the palace. What have you seen already?"

He guides me expertly around the maze of hallways and bridges. The city stretching beyond us is noisy and efficient, the rhythm of machines and chariots and voices like clockwork. It's very different from the cacophonous collision of noises on Wychstar; this rhythm is smoother, ordered, like musical notes: a machine's click and whir; a chariot's rumble; voices calling names in order; a machine's click and whir; a chariot's rumble; a servant calling another; and so on.

Rickard introduces me to courtiers and servants. He takes me to a private parlor decorated with emerald curtains and shows me the maps and battle plans hung along the wall. He takes me to the sentries' headquarters housed in one of the spiky towers to meet their chief. He takes me to meet the smith downstairs, and she puts my measurements into her printer to make me my own armor.

I've noticed that the soldiers around the palace wear very little armor. Their uniforms are simple, dark gray shirts or tunics with fitted dark gray trousers and flat, sturdy boots on their feet. Archers wear quivers on their backs. Soldiers, a vest of light, almost liquid chain mail, and vambraces of the same nearly weightless, nearly impenetrable material. Kali's army is a smooth, disciplined one, known across the realm for its loyalty to the king's word. It's said that when its soldiers move in formation, they look like moonlight reflected off the sea. It's true.

They say Alexi's armor is a pale gold these days, setting him a small but pointed distance away from the silver of Kali's fleets.

The smith's workshop is a noisy, clanking, beautiful mixture of the old and new: axes beside lasers, designs for swords sketched onto tech screens, hot forged steel works combined with the products of printing machines.

My vest and vambraces take shape in the printer, glossy and fluid and silver. The smith smiles at me. "They'll need another hour or so to finish," she says and points at my watch. "I'll send you a comm when they're ready."

I leave reluctantly; I wanted to watch them being made. Rickard chuckles at my disappointment, then takes me to an elevator and down several floors to a set of hallways that have a shinier, steelier look than the austere beauty of the rest of the palace.

"Simulation rooms," Rickard explains, stopping at a glass door so that I can see the enormous white chamber and controls inside. "They're exactly like the ones we used on Wychstar."

And I don't plan on stepping inside any of these. I didn't come here to train or to fight. Part of the reason I chose to come here to find my uncle's weaknesses instead of simply taking *Titania* to Alexi is because I want the war to end quickly. I want Alexi back on the throne, and I want them to pay, but I don't want to see this kingdom in ruins before that happens. I love what Rickard used to call the backstage of warfare—the history, the design and construction of weapons, the music of a war bugle, the flight paths of starships, the formations and strategies. I love gripping pretend wars in both hands and manipulating them like clay, seeking out different ways to win, but part of the joy is knowing those wars are only stories I can write and rewrite as many times as I like. I don't long for war itself.

We leave the simulation rooms behind and board the elevator again. This time, we travel even deeper below Kali, down and down until the spiky, woody feel of the city above gives way to the unadorned steel and grease and engines of the base ship. This is Kali underneath its forests and sharp towers and pretty lanterns, a hodgepodge of water pumps and air filters and gears. The walls are white and chrome with low ceilings and noisy air vents, the engines are loud, and the floors are stained with oil. There are areas devoted to every function the base ship performs, from sustaining the atmosphere to powering the shields to supplying the cities with electricity, and there are tech screens filled with data everywhere.

One of these screens catches my eye. It's behind a locked door, quiet and lit up like it's always powered on. A series of numbers whisks across the screen. They appear to be an entirely random sequence, but there are gaps. Nine numbers are missing.

"Emergency shutdown," Rickard explains. "That's the first of six different numerical sequences. Each one is missing the final nine numbers. Elvar, Guinne, Max, and I are the only people who know the complete sequences."

"The rulers and their most trusted adviser," I say. "Hasn't that always been the way?"

He nods. "If all six sequences are completed, Kali's systems will turn themselves off."

"Completely?"

"Completely. Shutting down the ship for good is the final step of permanent evacuation."

Such a measure is rarely necessary, but it was used once or twice in the days when there were more spaceship kingdoms in the star system. Most gave up and returned their base ships to their origin planets, but one shut down at the end of a bitter war and another evacuated its healthy citizens and shut down when a fatal disease spread too rapidly to be isolated safely.

Automatic doors open and close as we continue. The sheer breadth and scope of the base ship is extraordinary. We eventually reach a wide hallway with a set of sturdy doors at the very end.

"You know of Kali's storerooms, of course," says Rickard. "They're full. With these stores, Kali can feed, fuel, and power itself for five years if all supplies from the outside are cut off."

The only time such a thing has ever happened was about a hundred years ago, when Winter and Kali had an argument and Winter refused to supply Kali with food or fuel for six months. Winter's embargo could have meant the end of Kali, and so Kali did what it does best and went to war. A god eventually intervened, the war ended, supplies were flown in, and the world went back to normal. Still, these storerooms have been maintained ever since.

"Why am I here, Rickard?" I ask him. "Why are you showing me all this?"

"Because you may be queen of Kali one day."

I frown. Not this again.

"Elvar may name you his heir. You must have realized that after last night. He believes in blood, which Max is not.

He also knows that an heir who is one of Cassel's children is likely to be a more popular choice with the world at large. Either way, you could be queen. And if that day should come, you will need to know more than what I've shown you today to care properly for your realm."

"I don't want to be queen. I want to live on Kali, not rule it."

Rickard smiles. "Well, we'll see."

Footsteps clatter down the corridor behind us. I look back to see a palace guard stumbling to a halt.

"Master Rickard—"

He's obviously agitated. Rickard strides up the corridor to meet him. The guard glances at me before dropping his voice to a whisper. I try to read his lips, but he's speaking too fast.

Rickard looks concerned. He replies quietly, and the guard takes off again without another word.

"We've been sent for," Rickard says.

"Why? What's happened?"

"Your brother's here."

My breath catches.

"Bear. He's in a ship, just outside the inner shield, and Elvar is about to shoot him out of the sky."

CHAPTER FIFTEEN

I follow Rickard to the king's parlor at a run. I've seen what *Titania* can do. I've seen her turn three warships to ash in a single flash of white fire. What if we're too late? What if Bear's ship has already met the same fate?

Instead, we find Elvar in a state of such anxiety that he can scarcely speak. Guinne is tense and silent in a seat by the window. And Lord Selwyn prowls the room with a vicious smile that neither the king nor the queen can see.

"Why have they attacked us?" Elvar cries as we enter. "Their army cannot yet be big enough to take on our entire fleet!"

"Even if it is," says Lord Selwyn, "we could always persuade your niece to let us use *Titania*."

"They must think they can win. That's the only reason they would come. What do they know? What terrible plan have they conceived of?"

"They may not be thinking clearly, my king," says Lord Selwyn. "Whatever their state of mind, however, their aggression is unquestionable, and I would advise responding in kind—"

"Stop working him into a panic!" Rickard barks.

Lord Selwyn spins around, and his smile withers. "I was just—"

"I've been very patient with you, Selwyn, but I will not allow you to fill the king's head with such nonsense. Aggression, indeed! What exactly is aggressive about one boy in a solitary ship?"

"Rickard!" the king spins around and grasps the warrior's hand with both of his own. "Rickard, you must defend us—"

The door clatters open. Max gives his uncle a stony look, then turns to his father. "We are not under attack."

Elvar jerks his head in Max's direction. "We can't be certain of that. Selwyn has rightly pointed out that one ship could herald more. I must get my armor. I must prepare myself—"

Max gently eases him back into his seat. "You don't need your armor, Father. There is no attack."

"But Bear knows he is not to set foot on Kali!" Elvar bursts out, either unable or unwilling to let his son reassure him. "Why is he here if not to cause trouble? What does he want from me? Rickard, *do* something!"

"No," says Rickard flatly. "You're being absurd, Elvar, and I'll thank you to stop it immediately."

There's a ringing silence. Lord Selwyn opens his mouth as though to protest, but Rickard's glare stops him.

Elvar blinks a few times. "There's no threat?"

"None," says Rickard. His voice is deep and utterly confident. It's the voice that must have comforted me a thousand times.

Elvar calms down immediately. He may be a king today, but he never stopped being the boy who clung to his teacher's every word. It's unnervingly familiar.

"Max?" Rickard turns to him, puts a hand on his shoulder. "What do you think?"

I'm surprised by the trust and confidence implied in the question, by the easy affection that seems to exist between them.

Max frowns. His eyes are fixed on something beyond the window. I follow his gaze and see it for the first time: a lone, red ship in the distance, little more than a dot on the star-flecked horizon. Bear is in that ship.

"I suggest we ask him why he's here."

Lord Selwyn sighs. "Dearest nephew, I fear you are too tolerant. Surely your cousin has broken the terms of his exile, and the only option is to destroy his ship."

I can't stay quiet any longer. "He's just a boy!"

"He hasn't broken any terms, either," Max adds. "Kyra, Alexi, and Bear are not to enter Kali. Bear has abided by that command. He's not on Kali. He's outside the inner shield."

Max walks across the parlor to the tech screen above the artificial fireplace. He flicks it on, taps the communications icon at the bottom of the screen, and says, "Does he want to speak to us?"

A voice—a sentry's I assume—comes through crisp and clear from the speaker. "Yes. He says he won't budge until he's spoken to Master Rickard."

"Father?" Max says.

Elvar's jaw juts out. "Very well. Let's hear what he has to say."

Max keys in a few numbers and the speakers crackle faintly as they connect to Bear's ship. "Why are you here, Bear?"

"Oh." It's Bear's voice. He sounds almost sulky. "I don't want to speak to *you*."

"Don't be so foolish, you horrible boy," Rickard says in exasperation, "You have no idea how close you've come to a very unpleasant death, so I advise you to start spitting out useful words."

Bear's voice is noticeably happier. "Hello, Rickard! I know I shouldn't have come." There's a crackle, and then, "Is she there?"

"Is who here?"

"The girl who won *Titania*." All heads turn in my direction. "Esmae." He hesitates. "My sister."

I stare at the speakers, struck by pain and something else, something softer and more tender. *My sister.*

"She's here," says Rickard.

"I came because I wanted to see her. May I?"

Max cuts the connection. He looks at me, a question in his eyes.

"I don't like it," says Elvar.

"They must be furious that Esmae won *Titania* for us," Guinne adds. "And Bear always had a temper."

They all debate the point until I interrupt: "I'll meet him. I'll talk to him."

"But—"

"With all due respect, Uncle," I say gently, "I'm not going to be persuaded otherwise."

Elvar grimaces. He mutters something under his breath that sounds remarkably like, *Just like Cassel.*

"It's her decision, not ours," says Max. "If it'll make everyone feel better, I'll go with her. I imagine Esmae will want to take *Titania*. What could be safer than that?"

"And what, pray tell," says Lord Selwyn, "are we to do if the princess knocks you unconscious and makes off with her brother and the world's greatest warship?"

"However did you guess my plot?" I ask. "And here I assumed I was being so crafty. After all, why let Alexi win *Titania* in the first place? How much simpler and more straightforward to compete against him, win her myself, fly her to Kali, get word to Bear to come and knock at your door, and *then* make off with the ship!"

Lord Selwyn steps so close that I can see all the way into his cold, angry eyes, and the hatred there makes my skin crawl.

"Take care, dear princess," he says softly, "or someone may cut that clever tongue out one day."

Rickard's voice is low but thunderous. "Carry on, Selwyn, and it will be *your* tongue at the end of the blade." Lord Selwyn goes red. My old teacher turns away from him and to me. "And you will apologize, Esmae. You are a princess of Kali, and princesses of Kali treat others with courtesy."

"I'm sorry, Lord Selwyn," I say with icy politeness.

The expression in his eyes is anything but forgiving.

Max flicks the speakers back on. "Esmae says she'll see you, Bear. We're coming."

We don't speak as we climb aboard *Titania* and set off for the shields. I dig my fingernails into my palms, anxiety dialing higher and higher. I have no idea what Bear wants or what to say to him.

Titania glides to a halt and hovers. The two ships are nose to nose, with only the fine, faintly twinkling barrier of the inner shield between them.

I watch Bear climb out onto the ship's wing and approach the shield. A fierce pride fills me. Rickard once told me that battles typically take place between the inner and outer shields of spaceship kingdoms, and that's exactly where Bear is now. He knows *Titania* is deadly. He must know there are a dozen armed sentries ready to attack him if he makes a single mistake. He must know some of them are probably waiting for any excuse to cut him down. And yet here he is in enemy territory, high above safe ground, bold and exposed and alone, every bit as brave as everyone says his brother is.

"What did my uncle say to you?" Max asks me. "What made Rickard so angry?"

"He told me I'm too cheeky for my own good."

He doesn't believe me. "Did he threaten you?"

I don't answer, telling him all he needs to know.

Max's jaw locks. He doesn't speak for a moment. "My uncle likes to feel respected. He likes to be in control. He helped my parents get where they are. I think it's made him feel like he has to protect the throne on Father's behalf."

"And I'm a thorn in his side."

"It's more like you're a variable he didn't account for. It makes you a threat in his eyes."

"Why is he so interested in keeping your father on the throne?"

"He's loyal to him."

I bare my teeth in a smile. "I hope you're right about that. Betrayal has been quite the epidemic on Kali lately, and it would be a shame if it infected anyone else."

I turn away, but Max catches my elbow. "Don't say that in front of my parents or uncle," he says. "Not *ever*, Esmae. The only person they'll suspect of betrayal is you."

He releases me, but I'm rooted to the spot, too surprised by his warning to move. I want to ask him why he bothered, why it matters to him whether his parents suspect me of treachery. Why he doesn't just stand back and let me stumble right into the fire.

Instead, I turn and climb out onto the right wing. I walk down to the end of *Titania*, to the very point of the arrowhead, where Bear waits.

My heart misses a beat. I can't speak.

Bear doesn't have Alexi's confidence. His posture is more like mine: stiff, arms tucked close to his body like he's trying to protect himself from the cold. The wind buffets us, and my hair whips against my cheek. I brush it out of my eyes.

"You look like him, you know," Bear says at last. "Like Alex. I didn't notice the resemblance before, but it was so obvious the moment I found out you were my sister. I replayed the broadcast of the competition about six times and you looked more and more like him each time."

"You're upset," I say. "I'm sorry."

He brushes my words away. "It's not your fault. You didn't ask to be thrown into space. I can't believe she did that. I can't believe she never told us. She remembers, you know. You were wrong about that part. No one's memories were ever erased."

"I know. I found that out last night." My voice wobbles.

"I don't want to be angry with you," Bear says. "I don't hate you for taking *Titania* from us. I just want to know why. Why did you come here to the uncle who betrayed us?"

"I couldn't keep living in Alexi's shadow." Bear nods like he understands that. "I'm not sorry I competed, Bear, but I never wished any ill on you or Alexi. I have no intention of letting *Titania* destroy any of you."

He kicks at the wing of his ship. "That doesn't help me decide what to do, though."

"Do?" His childlike frustration makes me smile. "What do you mean?"

"You're my sister. You're as much my family as Alex. I owe you both my loyalty. How am I supposed to fight you?"

I can't believe he's even contemplating such a question. I can't believe he believes so deeply in the idea of family that he feels conflicted about me, the girl he thinks stole his way home. Our mother's curse made flesh and blood. He's more generous and selfless than I will ever be.

And it almost got him shot out of the sky today.

My heart breaks a little, but I can't let him come back here while Elvar's on the throne. I can't let him risk his life again out of some idea of loyalty to me. "You'll fight me if you have to, Bear, because Alexi needs you. Now you need to leave. You can't be here."

He frowns. "Don't you want to know me?"

"Of course I do. But you can't be on Kali, and it's where I need to be." I want him to know I'm on his side, but I don't dare with Max just a few yards away.

Bear nods like he's ready to leave. He steps closer, puts one hand up against the invisible wall between us, and says quietly, "One act of brotherly loyalty, then, before I go."

"What?"

"We won't give up on Kali. This is our home. We'll get her back one way or another. There are ways around *Titania*."

Of course there are. She's an unbeatable battleship, but there are means outside of battle. She can't save a prince from an assassination in the dark. She can't guard the perimeter of an entire kingdom alone. She can't take the throne from a king herself. That's why I'm here. I knew Elvar would have found ways around her if I'd taken her to Alexi.

But what Elvar would have done is not the point. Bear is talking about what *they* have done.

He winces, staring at me with worried eyes like he's wrestling with himself. Then, leaning so close to me that we can both hear the crackle of the shield, he whispers, "Don't drink the wine."

I freeze. "What's wrong with the wine?"

"Just don't drink it."

"Poison?"

I think of all the people who eat and drink at the palace. Anyone could drink poisoned wine by mistake. Including me. That's why Bear's here, after all. Why he really risked his life and rushed to danger as soon as he found out about my arrival. He knows I could tell everyone and ruin their trap, but he came anyway. He came to keep me from becoming one of the poison's victims.

My throat closes with emotion, but I still manage to summon a protest. "Alexi would never use poison. He'd never smash his honor to pieces like that, and he would never risk harming innocent people. He would never risk poisoning Rickard!"

Bear shakes his head, backing away. The last thing I hear on the wind is "Not Alex."

And I realize what he's really telling me but won't say out loud. Alexi wouldn't poison anyone.

But our mother would.

I watch my brother vanish into the dark, my ears buzzing with more than just the crackle of the shield.

CHAPTER SIXTEEN

The king and queen want to know what Bear wanted. I tell them the truth to a point. Max stays quiet. He doesn't tell them that there was a moment when my brother leaned close to whisper in my ear.

There's about an hour left before the procession. I wait impatiently until Rickard retires to his suite to dress. As soon as I can be sure he's alone, I go after him.

There's a part of my furious, wicked heart that doesn't want to follow him. That wants me to shut my mouth. *After the way they rose up*, says the little voice that hides in that part of my heart, *they deserve to be torn down. And it doesn't matter if they die like this.*

And maybe that's true, but I can't keep quiet. I have to tell Rickard. Maybe if Bear had given me some guarantee that Elvar was a sure target and no one else would be hurt, maybe then I could have kept silent. Maybe then I could have sat back and watched my uncle die. But anyone in the family banquet room could be served the same wine as the king. Any guest could drink a glass of it at a state dinner. Any servant could sneak a sip out of the bottle when they uncork it in the kitchen.

"Damn it all, Kyra," he says, once I've shared Bear's message.

I fidget while Rickard contemplates our options, tidying the objects on his mantelpiece: a knife and a bowl of lotuses in water and a wooden puppet. The puppet is on strings, a joker with a wide, eerie smile. I turn its head away so that it can't leer at me anymore.

I can't bear the silence another moment. "Please tell me I'm wrong."

"Why would I tell you that?" he asks. "You were one of the brightest students I ever had, Esmae, and you were very rarely wrong."

My heart sinks. "So you think my mother's capable of this."

"Kyra will do anything to protect her—" Rickard stops. He was about to say *her children*, but that wouldn't have been true. "She will do whatever it takes to protect Alexi and Bear."

"But she must know there's no way to guarantee that only certain people drink the poisoned wine—"

"Whatever it takes," Rickard repeats. "Make no mistake, Esmae. Kyra did not cast you out into open space because she was afraid you would destroy her. She had another child, and she was afraid you would destroy *him*. She will kill anyone and everyone if it means keeping her sons safe. I'm sure she would even accept Elvar's rule over Kali and try to persuade

Alexi to abandon his war if she could only be sure that that would keep him alive. But she's so certain Elvar and Guinne want your brothers dead, and as long as she feels that way, she will want them to die first."

"*Are* they trying to murder my brothers?" I ask.

"Esmae," he warns.

"Are they?"

"Of course not." But there's something in his voice, something that makes me wonder if it's not me he's trying to convince.

I let it go, for now. "The poison could be here already. It could be anywhere. What do we do?"

"*You* can't do much. You haven't even been here a day, you don't yet have any power here. You won't be able to warn Elvar without Selwyn finding some way to make it look like you're responsible."

"I know that."

"I could speak to the king myself, but I'm not sure that would be the best course of action either. I'm afraid of what it would mean for Kyra. Elvar is so terrified already. If he finds out about the poison, he'll take steps to ensure your mother can never be a threat to him again."

My mouth is dry. "I know that, too."

Rickard scratches his jaw, absently studying the tapestry on the wall across the room. That's how he thinks. At last, he says, "Tell Max. Ask him to find the poisoned wine. He's the only one with the authority to do so without consulting the king or queen."

"How is telling Max any different from telling Elvar?"

"Max will do whatever it takes to make sure no one harms his father, but he won't hurt your mother either." Rickard smiles faintly. "You don't trust him, which is understandable, but you can trust me. Max won't hurt her. And he can be persuaded to keep this quiet."

"Can *you* do the persuading?"

Rickard gives me a severe look. "I am not the one who wants the favor."

So now I have to trust my enemy to protect the mother who literally threw me out of her home. It's a moment of bitter irony.

Max is in his suite, surrounded by paperwork. His rooms are cream and brown, simpler than mine, as if he's stripped back a lot of the luxury, and there's not much else other than books, a desk, and two sofas in the outer room. Even his curtains have been removed, and a combination of real and false sunlight blazes in.

He's surprised to see me. "Are you okay?"

I summon my nerve, bobbing on the tips of my toes as if I might take wing and fly away if I wish hard enough. "Do you need a favor?"

"I'm sorry?"

"A favor. Do you need one?"

He frowns. I look away so he doesn't see how much I hate doing this. There's an awkwardly shaped paper hound on one of his bookshelves. Is it the one I left in the bowl at the altar? Why would Max have that?

"Why are you asking about favors?" Max wants to know, drawing my attention back.

"Because I need a favor in return."

"Esmae, there's no need to give me—"

"I think my mother is going to try to poison your father," I say in a rush. "I don't know when, I don't know how. I don't even know for certain if he's the one she wants to poison. I just know there will be poison in the wine."

"In the wine? Do you know which bottle? Which kind?"

"No."

"Everyone in the palace drinks the wine. Anyone could drink the poison by mistake."

"I know. Rickard told me to tell you because you can make sure no one gets hurt. So I'm telling you." I finish the rest quickly before I lose my courage. "The favor I want to ask of you is that you don't hurt my mother."

Max rocks back on his heels, but his eyes never leave mine. "How do you know about this?"

"Bear. He told me not to drink the wine."

Max nods. "I'll do what I can about the poison."

"And my mother?"

"She's safe."

"Thank you."

He nods again but says nothing more. He's probably trying to figure out how to keep his father alive.

Tentatively, I say, "You haven't told me what you want in return."

"You may have just saved my father's life. I'm in no position to ask anything of you."

"I don't see it that way."

He grimaces. "Do we really have to do this? Count favors to make sure we're always even?" I don't know what to say, so I stay quiet. He sighs. "It doesn't matter. There's nothing I want from you, Esmae."

The words tumble out before I can stop them: "You could ask me for *Titania*."

He laughs then. "I have a feeling I know how that would go, so I'll save us both the trouble."

I smile back, reluctantly, and turn to go.

"Wait." He pauses, scraping a hand through his hair like he's unsure. "When I was seven years old, I was playing in the conservatory when Kyra came in. I was supposed to be in a lesson, and I didn't want anyone to catch me, so I hid. She knelt on the floor and she called for Amba, but Amba didn't answer. Kyra cried. I remember because I'd never seen her cry before. I'd never seen her be anything other than hard as nails. When she left, I crept out of my hiding place and saw that she'd left something behind in the offering bowl. It was a pair of socks. Tiny socks."

"You think they were mine," I say softly.

"I do now, yes."

I swallow. "Why are you telling me this?"

"Just so you know that she cares. Somewhere in there, under her love for your brothers and her fear of you, she cares."

My hand clenches so hard on the handle of the door that my knuckles go white. "For all she knows, I could drink the poison she's sent to kill your father. So no, I don't think she cares all that much."

CHAPTER SEVENTEEN

The procession goes well, better than even Elvar dared hope, or so I assume from the look of joy on his face.

People have flooded the streets to watch us. Elvar and I are in a chariot. We've both had to wear our armored vests and vambraces in case someone lashes out, but no one seems angry. They chant my name, beaming. They throw paper ships shaped like *Titania* into the air. And I, who grew up in obscurity, find it enormously uncomfortable to be celebrated.

I smile and wave anyway. I am as responsible for these people as any other Rey, and they deserve my courtesy no matter how I feel about standing at my uncle's side.

Elvar touches my shoulder. "Look."

He can't see whatever it is himself, but his face is bright with real pleasure. I follow the line of his pointing finger to a statue. It's a man carved out of smooth, pale stone. He has a crown on his head, a sword by his side, and a shield across his other arm. He's on a stone plinth, and he looks like he's guarding the city.

"Cassel," says Elvar. "Your father. He was a good king. He always wanted what was best for Kali." Elvar's smile grows. "It seems only yesterday that we were boys, brash and brave."

I turn away from my father's face and look into Elvar's. There's no mistaking the expression there.

"You loved my father very much," I say, shocked.

"Of course. He was my dearest friend."

"But he took your throne!"

"Not at all," says Elvar. "He had about as much choice as I did. Our mother and her war council decided he would be better suited to the throne than I, and that was that. He tried to refuse, but they persuaded him to put Kali's needs first."

I'm too stunned by his steadfast loyalty and affection to reply immediately. I always believed his bitterness at what his mother did to him had twisted his feelings for my father into something black and sinister, but I was wrong. There was love and warmth in my uncle yesterday, when he touched my face and almost wept because I have my father's nose, and there's love and warmth in him now.

"Maybe you could tell me stories about him," I hear myself say.

Elvar's expression softens. "I'd like that very much."

At the end of the procession, back at the palace, a group of elders and generals is waiting for us. Everyone is thrilled with the results of our trip, and I hear Elvar speaking excitedly to some of the elders. I want to slip away, unnoticed, but that's easier said than done. I've barely taken two steps in the direction of the door when a bony hand wraps itself around my elbow.

"Ez-may," says the old queen, whisking me away from the door, but also away from the other elders, "Come and talk to an old crone for a moment or two."

This is quite frankly the last thing I want to do given my great-grandmother's fondness for thorny, scorching truths, but it wasn't a request, and I'm not inclined to thwart her at the moment. I'd rather have her as an ally than an enemy.

"I've just had a chat with Rickard," she says, and I tense, "And it left me with the impression that you have no desire to see your brothers killed in a war."

"Of course not."

"Excellent," she says and pats my hand. At least, I think it's supposed to be a pat, but it feels more like claws digging into my skin. "Then you'll be of great help to me."

I stare at her. "I'm afraid I don't understand."

"I have no wish to see my grandson and great-grandsons kill each other, and who knows how many others, in a futile war."

"I gathered that much, Grandmother. The part I don't understand is how I can help you avoid that."

She steers me farther away from the others. "What I need, my dear, is a vote I can rely on. And your arrival couldn't have come at a better time."

"What kind of vote?"

"A vote on the war council."

My bewilderment grows. "How can I vote on the war council? I'm not on it."

"You could be."

Wait, what? I stop walking and face her. "You want to put me on the war council of Kali?"

"Max is on it. Why can't you be, too?"

"But he's a ruler—"

She brushes my protest aside. "So? As one of Elvar's possible heirs, you have an equally valid claim to a place on the war council."

So this is why she brought up the subject of heirs at dinner: my great-grandmother was planting seeds that she fully intends to harvest.

"If you truly want to keep this family safe," she says, "the war council is the best place for you."

This is the perfect way to find out information I would otherwise have no access to, but I want to make sure I truly know what she's asking of me first. "And if you *do* get me a place on the council, what then?"

"You will sit in on our discussions whenever possible. And you will vote the same way I do on every issue. You needn't look so shocked," she goes on, with a chuckle. "Based on your sentiments so far, you'll likely agree with me on most issues anyway."

"And when I disagree? Do I still vote your way?"

"It's hardly a great deal to ask, is it? You may find this difficult to believe because I cursed your mother, but my only goal is to protect this family. Both sides of it. At the moment, that means putting a stop to the war that's coming. There are twelve members of the war council, including the king. Rickard and I can be relied upon to vote against aggressive strategies. Four others tend to agree with us, but are less invested and therefore less reliable. Selwyn, as you may have already guessed, always votes in favor of aggression against Alexi. Max often votes with Selwyn and the other three members tend to follow Max's lead. Elvar, who is the twelfth vote and also has the final say, can usually be made to see reason and abstain from open war. He tends to listen to Rickard or me."

I see where this is going. "But you're worried that as he grows more afraid of whatever Alexi is planning, he'll be more likely to vote with Lord Selwyn. The king's final say could ignite war. You want to avoid putting him in that position. You want another sure vote."

"Good girl," says the old queen.

"Isn't Guinne on the war council?"

"Guinne could have had a seat on the war council, but she didn't want it. She prefers to devote her time to the palace, the city, and a number of charitable works. She tends to side with Selwyn, so it's probably just as well." Cassela smiles, canines showing. "So you see why you'll be so very helpful to me."

I look her in the eye and smile back. "I think you'll be very helpful to me, too, Grandmother. So yes, by all means, let's use each other."

Her eyes twinkle wickedly. "Welcome to Kali, Ez-may. I think you'll fit right in."

CHAPTER EIGHTEEN

Cassela gets me that seat on the war council, of course. Not that I ever doubted her. I have a feeling failure is not a concept with which the old queen is familiar.

I gather with the war council when they meet. Suspicious looks are pointed my way at first, but I exercise all the restraint I have, keep my mouth shut, and behave so well for the first few weeks that even Lord Selwyn starts to act like he's forgotten I'm there.

The war council does not provide me with the answer to cut Elvar down once and for all, but it is a view into the very heart of the war that will come if it can't be averted. There are debates about routes and strategy, discussions about soldiers on both sides who have great skills, ideas tossed around about potential allies and friends in other realms and favors that can be called in. There's a lot of dismay over the fact that

Tamini has sided openly with Alexi, but there are other realms to consider and the voices of the advisers blend around me.

"Shloka, Sting, and Elba may join us."

"Elba's new king will only do so for a hefty price. He's difficult. He'd rather collect new wives than rule with good sense."

"We must do what we can to ensure Winter doesn't turn against us," says someone else. "We can't afford to lose that supply route."

"Has there been any news of the Blue Knights? They're bound to side with Alexi, given how fond their god is of him."

On and on it goes. I take it all in, hungry to learn as much as I can. When I'm not at council meetings, I spend most of my free time in the library and on tech screens researching the people, places, and alliances I hear about.

Not that there's much free time to speak of. It's wonderful, actually, to be kept so busy, and as the weeks pass, it's more and more difficult to keep the people here at a distance.

I expected to struggle with spending time with the people I've hated for years, but I find it's the opposite. The more time I spend on Kali, the harder it is to hold on to my hatred. Whatever their motivations, whatever they've done in the past, they've welcomed me into their lives, and they treat me as one of their own. They give me the duties of a royal princess and trust me to carry them out. In time, it's as though I've always been here and this is exactly where I'm supposed to be.

They didn't want you, Guinne told me that first day. *We do.*

The words are so easy to believe. It's so difficult to remember that I can't trust them. I mustn't ever trust them.

139

It's fortunate then, I suppose, that it isn't long before they remind me why I shouldn't.

The war council has gathered in Lady Su Yen's modest suite today. Lady Su Yen, one of the generals of Kali's army, serves us all glasses of wine. I politely decline. I always do. It's been weeks, and Max has made sure to test the wine every time it's served, and no one has been poisoned, but I'm not taking any chances.

Su Yen finishes serving, then takes her seat. Her suite is close to the base ship's power supply and we can all feel the low thrum of the engines. Everyone else ignores the sensation, but I pay attention to the rhythm of the revs.

"Are we ready?" asks Elvar.

"We are," Max replies, albeit reluctantly. "I still don't see why this couldn't wait until Rickard got back."

I frown. I assumed Rickard hadn't arrived yet, not that he wouldn't be here at all. This isn't good.

"There's no way to know when Rickard will be finished on Winter," says Lord Selwyn. "He may not be back for days. I, for one, don't feel we can afford to waste that much time."

"You would say that," says the old queen, her words punctuated by a loud and pointed snort.

Elvar looks uncomfortable, possibly because Rickard's absence doesn't sit well with him either. "If you'd rather not be here, Max, you're free to go."

Max's eyes narrow, but he doesn't budge.

"What are we due to discuss today?" asks Lady Su Yen. "Arcadia?"

Elvar winces. "Must we?"

"One could hardly blame you for your aversion to the topic, my king," says Lord Selwyn. "Discussing it is, however, a necessary evil. We cannot turn a blind eye to what that boy has done."

I look around the table, confused. "What's Arcadia?"

"We had word earlier today that King Ralf gave Alexi a piece of territory on Winter," Max explains to me. "He must have done it over a year ago, but they kept it quiet. They built a city there and named it Arcadia. Alex now rules it. It's thriving."

I have to work very hard to hide my glee. "Is that a problem?"

Lord Selwyn scowls. "Of course it's a problem. We exiled him. Our hope was that he'd crawl away into obscurity, not find somewhere else to rule."

It must be so galling for them. Alexi had the kingdom in his hands, but they took it from him and sent him away for good measure. He wasn't supposed to rise up again. He wasn't supposed to lose *Titania* and still come away the prince of a city they have no claim to.

My twin brother is good at winning even when he's lost. Golden as the sun, no matter what.

"More importantly," Lord Selwyn continues, "the existence of Arcadia indicates that King Ralf has chosen a side. If Alexi asks it of him, he could cut off our supply route."

"Ralf won't do that," says Max, "He's not the kind of man who would allow innocent people to starve."

Some of the other advisers nod in agreement, but Lord Selwyn frowns. "That's not the only concern. Alexi has been building an army for years. He's so close to being ready to strike."

"He's coming for us, Max," Elvar says. "This is your fault. *You* were the one who wanted him exiled."

"Father—"

"He wants to take the throne from me!"

"I told you I wouldn't let that happen."

"And how do you intend to stop him?" Elvar barks, banging his hand down on the table. Max doesn't even flinch. But the crack in Elvar's voice wasn't anger; it was panic. "You can't stop him, Max! He would defeat you in battle."

"There are other ways to stop him."

Elvar's shoulders sag. "You are not to blame for the fact that you cannot equal Alexi in battle, Max. Esmae could, I daresay, but she is a Rey and we Reys have always been exceptionally talented at warfare—"

I want to look away, to not see the expression on Max's face. Now I see who makes him feel like he's not one of us. Not quite *enough*. It's never been the people of Kali, nor the devoted Hundred and One, nor even the people across the galaxy who loathe him for what he did to Alexi. No: it's his own father.

The old queen reaches out and pats Max on the shoulder. It's a kind gesture I didn't expect from her.

Max clears his throat. "Whatever Alex's motives may or may not be, you need money to build and look after an army. Arcadia may indeed be a wonderful place, but it isn't going to provide Alex with that kind of silver." Max gestures to the map lying on the table, his finger circling Kali. "He'll need an enormous force to confront us."

Lord Selwyn shrugs. "Alexi's lack of funds is a valid point, but he's earned an enormous amount of goodwill across the star system. We have no idea how many realms have already promised to assist him with funds, arms, and troops if there's a war."

"Then we had better make a bigger push to win over our own allies," says Grandmother.

"A worthy option," says Lord Selwyn. "There are, however, alternatives."

Max looks at him warily, but most of the others simply look puzzled. Lady Su Yen speaks up. "Such as?"

"*Titania*," says Lord Selwyn. I stiffen. "It would be well worth our while to remind the star system of her power."

My skin begins to prickle. Lady Su Yen is still confused. "I was under the impression that Princess Esmae has refused to participate in further broadcasted events."

"Well, yes," says Lord Selwyn between gritted teeth. He refuses to even look at me. "The princess has certainly made up her mind about that."

I don't reply. Elvar and Selwyn wanted me to show off my skills in tournaments and take part in interviews about my past and *Titania*. I can tolerate attending processions and royal events, but the idea of giving myself over to Lord Selwyn's propaganda machine turns my stomach, and so I refused. Elvar recovered from his disappointment within days, but Lord Selwyn hasn't yet forgiven me.

"But if you're not referring to Princess Esmae, what—"

"Skylark is a relatively unimportant realm," says Lord Selwyn, "And it's vulnerable at the moment. Princess Shay is only sixteen, and quite inexperienced in matters of statecraft and warfare. It would be an easy victory, and one that would show the rest of the star system what *Titania* is capable of."

I draw in a sharp breath. The room feels small and claustrophobic. The hum of the ship's engines beneath us is suddenly loud, oppressive, and threatening.

Amba warned me. *Watch, Esmae.* That was what she said when she came to see me after the competition. *Watch the forest burn.*

One of the other elders is the first to recover. "You think we should take over Skylark? Invade a realm we have no quarrel with?"

"I believe it would be the most effective way to remind the other rulers in the star system that siding with Alexi would be rash," Lord Selwyn replies. "I would have suggested we use Tamini as a target instead, but they have too much fertile land that could be destroyed if we were to invade. Better to frighten their queen into rescinding whatever aid she has offered Alexi. Without friends or funds, he will have no army with which to threaten us. With which to threaten *you*, my king."

"That is true," says Elvar slowly.

I grip the arms of my chair tightly. "You speak of *Titania* as if you have free rein to use her, Lord Selwyn, but she is not yours."

"Do you refuse us the use of her to defend ourselves, princess?" he asks with exaggerated surprise.

"Invading a neutral realm is not *defending ourselves*," I snap. "You can't do that. The Forty Realms would never forgive it."

"You have been on the war council for only a short while, princess. I'm afraid you may not yet understand the intricacies of politics. With *Titania* on our side, it is utterly irrelevant who does or does not forgive us."

Titania is not on your side, I want to snarl, but I can't. I have to tread carefully. They won't be allowed to use *Titania*, but I can't let them think I'm not on their side either.

"It could completely backfire," I point out. "Instead of making the other realms afraid to ally with Alexi, it could scare them into banding against you."

"And?"

"And," I say, "Kali is not indestructible. Even if I were to let you use *Titania*, what if they wait until she isn't here? What if you send her to some faraway realm to fight a battle, and the others swoop in while she's gone? There are ways around her, and you're so eager to flex your muscle that you've forgotten that."

His face whitens. "How dare you—"

"Quiet," says Elvar. "Both of you."

Lord Selwyn grits his teeth, but obeys.

Don't let him do this, I silently beg my uncle. *Don't let him make you afraid enough to do this.*

"I don't like it," says Lady Su Yen. She gives Selwyn a defiant stare and I want to applaud her for it.

It doesn't look like it will take much more to splinter Lord Selwyn's temper. "Are you questioning the king, Su Yen?"

"I think we all know this was not the king's idea."

"We also all heard the king agree that—"

Max pushes his chair back from the table and stands. "The king can speak for himself. Father? What do you really think?"

"I think Selwyn makes a good point about how we can best cut Alexi off," says Elvar, but his voice isn't quite certain. "I also share Su Yen's discomfort with the idea of attacking a realm we have no issue with. It doesn't feel honorable. I—" And then, undoubtedly out of desperation, he swivels his body round toward the old queen. "Grandmother? What do you think? As the eldest in the room today, your opinion takes precedence."

Cassela doesn't even hesitate. "I think your son has something to say, Elvar."

Elvar's cheek twitches, but he nods. "Max?"

"Father, perhaps Uncle Selwyn has forgotten that Princess Shay's mother is King Darshan's cousin."

Lord Selwyn blinks. I'm impressed. Summoning the specter of the one thing *Titania* can't touch is genius.

"Darshan is unlikely to stand by and allow us to take Shay's realm from her," Max goes on, "and we all know the story. If *Titania* confronts Darshan, *Titania* will be destroyed. Do we want that? I don't consider it a risk worth taking."

"In any case," the old queen adds, with a sound that could have been a cough, but sounded suspiciously like a cackle, "no one can send *Titania* anywhere without Esmae's permission. Furthermore, even if Esmae were to agree, the war council would have to approve this hypothetical invasion. Shall we vote now?"

"There's no need," says Lord Selwyn, face white and lips thin with fury. "It was only an idea."

I seethe. Maybe he expected more support from the war council and has now been deterred. Maybe he'll go away and whisper in Elvar's ear until they find a way to get around the council's protests. I don't know. Either way, I can't sit idly by.

As soon as the meeting is finished, I race back to my suite. They will never persuade me to use *Titania* in an invasion like that, but I wouldn't put it past Lord Selwyn to convince Elvar to send Kali's armies to Skylark anyway, just to make a point. I have to make sure that never happens.

Unless—

I turn and shut the door behind me. What if this is a test? There's no doubt in my mind that Lord Selwyn wants to intimidate the rest of the star system, but what if he only suggested it today to test me? If he's looking for an excuse to get rid of me, showing Elvar evidence that I'm untrustworthy would help his case enormously. He may have spoken up today to see what I'll do.

And if that's true, Elvar will send me away. And where will I be then? I'll lose the home I've longed for all my life. Alexi and Bear still think I chose Elvar, I don't even dare wonder what my mother thinks, and I'll have no information I can offer them to use against him. All my work will be for nothing.

But what if it wasn't a test?

I close my eyes and make a choice. I say a name into the empty room.

You only have to speak a god's name out loud for them to hear you. Whether or not they choose to listen, however, is another matter.

When I open my eyes, Amba's there.

CHAPTER NINETEEN

She's perched primly on the edge of the sofa. "I didn't expect you to call," she says, regarding me with luminous, impossibly dark eyes. "I was under the impression you looked to lost gods for advice these days."

I blush. So she knows about the paper hound in the conservatory. "I needed a different sort of advice that day."

"I will recover from the insult eventually," she says. I can't tell if it's a joke; I can never tell with Amba.

"I need your help."

"I can't defend Skylark. That is a risk to my immortality I am uninterested in taking."

I wonder how much she knows. "I wasn't going to ask for that."

"Then what did you want from me?"

"I need to get word to Rama immediately."

Amba rises off the sofa, her eyes flashing like lightning in the sky. "You want a *goddess* to run an errand for you?"

Her annoyance is a gust of wind that knocks me back against the wall. I don't cower. "I can't use a tech screen. And I can't send a comm from my watch. They're probably monitoring all of my devices. I can't give Lord Selwyn any evidence to use against me. I need to speak to Rama, but I can't do it safely without you."

The wind stops. "They would still know you were the one who passed on the information," she points out.

"They might guess," I say, "which is better than if they had proof."

Amba nods. "Very well. Just this once, Esmae."

I thank her and write a hasty note. *Tell your father they might try to take Skylark. They need to know it's under his protection.* I don't know what else I can say. If I start telling Rama anything more, I'll open the floodgates and sit here writing to him for hours.

I put the folded note into Amba's hand. She closes her fist and the paper vanishes into smoke, ready to materialize when she needs it.

She considers me for a moment. "I told you not to fire that arrow."

"I know."

"I should have told you the truth." She sighs. "If I'd told you why I wanted you to stay away from your brother, maybe you would have obeyed."

I laugh without any real humor. "But you're so good at not telling me the truth, Amba. Remember that fairytale you made up about my heartbroken mother giving me up?"

Amba doesn't look sorry. "How does one tell a small child that her mother was so afraid of her, she almost killed her? It was kinder to let you believe she never wanted to give you up."

I don't know if that's true. Was it kinder to let me believe my mother loved me? Was it kinder to give me years of hope, only for me to end up with even more pain when that hope finally burned out?

"So what was it?" I ask again. "Why didn't you want me to meet Alexi that day?"

"My brother Kirrin is determined to help Alexi win this war, you know," she says.

"That's not an answer."

"Strive for a little patience, Esmae. Kirrin is important."

"He's the god of tricks."

"And bargains," she reminds me. "He doesn't like it when people forget that part. Kirrin loves Alexi. He was the one who gave him the Golden Bow."

The Golden Bow is the bright bow Alexi always wears on his back. I knew that it was a gift from a god given when Alexi was only ten years old. It's a divine weapon, one only Alexi can use. It's said that there's an incantation he can use to transform it into an explosion of radiance that will obliterate any mortal enemy he chooses.

As if that wasn't sufficient, Rickard gave all his students a gift when they passed his first test. Bear got Rickard's own mace. Alexi got an arrow that will always return to him. And I got the Black Bow, cut two thousand years ago by Amba herself.

"Kirrin's help may make all the difference between victory and defeat for Alexi," Amba says. "It's very difficult to defeat those who are so loved by gods, even with a god-graced ship."

"Lucky for me, then, that I'm not trying to defeat him."

She sighs, steps close to me, and touches my cheek. I see sorrow and calamity in her eyes. "You are loved by gods, too, Esmae, even if you don't yet know it."

I smile. "That's absurd. You're the only god I know, and you don't love me."

She frowns but doesn't reply.

"What could I possibly have done to make the gods see me as something out of the ordinary?" I ask her. "What could I possibly have done to make any of you love me? Was it the competition?"

"That is a scant part of it," she says. "Perhaps you can't see it, but you are more than your flaws and mistakes. You are more than the sorrows of your past. Your heart is as fierce as a lion's. You are loved by gods, just as your brother is. Remember that. Perhaps it will help you in the way it will help him. Perhaps it will help save you in the end."

I go very still. "What?"

She's silent.

The chill starts at the top of my spine and spreads out from there. "Save me from what?"

Amba turns away. "Time is different for gods. We see small pieces of the past and the present and the future all at once, like stars. We see what will be and what can be and what may or may not be. And what we see shifts as different choices are made. I've told you that before. What I may not have ever told you, however, is that sometimes we see fixed points. Events that cannot be shifted. We don't always know the how, we don't always know the why, and we almost never know what leads to a particular event. Mortals make their own choices, and we can't control them, but they inevitably lead themselves to their own fates—their own fixed points.

And those points, in time, will happen. One way or another, they will happen. They already *have* happened. You see? Past and present and future are all one and the same to us."

"Just tell me!"

She won't look me in the eye when she says it. "Four years ago, when Elvar took the throne from your brother, Kirrin and I both saw the same piece of the future. We agreed not to share it with either of you, but Kirrin told Alexi about it just yesterday. He told Alexi he would murder his twin sister one day."

My heart thumps unevenly. "No."

"We didn't know how it would come about, exactly, just that it would start on the day you met your brother. That's why I wanted you to stop training with Rickard. That's why I wanted to keep you away from Alexi. Then, when you went to the palace on the day of the competition, in spite of my asking you not to, more of the future became clear. Suddenly, I could see how it would start." The way she looked at me before I fired the arrow. "The moment you shot that fish, you sealed your fate. Made that event a fixed point."

"It's not true. He wouldn't. Alexi wouldn't. I'm his *sister*."

"He will do it. We've seen it. There will be a duel, a broken arrow, your eyes will grow wide with fear as you realize he's broken the rules. You will fall, and you will spit blood onto the grass beneath you before you die."

"You cannot seriously believe Alexi Rey would break the rules of a duel. That's even less likely than him killing his own sister."

"It is what it is," says Amba softly.

My fists clench and unclench at my sides. And in a dark, terrible corner of my mind, a little voice tells me not to forget Rickard and the curse he laid on me.

That's the day his curse will come for me. And Alexi will kill me.

"When?" I ask. "When is it supposed to happen?"

"Soon. Neither of you look any older."

"You and Kirrin must have made a mistake. The blue-flower jewel keeps me safe, Amba. Alexi *can't* kill me."

"I don't know how it's possible, just that it will be."

"He won't do it."

"He will."

"Tell the gods to watch us," I snap. "If I really am a favorite of theirs, like Alexi or Grandmother or Rickard, then my words should have power. So tell the gods to watch us, Amba. *That will not be our fate.* Alexi will not kill me. I will not die that day. I swear it."

I expect her to be furious with me for making reckless vows, but she simply smiles. For just one moment, her eyes shine as gloriously as stars. "Now you must keep that vow, Esmae," she says. "I do not believe you can, but I hope you will."

I will, I swear to myself. *I will.*

CHAPTER TWENTY

The Hundred and One will be killed.

They're just kids, and they're going to be killed. I know this because I'm watching them train right now—have watched them before—and they will not be able to beat Alexi, Bear, and the warriors I know my brothers have on their side.

It should reassure me, knowing that Max's force can't beat Alexi's, but it doesn't. They're not anonymous, faceless soldiers I can calculate the odds on from a distance. They're faces I see every single day.

Sybilla is on the training field with a handful of them, finishing up their evening session. The sun lamps have switched over to moonlight, the ship rumbles beneath us, and the field is a harsh landscape of rocks, perilous crevices, and short, prickly yellow grass. I'm in a tree, above them; I was reading when they came out and then I stayed to watch.

"Juniper, you're dead," Sybilla says in frustration. "I just got you in the back. How many times do I have to remind you to guard your back in battle? You *cannot* waste time making sure your brothers are okay."

This is true, but her brothers do the same for her. Ideally none of them would be in a battle because they'll just worry about one another and get distracted, but they would make an excellent stealth team for quieter, more devious attacks.

I open my mouth to say so but clamp it shut again. I'm not supposed to be making them *better*.

But what about just keeping them alive, Esmae?

I swear under my breath.

When the session is finished, the Hundred and One bound away with cheerful, youthful exuberance, chattering about what they're having for dinner and who's off duty tonight. Only Sybilla remains, collecting stray arrows across the field. She slots them into the practice quiver propped against the trunk of my tree.

"You can come down now," she says without looking up.

I had a feeling she knew I was there. She looked at the tree far too often. I drop lightly out of the tree.

"What were you hiding up there for, Princess?"

"I was *reading*, not hiding."

"And watching us."

"Yes, that too."

"And?"

"And what?"

"What did you think? Of them?"

I measure my words, then say, "I think you and Max have done the best you can, but none of you will beat Alexi without better techniques and a lot more practice."

I watch her to see if she's insulted, but she only nods. "I know. So does Max. But Rickard can't teach us and General Saka left. Everyone who is left has already taught us everything they know." She laughs, short and jagged. "Well. *Almost* everyone who is left."

"You want to know why I haven't offered to teach the Hundred and One," I say. No use dancing around it.

"No," says Sybilla. "Max says you didn't come here to train us. You're here because it's your home. You don't owe us anything. And I agree. You *don't* owe us anything. I just don't understand why you haven't offered. I saw you teaching one of the kitchen maids how to read the other day. I've seen you working on equations with Jemsy. So it makes no sense to me that the one place you haven't offered anyone any help is here. Battle."

"You've wanted to say this for weeks," I remark. "You've bit your tongue. But I don't mind. Honestly, Sybilla. Whatever else you have to say, say it." I'd rather know what I'm facing. If she suspects my allegiances lie elsewhere, I want to know it.

She crosses her arms over her chest, jaw clenched, bracing herself. "No one's seen you so much as touch a sword or arrow since you got here. I'm starting to wonder if it was all a trick after all. I've said it before, but where are your scars? How did you supposedly train under Rickard and yet come away unscathed? Maybe you have no battle skills and that's why you won't show anyone what you can do. Maybe you're not the real Esmae Rey." I blink, and she rushes on, defensively, "It's possible, so don't look at me like that. The gods used to cloak people in the old days by making them look like other people. A god could have done that for you. Maybe Kirrin, god of tricks. He's on Alexi's side. He could have sent you here to distract us while the real Esmae fights with Alexi. I know there are holes in this theory, but I can't think of any other reason why—"

"Sybilla," I say, almost laughing because I'm so relieved that *this* is why she doesn't trust me. *This*, I can fix. "Stop. Yes, the gods can cloak people. No, I'm not an imposter."

She kicks at the dirt beneath our feet. "I want to like you, Princess. I *do* like you. I would gladly be your friend, under different circumstances, but I can't get past this. I will protect you because it's my job and I will be courteous to you, but I can't trust you and now you know why."

I sigh. "Give me your bow and one of those arrows."

She's shocked. She silently hands them over. This is the first time I've held an arrow since I fired at a mechanical fish.

I unwind the bowstring, test it, and string the bow again. A small, sharp stab of pain shoots through my hand. I hold it open and show Sybilla the blood on my fingertips.

"Watch," I say.

In the bright, clear light of the moon lamps above, Sybilla watches as my fingers heal.

She gasps. "How?"

"It's a long story."

After a moment she asks, in a softer tone than I've ever heard her use before, "Does it hurt every time?"

"Yes."

"Even after all this time?"

"It doesn't matter how much time passes. This is why I have no calluses. No scars. I heal too fast." I pause, then reluctantly add a lie at the end of the truth. "And I haven't touched a sword or arrow since I got here because I don't want anyone to see the way I heal."

She lets out a breath, and with it her entire body seems to soften, losing the taut, suspicious posture she's always had in my presence. "I'm sorry. I was so sure you were lying to us, but this answers all my questions. Thank you for telling me. Esmae."

I grin. "So about that part where you'd gladly be my friend . . ."

She laughs. "Does Max know? About this?"

"If he does, he hasn't mentioned it to me."

"Speaking of," she says.

I look across the field and see Max standing on a palace balcony some distance above us, silhouetted. A woman is at his side.

"Who's he talking to?" I ask.

"No idea."

"I've never seen her before." And now that I think about it, that seems to happen an awful lot. "I often see him with people I've never seen before, and then I never see them again."

She chuckles. "Oh, yes, that's always been his way. No one knows who those people are. They come and they go."

It's unusual behavior for a crown prince. Are they spies? Assassins? But why would you talk to your spies in full view of anyone passing by? On the other hand, if they're just casual acquaintances or friends, why not meet them in a more social setting? And why don't they ever reappear? It has to be something more secret, yet he's not afraid of other people seeing his visitors' faces, which is an odd contradiction.

I scrutinize the balcony some more. Max and the woman are arguing. He makes a gesture of annoyance and strides back inside. The woman follows.

"Hey," Sybilla says, and I turn back to her. "There's this fayre down by the river. Great music, lots of food. Do you want to go?"

"I'd love to."

I've only ever left the palace by chariot, but this time we walk. It's a steep, winding path down into the city, a knotty set of side roads past little red-roofed houses and air vents hidden behind thorns. The woods creep over us, shadows blotting out the lamps. I shiver. The hiss of steel follows us, and every now and then I catch a glimpse of the source: a sword flashing in someone's hand or two people training with knives.

We go down into Erys, down back alleys, where voices and the clang of steel periodically burst out of windows. The calm electronic voice of the base ship's systems crackles over hidden intercoms a few times along the way.

"There," says Sybilla, as we step out of an alley and into a labyrinth of courtyards. "The fayre."

The courtyards are cobbled, surrounded by gurgling canals from the artificial river and connected by picturesque little bridges. The only knives in sight are the ones used to slice meat, and swords are either absent or sheathed. It's a glimpse of the Kali beyond the reach of warfare and discipline, a world where mayhem and joy are allowed to thrive. The fayre itself is not unlike the noisy, bustling markets of Wychstar, but smaller and more intimate. Children perform cartwheels across the cobblestones and puppeteers put on a show at the far end of the street. The stalls are crammed with food and trinkets. Somewhere, someone plays melancholy music. Sybilla and I find an empty bench. I wander off to buy us a loaf of warm bread with cheese and walnuts, and when I return, I see that a girl has joined Sybilla at the bench. They seem to know each other. I wait a short distance away so that I don't interrupt them, but Sybilla doesn't seem interested in whatever the girl's asking her. She shakes her head and the girl leaves with a graceful shrug.

"So you said no," I guess, dropping onto the bench.

She breaks off a piece of bread. "I said no. We've been out before and I don't do second dates. Second dates lead to attachments."

I smile at her prickly tone. "If you say so."

"What about you, then? Do you like girls?"

"Boys, I think." I let a laugh out of my nose. "Not that there's been many to speak of. There were a couple of boys I liked for a little while on Wychstar, and several sloppy kisses, but romance wasn't exactly my priority."

"It's not mine either," she says, jumping to her feet. "Let me go get us some drinks. You haven't yet tried our terrible gooseberry wine, have you?"

She saunters off. I'm tempted to tell her that gooseberry wine is even more terrible when there's a possibility it might be poisoned, but of course I can't say that.

I shift my attention back to the fayre, listening to the music, which has shifted from melancholy to something harder, more energetic, *defiant*. It works its way into my heart like a blade between the ribs.

My watch pulses on my wrist. I slide an earpiece into my left ear and answer the comm. "I'm out in the city, so you may have trouble hearing me."

"Out in the city?" Rama repeats. "On Kali? Do they do that?"

I grin. "It seems so."

"Is that music? I can hardly cope with my shock."

His lazy voice is so comforting, so *known*, like a favorite story. I describe what I can see, and he tells me he's hiding from the royal sword master, and we talk like we're sitting side by side.

"Are you happy there, Ez?" he asks.

I wish that were an easy question to answer. I came to Kali for one reason and one reason only, but there are days when I almost forget about war. In spite of my hatred and mistrust of many of the people around me—hatred and mistrust I'm certain aren't as vivid as they were a few weeks ago—I like my life here.

I had some idea of what to expect from royal life because I often saw Rama's brother and sisters busy with their obligations on Wychstar. (Rama himself refused to contribute to tasks he deemed either too strenuous or too tedious, but he would frequently sneak away to read stories to the children at the hospice. He still thinks he's kept that a secret from me.) I haven't been surprised by my new responsibilities and I've taken to them well. I learn about other realms' customs and rulers. I help Guinne plan state dinners. I check menus. I visit new babies in the city. I sit in with Elvar and Max in the throne room each afternoon while a steady stream of citizens come to bring gifts of respect or ask for help. Rickard and I drive around Erys in a chariot so he can show me the city. Elvar walks with me in the palace gardens after dinner and tells me stories about my father. Asteroids rock the base ship and starships fly in and out of the shields. And for now, at least, *Titania* remains safely in the dock.

"Ez?" Rama says again. "Are you still there?"

And then there's the vision. My supposed death at my brother's hands. Impossible, absurd, yet nevertheless disturbing. I haven't told Rama about it, partly because I don't want Lord Selwyn to find out if he is indeed keeping an eye on my tech, but also because it's such a bleak idea that I don't know how to share it with even my best friend.

"I think I could be happy here," I finally say. "I think I am sometimes. Sometimes I can trick myself into believing this mess will all turn out okay. Sometimes I can ignore the hole in my heart where my mother and brothers should be." I blink back tears. "Sometimes I even forget I miss you."

"What a terrible friend you are, you brat."

"I love you, Rama."

"And I love you, Esmae." I can almost see him rolling his eyes, and it makes me grin. "Gah, I wish you'd just come back, you know. There is no one interesting left in this palace. You've left, Radha's left, Ria left years ago, Rodi's always busy, Father's perpetually grumpy—"

The fact that his brother is busy or that his other sister left two years ago to study archaeology on Shloka is not new information to me, but I had no idea Princess Radha had left. "Where did Radha go?"

"She's off doing diplomatic work for Father," Rama grumbles. "I'm not sure where. He says it's sensitive information and won't tell me."

"That must be enjoyable for you."

"I object to the amusement in your voice. You know I hate secrets at the best of times."

"You'll survive." Nevertheless, I listen patiently to him as he complains bitterly about his father's determination to keep secrets from him and the palace cats' determination to pester him ceaselessly and any number of other inconveniences that annoy him on a daily basis.

It's not Rama's fault, but I probably would have seen the shadows sooner if I hadn't been distracted.

They fall over the courtyard from high above, black like crows, their shape so unnatural that I look up. A pair of starships dart across the sky. They have narrow, pointed wings like curved knives and they're small, but fast. I've seen starships like these in books. They're called them corpse ships, because that's what they leave behind.

I say an unceremonious good-bye to Rama and stand. Sybilla returns. Her eyes are on the sky, too, watching the ships slide out of sight. She looks worried.

"Where have they gone?" I ask.

"I don't know."

I run as fast as I can up the thorny wooded paths to the palace. Sybilla is on my heels, but I'm faster, and she doesn't catch up until I'm already at one of the sentry posts.

"The corpse ships," I say, breathless and afraid. "Where have they gone? *Why* have they gone?"

Two sentries look at each other. "I don't think they've gone anywhere, Princess," says one. "We were told the crews need to train."

They're training. I walk away, heart stuttering, and sit on the plinth of a statue by the palace gates. My legs feel wobbly. I look up at the sky and watch the ships with their sharp, wicked wings do another circuit of the city.

No one is about to die yet.

Yet.

"Esmae." Sybilla's next to me, her voice not entirely unsympathetic, and I realize how close I've come to giving away the truth of my loyalties. "No one begrudges you your concern for your brothers' lives, but what did you expect? The ships have to train. They have to be ready for when the war comes."

If the war comes, I want to say. *If, not when.* War feels so close, an oppressive presence in the air. I want more than ever to win, but more than even that, I want to win *quietly*. I don't want to rip my uncle's throat out anymore; I just want him to go quietly so that Alexi can have his home and crown back. It's an unrealistic hope that's doomed to disappointment, but it's what a few weeks here on Kali have done.

"You don't really want to see this world burn down in a war, do you?" I ask.

Sybilla scuffs her foot against the ground. "War doesn't have to burn the whole world down. I don't want Kali ripped apart, but I'm not afraid of battle. From the very moment I was born, I've battled against *everything*. War is what I do. I don't know what I'd be without it."

I think of the way she said she doesn't do second dates, and I wonder if part of it is because she's afraid of happiness, of anything that might make her stop fighting for even a minute.

I remember what she told me the day we met, the way she said she had once been one of the unwanted children left to the palace's care. "Have you always lived here? On Kali?"

There's no way to really tell. Accents don't vary much across the planets and space stations of the star system anymore, and centuries of people traveling more or less freely between realms now means a certain kind of name or skin color or other physical feature is not a certain sign of where a person is from.

"My father moved us here six years ago," she says. "We lived in Sting before that, but then he found work with one of the finest smiths here." Sybilla pauses, sees the question on my face, and answers. "My mother died when I was born. He never forgave me. As soon as he found out about the queen's school at the palace, he sent me away. We haven't seen each other since."

"I'm sorry." It's no wonder she behaves like she's made of thorns and broken glass.

"I'm not," she replies. "I have a better life here than I ever had with him. Don't you feel the same way?"

The abruptness of the question catches me off guard. "I suppose I do have a better life here than I did on Wychstar, but I had Rama when I was there and that counted for a lot."

"You may not have Prince Rama here, but you have us. And you could make such a difference."

I think unexpectedly of little Juniper, who keeps dying in training because she's too busy making sure Jemsy and Henry are okay. I think of the others, a hundred and one faces.

I could teach them a trick or two that could save their lives.

A trick or two that they'll use against my brothers.

Sybilla is still watching me, and it's the hopeful look on her face that decides it for me.

"Gather the Hundred and One tomorrow," I say. And wonder if I'll live to regret it.

CHAPTER TWENTY-ONE

It's the post-dinner lull, when we usually all sit in the warm, snug, book-filled family parlor and read or talk or walk outside in the terrace gardens. I have a spot by the window and I look out at the star-stained sky, the red and gold of the Scarlet Nebula, the orb of the planet Winter. My mother and brothers are in a city somewhere on that planet preparing for a war.

The mother who wanted me gone. The brother at least two gods believe will kill me.

I rub my arms to keep warm.

I sense Rickard behind me before he speaks, his voice deep and gentle. "What is it, Esmae? What's happened?"

How can I tell him? Here is where the broken trust between us shines brightest, like light so sharp it's unbearable to look at. How can I tell him that my choices and his curse could soon have me spitting blood onto grass as I die?

And so I don't.

"Esmae," Elvar says from behind us, "would you like to join an old man for a walk in the gardens?"

I help him to the doors, my hand on his arm to guide him across the room. Rickard goes to play dice with Guinne and Sybilla. Beyond them, the old queen dozes ungracefully by the artificial fire and Max is mostly hidden behind a copy of *The Three Stolen Queens*. It's a peaceful time of day, so peaceful that I can't quite believe there are so many thorns and such bitterness buried just under the surface.

The gardens outside the parlor are built on an enormous terrace, a maze of wild hedges with beautiful flowers strewn across the paths. Above and around us, the skies seem endless, a harsh black-blue dotted with stars and stained to the east with the crimson of the nebula. Starships zip across the skies.

"Have I told you about the time your father and I stole a starship and tried to fly to Tamini?"

I smile. "How far did you get?"

"Our mother found us before we left the dock."

We laugh. After a few minutes of walking, we stop to rest on a bench. Elvar turns his face toward the stars. "We were so brave as boys, Cassel and I. I sometimes wonder if everyone grows afraid as they grow older. Kali is not a place for the old and the tired and the fearful."

"You are none of those things, Uncle Elvar," I say, but we both know that's a lie.

"May I ask you a question, Esmae?"

I nod out of habit, then remember he can't see me. "Of course."

"You lived on Wychstar almost all of your life. You knew the royal family well. Do you think King Darshan will join

Alexi's army? Do you think he'll come here with him just to render *Titania* useless?"

So that's the new terror plaguing his mind. I wonder what Lord Selwyn hopes to gain by putting it there.

"King Darshan is too clever and too fair to do that, Uncle. He may offer Alexi silver or troops if he thinks it's worth his while, but he won't involve himself directly. He won't come with him, just to make *Titania* useless. He won't try to destroy the ship he built just because he can."

"And yet he does favor Alexi, doesn't he? Some believe Darshan deliberately rigged the competition."

I hesitate. I have to be careful about how much I lie. "I don't think there was any specific plan for Alexi to win. Darshan constructed the competition as he did because he was inspired by a display of Rickard's he'd once seen."

"Yes, they knew each other years ago," Elvar agrees. "I remember when they fell out."

I'm puzzled. "Fell out?"

"I was only a boy then, which means Darshan must have been twenty or so, long before Rickard had made his vow to Cassel. Darshan was one of Rickard's students, you know."

"Was he? His son seemed to think he never made the cut."

"He might have let him believe that to avoid explaining what really happened. He had only been training with Rickard for a few months. Then they argued. Darshan had promised Rickard half of Wychstar's wealth in return for his lessons, you see. Rickard had no interest in Wychstar's wealth, but he wanted to see if the boy would keep his word. He asked him to deliver on his promise. Darshan panicked and threw a fit."

I wince. "I'm sure Rickard wasn't impressed."

"No. I would die for Rickard, but even I have to admit he can be very harsh." Elvar sighs. "In front of everyone present,

Rickard turned his back on the boy. He told him that he could give up his lessons or give up half of Wychstar's silver, but he couldn't keep both. Darshan was humiliated. He left. Word has it he's never gotten over the incident."

"Do you think that's why—" I remember who I'm speaking to and abruptly bite my tongue. I was about to speculate about *Titania*, and the god who told Darshan that the ship would get him what he wanted, but Elvar is not the right person for that.

"Esmae?"

"Sorry." I shift the conversation back to a safer topic. "You have no need to be afraid of Darshan, Uncle. I truly don't believe he would try to destroy *Titania*."

"You are kind to try to reassure an old man," he says fondly. "I'm so happy you came to Kali. Your presence has made a world of difference to me."

It's difficult to cling to my hatred of him. It's just as difficult to understand how a man who can be so gentle with me can be so cruel to his nephews and so dismissive of his son.

I guide my uncle back into the parlor. Grandmother is still asleep in her chair and Max is still hidden behind his book, but Sybilla, Guinne, and Rickard have all left the room. Elvar stops to talk to Max for a few minutes before retiring, trailed by his usual escort of royal guards.

I return to my seat by the window. The sight of Winter below takes my mind immediately back to Amba and her terrible certainty about my fate.

A movement makes me turn. Max has abandoned his book and crossed the room. He leans against the window beside me.

I look away. I've started to see him differently since I joined the war council. He supports his uncle on a lot of issues, yet simultaneously avoids escalating the war wherever possible. He speaks of Alexi and Bear dismissively, bitterly, but argues against attacking them prematurely. He's the jealous prince I expected but also so much more than that. Max is the reason Elvar has kept hold of the throne. Max is the reason Kali hasn't fallen to pieces.

The realization should make me happy, the discovery of a chink in Elvar's armor. The usurpers' hold on Kali would crumble if Max were removed from the equation. And I could easily remove him from the equation if I wanted to.

And yet I haven't. I don't want to.

"Father told me what you said to him in the garden just now. You've made him feel better about Wychstar's possible role in the war. Thank you for that."

"Your father should never have become king," I say bluntly. "It's making him sick with worry."

There's a heartbeat of silence, then Max says, "I know."

It's more honesty than I expected, and it clearly wasn't easy for him to say. I want to push the issue, but I don't have the heart to. "You and Rickard are very close," I say instead.

Max nods. "He was never able to teach his grandson or me, but he treated us just the same as he did Alex and Bear. The four of us were excitable and reckless and sometimes very badly behaved, but Rickard would only laugh at our angry parents and say 'Can't you see into their hearts? They'll grow up well, I promise you that.'" A faraway smile lights Max's eyes. "He loved us."

That, I understand. In a world where they were raised to be warriors and meticulously disciplined by ambitious, ruthless parents like Elvar, Guinne, and Kyra, who loved them but probably offered them very little in the way of affection, they must have been starved for the warmth and merriment that Rickard brought to their lives.

"He let us cry when we fell down," Max says. "He hid cakes in our rooms when we were punished. He let us travel across the galaxy with him."

Touched, and more than a little envious, I look at Max and look past the cousin who helped destroy us. I notice the way his eyes crinkle at the corners when he smiles, and the way he pushes his sleeves up past his elbows whenever they slip down, and the way his dark hair sticks up at the back. Small parts of him that I can look at without prejudices or preconceptions, parts of him that aren't tainted with history.

His eyes crinkle in a smile now, and there's something about the way he looks at me that flusters me. I turn away again. "I sometimes tell myself to trust you because Rickard does," I hear myself admit.

"That's not a good reason."

"I know. I tell myself that, too."

"He means the world to you," Max says.

I nod, my eyes fixed on Winter once more.

"Then why doesn't he teach you anymore?" he asks quietly.

To my own surprise, I tell him.

CHAPTER TWENTY-TWO

I was Rickard's student for almost seven years. He flew to Wychstar every week for two days, and we crammed in as many lessons as we could. I don't know how he explained those absences to the war council on Kali, but he always came.

For four of those years, I was happy. He told me stories about Kali and the star system. He made me see the world in brand new ways. He found the best parts of me and amplified them, and he found my weaknesses and tried to teach me how to use them. He loved me like I had been his own child and better than my own parents had. He understood how much I wanted to be like Alexi, as good as Alexi, how much I wanted to show my family I was worthy of them.

And it was he who first told me I didn't need them to be worthy. That I didn't have to define myself by my mother or father or brothers. *You are more than Alexi's sister, Esmae.*

Then, when Alexi, Bear, and our mother were exiled, Amba stepped in. She told me only disaster would come of my lessons and that they had to stop immediately. I understand now what she was afraid of, now that she's told me about the vision of my death, but at the time it made no sense. She spoke to Rickard. Whatever she said, he promised her that he would stop teaching me.

I couldn't bear it. Without Rickard, my tenuous link to Kali and my family was gone. Without Rickard, *Rickard* was gone.

I was convinced, utterly convinced, that home and love and family would only be possible for me if I was better than I was—less me, more Alexi. My lessons were the only way I knew how to chart a path across the stars back to my family.

And so I did the unforgivable. After everything Rickard gave me, I repaid him with a lie.

I waited until Amba said she'd be spending some time on Anga, the celestial planet where she rules the great beasts and forges the gods' divine weapons. Time passes differently there, and what was only weeks there could be months in our time. Once she was gone, I contacted Rickard over one of Rama's tech screens. I told him I had pleaded with Amba and she had relented. She had released him from his promise to her.

He didn't doubt me. Rickard never lied, and he believed his students never would either. Certainly not to him.

Amba was gone almost three years, an unprecedented absence. I got three more years with Rickard.

Then came the day it all went up in flames.

I went to see him without the slightest expectation of what was to come. He looked at me, so calm and steady. "Is there anything you'd like to tell me, Esmae?"

Perhaps he would have been less harsh if I had confessed.

I shook my head and I watched as his eyes turned to fire. "You tricked me into breaking my word. Amba is a war goddess and I am a warrior. I owe her loyalty, I owe her truth. You made me break my promise. You lied to me. Not once, not twice, but every day I've laid eyes on you for the past three years."

His voice rumbled like thunder and I shivered all the way down to my bones as I felt the crack of a curse. And then I remembered the old saying: *The gods' favorites can wreak havoc with just a handful of words.*

"You stole knowledge you weren't entitled to, so when you need it most, that knowledge will fail you. When you are at your most helpless, you will forget every lesson I ever gave you."

I told him how sorry I was. I begged him to take it back.

As he left Wychstar for good, Rickard looked back at me one last time. "I understand why you did it, Esmae. I understand it was not out of malice or greed. You will always have a place in my heart."

And he's always had a place in mine.

"That day you won *Titania* wasn't the day the curse came to pass," Max says. His eyes are kind. "That would have been an ideal time for the curse to take effect."

I shake my head. "It must not have been the time of my greatest need."

"So then it's still to come."

A duel. A broken arrow. Blood on the grass. "I suppose so."

"I can't believe he did that," Max says. He can't reconcile the Rickard who cursed me with the one he's known all his life.

"He loves us," I explain. "And that's as irrefutable as the existence of the sun. But so is the fact that he'll never break his word. His promises will always come first."

There's not much either of us can say after that.

CHAPTER TWENTY-THREE

I'm halfway to the seamstress on an errand for the queen when an asteroid hits the shields and the elevator comes to an emergency halt. The floor trembles, but I keep my balance.

The elevator opens at the floor where it stopped; it won't go any farther until the rock assault has passed. I'll take the stairs.

The hallways here are quiet, lined with stone and wood. It's a part of the palace I haven't been to before, up in one of the sharp spiky towers, and I don't know where to look for exits and stairways. My feet clatter across the floor, noisy and lonely in the silence. I search the hallways until I come to a door that must have been slammed open in the rock assault.

I stop in the doorway. It's a simple room, warm and woody. Bookshelves line all the walls, loose sketches are scattered on a desk, and I spot a worn, tattered armchair. A long worktable stretches out beside one of the windows. The furniture is bolted to the floor or to the walls, but a number of objects have tumbled to the ground—birds and miniatures of starships and a bow with no arrows. Except, when I look closer, I see that these models are more than they first appear. The birds have been sculpted out of feathers and buttons; the starships have been built from twigs; and the bow is thorny twine that would cut you if you touched it.

It's at once beautiful and terrible, lovely and brutal. There's quiet fury and loneliness in this room, as real as if it were flesh and blood.

So I'm not entirely surprised to see that the person in the middle of the room, picking objects up off the floor, is Max. *Beautiful. Terrible. Furious. Lonely.* Words I wouldn't have expected I'd ever use to describe him, and yet they fit.

"Are you lost?" he asks.

"A little."

I don't ask him for directions, and he doesn't offer any. A miniature of *Titania* is on a table close by, a patchwork of scrap metal fused together into her distinctive arrowhead shape. I want to touch it, to touch *everything*, but I resist. It doesn't feel right. It would be as though I'd put my fingers all over his soul.

"Why are you shut up here in a tower like a gargoyle?" I ask. "Don't you have a study downstairs near your father's?"

"That study is for Max Rey, Crown Prince of Kali, commander of the Hundred and One, secondary ruler of the realm. This is where I come when I don't want to be that version of myself anymore."

I look at him in surprise. He looks surprised, too, like he didn't expect to admit that to me.

"These things you make are beautiful," I say, changing the subject quickly. "Why have I never seen any of it before?"

"I don't show them off. Most people don't know I make them."

"Why not?"

"It's not approved of."

At first, I think he means he feels like he has to hide the rage, the loneliness, but then I realize he means the actual literal act of making objects out of scraps.

"What possible reason could the king and queen have to not approve of your work? Wych folk would call you a genius if they could see this."

He looks amused. "Is that so? The people of Wychstar would call the thief prince a genius?"

"Well, perhaps not you specifically. You're not very popular there."

He lets out a sharp, thorny laugh.

I look again at the model of *Titania*, scraps of metal layered like armor, like there's something precious inside that needs to be protected. "There's an awful sort of beauty here," I tell him, more honestly than I intended. "It makes me wonder what it is that goes on in your mind."

He's silent for a minute, then says, so quietly I almost miss it, "I'm tired. It's that simple."

"None of this says *tired* to me."

"I'm not the kind of son my parents wanted, as I'm sure you must have realized by now."

"So? You don't have to be something you're not just for them."

"You should have seen their faces when I first spoke with them after the competition. Mother tried the whole *You did your best, Max* thing, but I could hear the disappointment in her voice. Father didn't even try to hide his." Max makes a sound in this throat. "I'm not a child anymore. You'd think I would be able to just not care that I'll never be what they want. The problem is, I do."

My teeth snap together. "You spend too much time breaking yourself for your parents' sake."

"They're all I have left." His eyes are dark and faraway. "I'm not what they need me to be, but still I try to get as close to it as I can. And I know you understand that, Esmae, because you gave up years of your life just to prove yourself worthy—"

I take an involuntary step back. "That's not true."

"What's not true?"

"That I gave up years of my life. I didn't *give up* that time. I loved those years with Rickard—"

"I know that. It still doesn't mean it's how you would have chosen to spend your time if you had been allowed to live your life as Alexa Rey."

"How do you know what I would have done with my time?"

"It's an assumption. You don't seem to enjoy battle much. You spend more time in the library than in the simulation rooms or out on the training fields with the Hundred and One."

My mouth feels dry, my heart squeezed inside a fist. The look in his eyes is unbearable, so I look away. "Your assumption isn't incorrect. I loved my lessons with Rickard, but I didn't enjoy battle. My heart wanted the games and theory, not the blood and glory. Rickard, the perfect warrior, would talk about how he hoped he would die with honor in battle instead of peacefully in his bed. I was a pitiful excuse for a Kalian and hoped for the opposite." I risk a glance at Max and see that there's a smile in his eyes. "I loved the books better than the swordplay. I wanted to see the stars, not fight battles across them."

My voice fades into silence. I can't believe I admitted all of that to him. *Him*, of all people.

"We're not so different," says Max, an echo of the first time he said that to me. "We've both done whatever we had to for the sake of our families."

"Yes, I suppose we have."

It's a raw, naked moment. And then, just when I think I have to leave before the electric energy in the room becomes too much to bear, there's a rumble in the distance like thunder, and the room tips. Books rattle on the shelves. I retreat to a spot on the floor, up against the wall, and wait out the tremors.

Max has done the same across the room, his eyes fixed on the window. I can see the nebula reflected in his eyes.

"What will you do if this impasse turns into open war?" he asks me unexpectedly.

"I'm here, aren't I?"

"You're not here to fight for Father, Esmae."

So dangerous. How much has he guessed? Does he know about the pages and pages of cyphered secrets in a little blue notebook that I've hidden away? Does he know I plan to hand them over to Alexi as soon as I have a chance?

"I suppose not," I admit. Give a little of the truth to hide the lie. "I don't want to fight at all."

He nods. "Neither do I."

"Maybe you should try to persuade your father to give up the throne," I suggest, keeping my tone light like a joke. "It would solve the war problem."

"He won't give it up. He's wanted this all his life. He didn't feel like he was worthy of respect until the day he wore that crown. I can't take that from him."

"And Alexi won't let it go either, I assume?"

Max is silent for a minute or two, as though he isn't sure how much to say. "Alex's greatest pride is in his identity as a warrior. He believes his talent and his honor define him. He has too much pride and love for this kingdom to let it go."

I nod. "So neither side will back down."

"Not at the moment."

Not at the moment is a ray of hope. It tells me carnage isn't the only possible way this will all end. *I'm supposed to be that other way*, I remind myself. *I need to find Alexi the means to win his crown so easily that there won't be any more bloodshed.*

"If there is a war," Max says, "you could still remain apart from it. You could stay here or go back to Rama on Wychstar until it's over."

"If there's a war over Kali, my home, do you really think I could just stay out of it?"

"For your own sake, I wish you would."

I almost smile. "Then make it easy for me. Don't let it get that far."

"I'll do my best."

Another rumble like thunder and more vibrations in the walls. I pick up a book that's fallen off its shelf and run my thumb over the embossed text on its cover—a copy of *The Gods' Codex*, a history of the major gods.

"When I was ten or eleven," I say, still tracing the letters of the book's title, "Amba told me the story of her birth."

Out of the corner of my eye, I see Max look up in surprise. "And what was this story?" he asks, but his tone is careful, unsure.

"The god Ness was a wind god, a force of nature, capricious and cruel. Many centuries ago, he was told that one of his children would kill him one day. He wasn't too concerned about this prophecy at first; gods mate with stars all the time, and only very rarely are new gods born out of those stars."

Max smiles slightly. "But then a god was born after all?"

"Yes. The sun god Suya. Angry and determined to circumvent the future that had been foretold for him, Ness went after the godling, who was just a few days old at the time and had not even fully taken his true celestial form. Ness swallowed him to prevent him ever growing up, so he could not kill him." I trace the letters, over and over, again and again. "After Suya came Valin, a god of wisdom and choices, and then came Kirrin, god of tricks—"

"—*and* bargains," Max reminds me.

"Yes. Apparently, he doesn't like it when people forget that part. And after Kirrin came Thea, a goddess of hearth and home, and after her came Tyre, a god of justice. One by one, Ness swallowed them all and grew more confident, more smug, certain he had defeated his prophesied future." I glance up at Max. "And then Amba was born."

"The child who rose up."

"A war goddess. Fitting, really. She would have been swallowed up, too, had it not been for the great beast that happened to pass by the star from which she was born." Majestic, glorious, the great beasts are all but gone from the world—the last few live only on Anga. Once, they were everywhere, dragon-like and powerful, and they could fly across space just like ships, gods, and demons. "The beast took pity on the new godling and hid her under one of her wings. Then she devoured the star that Amba was born from. When Ness came, the great beast lied and said she had swallowed the star before Amba had even come out of it. Ness left without suspicion, and the great beast flew back to Anga to raise Amba in secret."

"And the war goddess told you all this?" Max asks curiously, his eyes alight with fascination. "I know *The Gods' Codex* chronicles part of the story, but some of those details must be hers. It's a very private story to tell a mortal."

"She knew I liked stories." I suppose I'm so accustomed to Amba flitting in and out of my life that I sometimes forget it's unusual for a mortal to see so much of a goddess. I think she cares about me, but I can never be sure. Maybe she feels responsible because of her role in my mother's past. Maybe I just entertain her.

Max asks, "What happened next?"

"Amba grew into her godhood in the care of the great beast who told her the story of her father and her devoured brothers and sister. Taking heart in the fact that Ness swallowed his children instead of murdering them, Amba decided there was a chance that they were still alive and resolved that she would save them. When she was grown, she faced off against her father, and she won. She split him open with an arrow from a divine bow she had forged herself—the Black Bow." *My bow.* "When Ness died, his godling children tumbled out of him. Suya, Valin, Kirrin, Thea, and Tyre, all of them, still alive, still unformed. And Amba, who had been born last, was now the oldest. The others grew into their godhoods in turn and—" I shrug, somewhat at a loss because the story doesn't really have an ending. "And all was well, I suppose? The end?"

"Creative."

I flash him a smile, but it doesn't last. "I told you that story because I wonder about Ness. If he'd left his children alone, if he'd ignored that vision of his future, would they have ever had reason to rise up against him? Would that future have been avoided?"

"Maybe," Max says, "or maybe one of his children would have found a different reason to kill him somewhere else down the line."

I try not to show how important this is to me. "So you don't think it's possible for such a vision to be averted?"

"Is this about your mother?" he asks gently. "You wonder what would have happened if she'd ignored Grandmother's curse and kept you?"

I can't tell him that it's about something else entirely, a future in which I bleed to death because my brother has chosen to kill me. And so I lie. "Yes."

Max sighs. "I don't believe things like that can be averted forever, Esmae. I think the *what* is already in place, and we just control the *how*."

I swallow. Am I really so crazy to believe I can prevent my own terrible future?

It's gone quiet outside. Max stands. I do, too, then take a step back in the direction of the door. "I should go."

"Will you come back?" He isn't looking at me. I get the impression that it wasn't an easy question to ask.

I give the model of *Titania* another wistful look, then turn away before I find the urge to touch it irresistible. "I'd like that."

"Why don't you just pick up the model? I don't mind."

"I don't dare."

"Why not?"

My cheeks redden. "Do you remember when the archaeologists on Sting found the fossil of one of the great beasts? Rama's tutor took us to see it." I can still picture the old bones, white and stained with dirt. "There were dozens of people there and they all touched the bones. I could see the smudges of their hands and their fingerprints. I wanted to touch the fossils, too, but I wouldn't let myself. They were beautiful and raw, still partly buried in the dirt, and I was sure I'd ruin them if my fingertips so much as brushed them."

Max regards me silently for a moment, and then he crosses the room and puts the model of *Titania* in my hand. "Take it," he says.

"But—"

He closes my fingers over the metal. "Get your fingerprints all over it." His eyes meet mine. "Otherwise, it's just another fossil in the dark, waiting for someone to find it."

CHAPTER TWENTY-FOUR

My hands are clenched together. *Titania* grumbles about the trauma of being forced to fly in the rain. We're about to land in Blackforest, the capital city of Winter.

The invitation to Princess Katya's wedding came months ago, but the first I heard of it was when Max asked me if I wanted to go with him yesterday.

"Alex and Bear will be there," he said to me. The look in his eyes made me wonder if he knew just how badly I wanted to see my brothers again.

There was no way in the whole, wide universe that I could pass up such an opportunity.

Now I'm here, and all I can think of is the look on Alexi's face when I won *Titania*. Suddenly, I wish I'd stayed on Kali like Elvar and Guinne, who never leave Kali for any reason.

"I have suffered a great many indignities in my time," *Titania* informs us. "No words can do justice to the atrocities I have endured. Yet this is, by far, the worst horror to befall me. What kind of demonic activity is this?"

Having only ever flown across spaceship kingdoms and through deep space, *Titania* has never encountered rain before now. She's not happy.

"I think it's beautiful," I say.

"I liked you until you said those words," says *Titania* bitterly.

Behind me, Sybilla is nearly doubled over in fits of laughter. She's come with us under duress, reluctant to let us go without extra protection, yet simultaneously irked because she despises celebrations. Funerals, she claims, are more to her taste.

I watch Blackforest draw nearer. Like most of Winter, it's a cold place, with powdery snow dusted across the rooftops and between the cracks of the streets' paving stones. It's a densely packed, rocky city of harsh lines and grim cathedrals, lovely in a bleak, gray, cold way, but I prefer Kali's austere, whimsical beauty.

The dock is a set of numbered holes punched into a cliff face. Beyond the dock, I can see King Ralf's palace, a pyramid of snowy gray stone with a tower at each of its four corners. A blue wedding flag waves from the top of each tower.

I look past the city, past the snow and the forests and valleys. Alexi's city is somewhere in that direction.

"Look at them cower," *Titania* crows, tugging my attention back to the dock.

This is an exaggeration. Blackforest's sentries are wary as they watch the unbeatable warship descend, but they aren't exactly trembling in their boots.

I reluctantly abandon the luxury of bare feet and put on the heeled slippers Guinne's seamstress thrust at me when she gave me my dress. "Only tall heels for you, I'm afraid," she'd said. "You're small, for a start. More importantly, the size of the heels will allow you to fit a tiny dagger in each one."

"Why would I need to hide knives in my shoes?" I'd demanded.

"One can never be too cautious," had been her enormously comforting reply.

Titania swoops out of the rain. Her main doors hiss open as she comes to a stop. "Good luck," she says a little sadly.

Max pats the console. "I'm sorry you can't come."

"*Hmph.*"

"Could someone remind me of what our story is today?" Sybilla asks, picking up her array of extremely impressive weapons.

I frown. "Story?"

"Story," she repeats. "Lovers? Or just Elvar's son and niece?"

"Don't," Max warns.

I'm still confused. "What are you talking about?"

"Ah." Sybilla looks like she has well and truly put her foot in it. "So you don't know what people are saying."

"How can she not?" *Titania* demands. "Even I know! Is it not true?"

"Is what not true?"

"Have you put filters in your tech to make sure you don't get any news stories about yourself?" asks Sybilla.

"Of course I have. Why would I want daily updates on what people are saying about me?"

"People want to know why you competed for *Titania* against your own brother and then took her to Kali," says Max.

Realization hits. "And naturally, the conclusion they've come to is that you and I must be—"

"Yes."

My face grows hot. "I'm a princess of Kali," I say bitterly, "I'm one of the finest archers alive today. I won the greatest warship in the world. I saved the life of a prince of Wychstar when I was twelve years old. And all they care about is who I may or may not be sharing a bed with?"

"To be fair," says Sybilla, "they may not know the part about you saving a prince's life." Max growls at her. She shrugs sheepishly. "Did you really?"

"I knew that, too," *Titania* says. "Rama told me himself the day you left Wychstar. He said, 'Take good care of her, *Titania*. She's as much my family as my brother and sisters. She once saved my life and she's made me laugh every single day I've known her. Don't let me lose her.' I've always been fond of Rama. I promised him I would do whatever I could to ensure that he did not lose you."

The memory of Amba's vision rises again before I can stop it: *A duel. A broken arrow. Blood on the grass.* Poor Rama, destined to lose me after all.

No, I can't think like that. I swore that wouldn't happen. I won't die that way.

I squeeze my eyes shut, then open them. "We're going to be late."

Max doesn't question my abrupt change in tone, but something in his narrowed eyes tells me he knows there's more going on here than I've told them.

My knees wobble as I step onto the solid ground outside *Titania.* I never get over this, how *still* the ground is. You don't appreciate how much a spaceship kingdom moves until you're not on one anymore; you don't appreciate how much your body has adapted the way it moves to accommodate such an existence. Here, there's no constant, almost imperceptible hum beneath my feet, no gentle tilt when the ship shifts a fraction, and there's certainly not likely to be a rock assault. My feet don't need to prepare to compensate for those movements. The sensation is alien to me.

So is the feeling of natural sunlight directly on my skin. It feels crisper and harsher than the softer, carefully filtered light of the sun and moon lamps on Kali and Wychstar. I blink at the bluish white clouds, breathe in raw air. I find it hard to believe that millions of people live their lives completely grounded. I can't fathom a life away from the sky.

Aircharriots wait outside the dock for the guests, suspended a foot off the ground. I climb into one, along with Max and Sybilla. Max is quiet as always, but Sybilla is completely unfazed by the sensations of solid ground and natural sun. She probably still misses them, even after six years on Kali.

We join a stream of other chariots drawing up outside the enormous palace doors as guests from all over the star system make their way inside. There's a procession of gowns and dresses, dark formal jackets and ties, robes and saris, guests and guards and servants.

We get more than our fair share of attention, an unfortunate side effect of being a thief prince and the girl who won the greatest warship of all time. A lot of it isn't friendly. I keep my eyes open, watching how people react to Max. The royals from Tamini don't look pleased to see us, no surprise as we already know whose side they've chosen. King Ralf's polite but cool manner seems to reinforce the war council's view that he and Winter are inclined the same way. On the other end of the courtesy spectrum are King Darshan and his older son Rodi, who are too far away to speak with but who smile at me across an enormous wedding hall lit by blue glass windows and an arched glass roof etched with crystals of ice.

I can't calm myself. There are so many guests that it's impossible to search the crowd during the actual ceremony, but after the birds have been let loose and the horn has blown the wedding call and the princess and her new husband have been blessed with fresh snow, the guests disperse into the banquet hall for the feast. Movement is freer and flows more quickly here, so it's easier to pick out faces.

I don't know if I'm more afraid that I'll see him, or more afraid that I won't.

"Princess Alexa," says a voice beside me.

"That's Princess Esmae, thank you very much," Sybilla snaps.

"This is Rama's brother," I tell her, "Rodi, Crown Prince of Wychstar."

"Oh," she says but is only a little mollified. "Nevertheless, sir, you will address the princess by the name she now officially uses."

Rodi grins. "I'm so very sorry, my lady."

"Lady?" she snorts, then remembers to be polite. "You may call me Sybilla, Prince Rodi."

He shakes her outstretched hand, smiles at her, is surprised when she appears utterly unmoved by his smile, and then searches the room for Max, who is about ten feet away talking with a young couple from Sting. Rodi turns back to me. "My brother," he says, "who I need hardly add felt unequal to the strenuous task of making the journey, sends his love. And how are you?"

"Overwhelmed," I tell him frankly.

"I don't blame you. We miss you on Wychstar, you know. Come and visit soon." He catches his father's eye from across the room. "I'll leave you to it. It's been good to see you, Esmae."

He leans down to kiss me on the cheek. At least, I think that's why he leans down, but as his mouth brushes my cheek, he whispers, "Rama asked me to tell you Skylark should be safe now."

I freeze. "Really?"

"A ship came close in what we think was an attempt to assess the defenses," he says, as quickly and quietly as he can. "It disappeared when the pilot saw that some of Wychstar's ships were present in those defenses. If they didn't know Father would extend his protection to Princess Shay before, they do now. Thank you."

And then he's gone. I turn back to Sybilla. She's giving me a wry look. "Is that a Wych custom? Kisses on cheeks that take all day?"

"He wasn't kissing me the whole time."

"Oh, I know," she says. "I could see you both whispering. Don't worry, I won't tell."

"Why not? What if I were plotting against Max?"

She laughs so hard that tears actually fill her eyes. "I wish you would. I'd like to see that." She wipes her cheeks. "Max can take care of himself. As long as no one tries to murder him on my watch, I'm not worried about anyone plotting against him. And while we're on that subject," she says with a wicked grin, "I'm not convinced it's polite to be cozying up to other princes when your lover is only a few paces away."

"You're a real thorn in my side, you know that?"

Max walks back toward us. "What's so funny?"

We just giggle harder.

And then I see Alexi, and my laughter sputters into silence.

He's just a boy. I've never looked at him that way before, but that's what I see now. A boy with a heavy, invisible crown on his head and a golden bow on his back, almost lost in a sea of faces.

Max's shoulders tense as he sees him, too. There's a heartbeat of stillness, in which no one seems to know what to do, and then Alexi moves our way. Sybilla's hands twitch at her sides.

Alexi ignores Max completely, addressing only me. "May I have a word, Esmae? Alone?"

I blink. Behind him, Bear gives me a quick, shy smile, while General Saka scowls. She's not the only one; glaring at Alexi like she suspects him of some nefarious scheme, Sybilla opens her mouth to argue, but Max gives a small shake of his head and she clamps her mouth shut again.

My heart begins to race. It won't go down well with Elvar and Guinne when they find out I spoke to Alexi alone, and Lord Selwyn certainly will talk about it for months, yet I can't pass up this opportunity. I don't know what Alexi wants, and I have no idea if he'll ever forgive me for what he thinks I've done, but this is finally my chance to tell him the truth.

"Where would you like to speak?" I ask.

He gestures to a doorway at the end of the room. I follow.

CHAPTER TWENTY-FIVE

As we pick our way across the hall, I study the faces around us, looking for gray eyes and brown hair.

"She isn't here," says Alexi. I flush at how obvious I must seem.

"Why not?"

"When she found out you would be in attendance, she refused to come," he says. "I'm sorry."

I blink away tears. What did I expect? Did I really think she'd want to see me?

Alexi is obviously familiar with the palace because he leads me directly to a small library. He couldn't have picked a better spot; I feel so much more at ease here, away from the crowd, with books as my allies and the smell of paper in the air.

Alexi closes the door behind us. He ignores the chairs and sits on the floor, his back against a bookshelf. I hesitate, then take a seat opposite him.

"Mother thinks you want to ruin us. She thinks you were born to destroy us. Bear says she's wrong."

"What do you think?"

"I don't know what to think. That's why I wanted to talk to you. The things you said on Wychstar made your allegiances pretty clear, but then I can't help but wonder how much of that was for Max's benefit."

My fists loosen and my breath flutters in relief. "You don't believe I'm on Elvar's side."

"Let's just say I'm having a really hard time believing my own sister would choose our enemy."

"And you would be right."

His face breaks into a smile. "So you *were* putting on a show because of Max."

"Of course I was," I say, my words tumbling out as the dam finally breaks. I get to tell the truth at last. "I needed him to trust me. I wanted him to want me on his side. I competed against you so that no one would think I was on yours, but I've always been fighting for our family."

"I knew it," Alexi says quietly. "I knew you were one of us."

I don't reply. I can't. My throat has closed up and my heart trembles with the sharp, keen ache of joy. I've wanted to be one of them all my life.

There's a moment of silence and then Alexi says, "You're my twin sister, the other half of me. I don't think I ever noticed the emptiness where you were supposed to be before I knew to look for it, but I can't *not* see it now. I've rewritten my entire life with you in it. It's what I do when I can't sleep. I try to picture what it would have been like if Mother had never sent you away. Would we have become warriors together? Would you have teased Bear with me, or would you have taken his side? Would Max have betrayed us if he'd known you? Would Elvar have hesitated if there had been three of us to contend with instead of just two? I think of birthdays, banquets, my first day of training, my first day in the schoolroom, the first time I ever kissed a girl, the first time I ever kissed a boy, the first time I held a sword, the first time I won a fight, and I think of how it might have all been if you had been right there with me."

"I've pictured our lives like that, too," I say. "We can't get that time back, but I'm here now. We're together and we can win."

"Why didn't you tell me? And join me? We could have had *Titania*. We could have fought them together."

"Have you won yet?"

He gives a rueful laugh. "No."

"Why not? Because you don't have *Titania* on your side? Or because Elvar and Max are able to stay one step ahead of you?"

"The latter," Alexi admits, reluctantly.

"On Kali, I'm learning their secrets. I know battle plans and the names of spies. I even get a vote on how to move against you. I don't have an easy way to cut Elvar down yet, but every single thing I learn is useful."

His eyes are full of anguished hope. "I want so badly to trust you."

"It's all right if you still aren't sure you can. We don't know each other yet. Trust doesn't appear like magic."

"How will you give me the information you have? You can't exactly call me on your tech."

I glance at his wrist. "Your watch can record voices."

"Yes. So?"

"All the information's in my head," I say, and grin. "Start recording."

It takes half an hour. Muted noise and music from the feast drift into the library. I speak as quickly as I can because I know Max and Sybilla will start to wonder what's taking so long. When I've told Alexi everything I know, we agree that I'll share future information by making trips to Winter under the guise of spending time with Princess Katya, who I will make sure to befriend before I leave the wedding.

"King Ralf and Princess Katya will be happy to give us cover," Alexi explains. "Everyone on Kali will think I'm busy in Arcadia, nowhere near here, and they can hardly begrudge you a friendship with the princess of the kingdom they rely on for most of their supplies."

"It could work," I say.

Alexi's face darkens. "Watch out for Max. Our cousin is as clever as he is treacherous. If anyone's likely to figure out what you're up to, it's him."

"He's not quite the monster I expected," I say cautiously.

"And our uncle is not the cruel villain you expected either, I imagine," says Alexi. He laughs at the surprise on my face. "It's hard not to warm to them, Esmae, but that doesn't mean you can trust them. I'm sure our uncle cares very much about you, just as he once cared a great deal about me. That's who he is. He cares until he thinks you're a threat, and then you become his enemy."

I want to protest that Elvar isn't that fickle, but then I think of how certain he is that people like King Darshan are out to destroy him. I think of that first dinner on Kali, and how easily Lord Selwyn put that look of suspicion on Elvar's face, and how there's no way to tell what he whispers in the king's ear.

Alexi uncurls and stands, quick and nimble. I follow. He holds a hand out to me, and I take it. "Thank you," he says quietly.

"We will win, Alexi."

He smiles, young and hopeful, his gray eyes bright as the sun. "I know we will."

"The gods are wrong."

"You mean the vision," he says, smile fading. "The one Amba and Kirrin saw. The one that makes me your murderer."

"I don't believe it."

"Neither do I. You need to know that, Esmae." He's earnest, his wounded honor written across his wide eyes. "You need to know I would never betray you or myself that way. I don't want to hurt anyone, let alone my own sister."

"You'll do what needs to be done to win this war," I point out.

"But this vision wasn't about open war. It was a duel. I would never breach the honor of a duel. And why would we duel, anyway? What would be the need? It makes no sense. How can what they saw possibly happen?"

"It can't. And yet they saw it."

His fists clench and unclench. I look down and see that mine are doing the same. "I can believe that we could be forced into a duel somehow," he says, "I can wrap my head round that. But no one can force me to hurt you. I won't be my sister's killer."

"I told Amba it wouldn't come to pass. Swore it, in fact. Swore I wouldn't die that way."

Alexi smiles. "Good."

I smile back, oddly comforted. The possibility of my blood on that grass is so much less terrifying now that I know there are two of us working against it. *Loved by gods.* Wasn't that what Amba said we are? Surely there's nothing, then, that we can't do together?

"We should return," Alexi says. "What shall we say we were doing all this time?"

"Arguing. We'll say you tried to persuade me to join your cause so you could have *Titania* and I refused because of what our mother did to me, so we argued about the way I've betrayed our family. They'll all believe that."

When we return to the feast, it's difficult to watch Alexi's face shift into a more mutinous expression as soon as eyes of others can see us, but it's necessary and I keep my posture just as stiff. Alexi marches off to find General Saka and Bear, and I go back to Max and Sybilla. I look back once, watching them go, my two brothers with copper in their hair and battle scars across their skin, and feel like a part of me has gone with them.

Sybilla raises her eyebrows at me. "That went well, then? Nice bit of family bonding?"

"Don't ask."

We leave early. The airchariot glides over the snow, sending clouds of white into the air, and a moon winks down at us from above. It's a half joker moon, the moon that laughed when the god Gann slipped on a banana peel and was consequently punished with a curse. *You will be the joker moon forevermore*, the god said in the story. *Only to appear when tricks are played and treachery is afoot*. It's bad luck to look at such a moon. I shiver and turn my face away.

We're about ten minutes into the journey back to Erys when *Titania* informs us that there's a screw loose in one of her controls. Max goes down to sort it out.

As soon as he's out of earshot, Sybilla turns to me. "Are you going to leave us for your family?"

I've started to understand the sharpness in her voice, and I can see now that that curt, brittle tone is a layer she uses to cover her fear. "Of course not. What would I gain from joining my entitled brothers and the mother who literally threw me out of our home? If I went anywhere, it would be back to Wychstar, but I don't plan on doing that anytime soon, either. And anyway, no matter where I went, I wouldn't leave *you*. We'd still be friends, wouldn't we?"

She nods, relieved, but we both know friendship wouldn't make any difference if we had to face each other in battle.

Sybilla scuffs a boot against the floor, making *Titania* grumble. "I told Max we shouldn't have let you go off with Alexi," she admits.

"Did you both expect me to go with my brother and, what? Never come back?"

"We didn't think you would. Just that you could."

A question sticks in my throat, but I ask it anyway. "Does Max *want* me to go?"

"Between you and me," she says, "I think he'd give almost anything for you to want to stay."

I look away so that she can't see the pain on my face. "I do want to stay."

For more reasons than I dare admit even to myself.

CHAPTER TWENTY-SIX

I let a couple weeks pass before I dare to fly *Titania* back to Winter.

It's a quiet day with not much on the royal schedule. I sit with Grandmother in her decadent private suite, sipping spiced wine and nibbling on kaju sweets while some truly abysmal music wafts from the tune player, and listen to her plot new ways to skew the war votes in her favor. It seems to be as good a time as any to leave.

"Grandmother," I say without ceremony, "I can't listen to this awful music a moment longer. I'll see you at dinner."

"Rachki is not awful, you blasphemous whelp!" she shouts after me. "She was one of the greatest veena players of all time!"

"There's a reason no one plays the bloody veena anymore," I mutter under my breath.

There's a comet shower deep in space. I have to wait for two engineers to finish a routine check on *Titania*, so I stand in the dock and watch the comets flash like fireworks over Kali.

That's when I see them, the two shadows standing on a maintenance ledge just below the ceiling of the dock. I recognize Max's profile. He seems at ease. The other shadow is unfamiliar. It looks like a man with stooped shoulders and a shock of hair.

Another mysterious visitor, never seen before, and probably never to be seen again.

I glance back at the engineers, one of whom raises both hands when she sees me looking. At least ten more minutes before *Titania* is ready.

There's a spiral stairway at the far end of the dock. I should be able to use it to get within earshot of the shadows on the ledge. I climb quickly, higher and higher. As long as I stay beneath the level of the ledge, I should be able to get close without being spotted.

I reach the top of the stairway and press against the wall of the landing, a few feet beneath the ledge. Snatches of voices float down to me—

"Do you remember how angry I made him that day?" the old man asks. "I thought he'd break the sun in a fit of temper—"

"It wasn't one of your better days. Mind you, it's not as bad as some of the other tricks you've played in your time—"

The old man laughs, and Max joins in. I'm bewildered. Their conversation sounds so relaxed, so normal. Why the secrecy then?

"I keep wondering how much I've forgotten," Max says, quiet now. "It feels like it's all still there, at the back of my mind somewhere, but the human brain can only store so much."

"Ah, but I'm always here to remind you of the pieces you've lost."

I wonder if they're talking about Max's biological parents. If he's afraid sometimes that he's lost even his few memories of them. I wonder if the old man knew them.

"Were you ever going to tell me about Esmae and the blueflower?" the old man asks.

I freeze.

"Why would I?" Max says. "What difference does it make to you?"

The old man doesn't answer that. "I saw her at the wedding. I saw the jewel in her hair. It looks like a gemstone, but it would be a travesty if I didn't know a blueflower when I saw one. I assume Amba blessed it before she gave it to her? Turned it into armor?"

"You'll have to ask her."

"Is there a particular reason you won't talk to me about this?"

"I'm not going to talk about Esmae." Max's voice is still friendly but implacable.

Unnerved, I flee down the stairway before I can be discovered. I don't know what to make of what I've just heard. I've always suspected that Max must have guessed about the blueflower at some point, but I have no idea why the old man is so interested in it, not to mention the fact that I've never seen him before, yet he has apparently been so close to me that he was able to spot a jewel in my hair.

I climb aboard *Titania*, still feeling troubled. She, of course, notices. "What's the matter with you?"

"It's not important. Can you put a call in to King Ralf's palace and ask for Princess Katya?"

"I didn't know Alexi changed his name," *Titania* says, dry as dust. I laugh.

When Princess Katya answers, I choose my words carefully in case anyone on Kali has intercepted the signal. "I'm at a loose end today and thought I'd take you up on your very kind offer to explore Blackforest. Are you free?"

"Of course!" she says enthusiastically, just the tiniest gurgle of mirth in her voice. "It would be my pleasure. Let me send you the coordinates of one of my favorite spots and I'll meet you there."

The coordinates she sends are, of course, in the new territory now known as Arcadia.

"Can you cloak us so that no one will know which part of the planet we've gone to?" I ask *Titania*.

"Already done. And the engineers will check my past journey logs, but they'll only see the coordinates I wish them to see."

She rises into the air and zips out of the dock. As we fly, she tells me about the newest book she downloaded from the tech library, a fascinating story about seven minor gods who were reborn as mortals as punishment for a crime.

"Do you miss Wychstar?" I ask her when she's finished.

"I don't know," she says, "What does it feel like, missing something?"

I don't know how to give words to such a feeling, so I ask a different question. "Do you know why King Darshan wanted Alexi to win you?"

"I know he wanted Alexi to know he had set up the competition for him," she says. "He wanted Alexi to be grateful.

Darshan wanted to ask favor of your brother and wanted him to feel unable to refuse."

"What was the favor?"

"I don't know."

What could Alexi have given Darshan that no one else in the world could? "I do know this much," *Titania* says. "He was very upset when you won me instead. He considered asking you for the favor, but decided in the end that because you would not feel the same gratitude Alexi did, you would be unlikely to grant it."

It's a favor he believed either of us were capable of granting. So then what do I have in common with Alexi that no one else does?

While I think about it, Titania says, "The goddess Amba is fond of you, isn't she? She was one of the gods who made me."

This is news to me, but it does make perfect sense. Why wouldn't a war goddess contribute to the creation of an unbeatable, unbreakable warship?

"Why do you want to know if she's fond of me?" I ask.

"No reason."

"Which means there's a reason. Are you going to tell me what it is?"

"We chat sometimes," *Titania* explains, "and she speaks of you in the tone of one who is fond. That's all."

I can't help feeling disquieted by this. Regular conversations between a war goddess and a sentient warship can't possibly bode well.

"Look!" *Titania* practically shrieks, making me jump. "We're here!"

It's a good distraction, I'll give her that. I drop the subject of Amba and cross to the glass to gaze down.

The first thing I notice is how green Arcadia is under patchy layers of snow and ice. It's a lush paradise, simultaneously rustic and modern, with forests and rolling hills. The palace is small and spiky, half-hidden by the woods around it, and the city is a maze of reddish rooftops, cobbled roads, smoky chimneys, aircharriots, and armorers' workshops. The fields are dotted with sheep, cows, and farms. There are sentries and riverships and spaceships and a nearly invisible shield around the palace.

It's beautiful, peaceful, and very carefully guarded.

A small river twists across the city and vanishes into the yellow woods on the western border. *Titania* flies there, then swoops low to find a spot to land beneath the drooping, weeping trees.

"Be careful," she says. But the way she says it makes me wonder if Amba has told her of the prophecy.

I pick up a coat, open an exit hatch, and climb onto *Titania*'s wing. There's a sharp, icy nip in the air. I cock my head and listen, then recognize what sounds like Bear's voice in the trees about twenty yards away. I jump off the wing, put my coat on over my inadequate summer dress, and follow the voice.

I find them by the river, just my brothers, barefoot with their trouser legs rolled up like they're children on a fishing trip. Bear has a staff in his hand.

I swallow down my nerves, toe off each of my boots, and try not to wince as I curl my feet into the icy grass. "And what are we doing?"

Bear bounds toward me, all boyish enthusiasm. "I'm so glad you came," he says, unceremoniously thrusting the staff in my direction. "Here. Let's spar."

"Don't even think about it," Alexi warns him.

I give him an annoyed look. "Don't write me off just because I'm smaller than he is."

Alexi's amused. "It's not you I'm worried about."

His words surprise a laugh out of me, but Bear is deeply offended and grumbles about being treated like the baby of the family.

"Why *are* we barefoot?" I ask. "Not that I'm complaining. Except I am. I can't feel my toes anymore."

"Come here," Alexi says.

I approach him. He's standing on a rock next to the water. This isn't the river I saw disappear into the woods from above; it's a deep pool. Steam rises from the surface.

"A hot spring?"

"They're all over Winter," he explains. He sits down on the rock and kicks his bare feet in the water.

I tentatively do the same and yelp when the heat hits my near-frozen feet. "Do you come here often?"

"It's our favorite place in the city," he says.

I stare at his profile for a moment. I don't know if it means anything that they invited me to their favorite spot, but I'm touched all the same.

Bear joins us, bringing bottles of fruit ale. He hands me one and opens his own with his teeth. "I forgot the honey cakes," he says. "They're in the box under the tree, Alex."

Alexi rolls his eyes and goes off to find the sweets. As soon as he's out of earshot, Bear drops his voice to a whisper: "You haven't been drinking the wine, have you?"

"Of course not." So Alexi doesn't know. Neither Bear nor our mother has told Alexi of her plans. Because his honor wouldn't abide it? Because he'd try to stop her? "I'm not sure it matters, anyway. Max tests every bottle of wine and every dish served. He keeps a syringe full of stasis serum with him at all times so that he can save Elvar's life if the poison *does* make its way in. Whoever has been helping our mother will have seen how careful he's been. They've probably already told her that poison is a waste of time."

"Just stay away from the wine anyway," says Bear stubbornly.

Alexi returns with the honey cakes. He gives me one, and when I taste it, the warmth and moisture floods my mouth. He grins at the joy on my face. "There's a local woman who makes them. Bear visits her at least three times a week to replenish his supply."

"Can you blame me?" Bear demands, except it sounds more like *caoobaymee* through the cake stuffed in his mouth.

I eat the crumbly edges of the honey cake first, then swallow the moist middle whole. I glance at Alexi in time to see him do exactly the same. He notices, too, and quickly looks away.

I give them my latest updates from the war council, including details of a plan to intercept one of Alexi's supply ships. It's frustratingly not quite what we need. Without open war, the council's current plans are mostly defensive, with a little trickery thrown in for good measure: reinforce this part of the perimeter; reach out to this ally; cut that supply route. Nothing I can use to end the war altogether. The names of spies are helpful, of course, but even the war council doesn't discuss those details openly, and there's a great deal I still don't know. I need to get more out of Elvar, but trust takes time and, despite his fondness for me, he hasn't yet revealed any convenient dark secrets. Perhaps he doesn't have any.

Once we've hashed the subject of war to death, we fall into awkward stilted conversation that gradually flows more easily. We talk of our childhoods—I tell them about Wychstar and they tell me about our father. We talk about places we'd like to visit, our favorite battle formations, our favorite weapons. Mine's my bow, Alexi's is his, and Bear's is his mace.

At some point, and with some difficulty, I ask about our mother.

"She's fine. She keeps herself busy."

"Would she see me if I asked?" I want to kick myself for the tiny note of hope in my voice.

They shake their heads. "Sorry, Esmae," Bear says, looking as ashamed as if he were personally responsible for her choices. "She refused to come with us today. She was wild as fire when she found out *we* were coming. She thinks we should have nothing to do with—"

"I think Esmae's gotten the idea."

Bear darts a guilty look my way. I rub my nose to hide how deeply his words have cut into my heart. "It's fine," I lie.

I finish my bottle of fruit ale and a few more honey cakes. The sun, so harsh and real, creeps lower in the sky. The ground is utterly still. I find myself missing the engines and spiky towers and colored skies of Kali. I think of how I'll return to Erys today and how my brothers won't. They'll stay here, with real sunsets and natural forests and ground under their feet that doesn't constantly thrum. They'll stay here with our mother. They get her, I get Kali.

And we'll all feel the desperate ache of what we can't have.

CHAPTER TWENTY-SEVEN

Max's dark head is bent over an object on the desk. I look over his shoulder and see that it's an old-fashioned sort of clock, dismantled. He has a knack with machines that he doesn't have with bows and arrows. Sometimes I think that in spite of all the bloodshed and betrayal littered across his past, he's better at putting things together than he is at ripping them apart.

I watch the way he coils a copper wire around his thumb to keep it in place. Unexpectedly, I think of a lock of my coppery hair twined around his fingers that way.

Does Max want me to go?

I think he'd give almost anything for you to want to stay.

The memory keeps pushing itself to the forefront of my mind, filling me with guilt and hope and *wanting* every time. It's as absurd as it is infuriating. Of all the people in all the worlds, why is *he* the one I want?

"Esmae, you were kind of in the middle of a sentence?"

"I was just saying I'm on my way out. I want to take *Titania* off Kali for a few hours. She doesn't get to fly half as much as she wants to."

"That's a good idea. I'm sure she needs it."

I hesitate. Then, for no fathomable reason whatsoever, I say, "Would you like to come with us?"

His eyes flash up to mine. He takes a minute to reply, and when he does, his voice is cautious. "Where are you planning to go?"

"I didn't have anywhere specific in mind. You're welcome to choose."

He hesitates, then nods and follows me out the door.

Titania wants to know where to take us.

"I don't know," says Max. A grin crooks the corner of his mouth.

"How helpful," she snipes.

"You're missing the point," I say, catching on. "You get to pick."

"Me? Really?"

"Anywhere you like," says Max.

"I'm going to show you something beautiful!" She bursts out of the shields so fast my head spins. We hurtle into open space. Once she's steadied her pace, I unbuckle myself from my seat and sit down on the floor beside the wall of unbreakable glass. Vast stretches of galaxy twinkle beyond. I count the stars but quickly lose track.

Max comes closer. I study him for a moment and see stars and moon rocks in his eyes.

"I want Alexi to win this war." It's my voice, but I almost can't believe I've said the words.

"I know."

"How could you possibly know that?"

"I can see it in your face when people talk about him. I can see how badly you want your family to come home."

I swallow. "How do you always see me exactly as I am?"

"I don't know." There's a pause, and then he asks, "What made you decide to tell me?"

I wish there was an easy answer, but I don't know why I said anything at all. "Why did you let me stay on Kali if you knew I want your enemy to win?"

"The alternative was to ask you to go, and that wasn't the alternative I wanted."

The moon rocks hurtle in and out of his eyes. I turn my head to the glass and watch a distant green nebula glowing bright against the void of space. Closing my eyes, I try to picture myself as an infant, surrounded by that void. Did I wail into the dark until my cries grew thin and tired? Did I lie quietly in my sealed boat entranced by the stars? Was I consumed by hurt and longing or was I captivated by the beauty? I don't know. I don't remember. Perhaps it was a little bit of both.

When *Titania* slows at last, I bolt to my feet; I know exactly where we are. The mass in front of us is uneven, wickedly jagged, gray-blue, cold, and almost translucent. It looks like an enormous piece of dark ice. And *Titania* is right. It is beautiful. Deep shadows cross its seas. A soft, haunting sound rises from the form and creeps into the ship, the eerie song of the hounds in the shadows.

"The Empty Moon," I whisper.

Ruled by the god Kirrin, it's one of those places mortals rarely go. Most would be too afraid. The seas are fathomless and terrifying. The creatures are deadly. Unlike the great beasts of Anga, born from the blood of the first *raksha* demons and typically peaceful, the creatures of the Empty Moon were bred by gods and they are supposedly without pity or mercy. The stories say there is a garuda that guards the palace; the hounds are as big as bears and will tear you apart if you fail their tests; the water beasts have three rows of teeth and tails as wickedly sharp as thorns.

Max's hand isn't quite steady as he reaches out and brushes the glass, like he wants to touch the Empty Moon. "Why are we here?" There's an edge to his voice.

"It's lovely to look at," says *Titania*, "and it means something to you both. This where Esmae's mother dove deep into the seas to find the blueflower."

The blueflower jewel burns in my hair as she says it, as if it knows how close it is to home. I watch the Moon and try to envision the rare, beautiful blueflowers deep in its sea.

"And as for you," *Titania* continues on, "You know what this place means to you. This is where *you* once—"

"Don't."

"You've been here before?" I ask.

He nods, his eyes fixed on the Empty Moon. I've never seen his face so completely raw. I can't decide if the expression there is pain or longing. Both, perhaps. I reach for his hand, then realize what I'm doing and drop my own back to my side.

"I was here with my family once."

"Weren't you afraid?"

"Oh, we were safe." He hesitates. "I was different then. I was better than I am now. Proud and brave. Too much of both, in fact."

"You can't have been so very different," I say. "I see those things in you. Whoever the other you was, he's still here."

He looks at me, surprised. The intensity in his gaze makes me look away, but this time I do reach for his hand. He startles, like my touch has set fire to his skin, and stares at my hand in his for what feels like eternity. When our eyes meet again, I know—I *know*—what he's about to do.

"Sometimes, I wonder if I'm still the same," he says. His other hand slides to the back of my neck. My heart gives a jolt. He waits to see if I want him to stop, but I don't. "Times like now. When I remember what it's like to be brave."

The kiss is just a touch at first. Then I let go of his hand and grip fistfuls of his shirt and it's like an entire universe has been blown apart. He kisses me deeper and one hand coils in my hair like it coiled in the wires of the clock. I want his hands all over my skin. The kiss is fierce and bitter and full of wanting and it's so very brief.

I don't know who pulls away first. At first, I can't quite think, and my body thrums with electricity, and then the disbelief hits.

How could I? *After everything he's done, how could I, how could I, how could I—*

He sees it on my face and steps back at once. I think I see hurt before he schools his features into a perfectly blank mask.

"I'm sorry," he says, "I shouldn't have—"

I try to tell him he doesn't have to be sorry, but no words come out, and I watch him retreat.

He steps away from the glass panel, away from the Empty Moon, away from me.

When he speaks again, it's to *Titania*: "It's time to go."

And she throws us back into the stars and shadows of the galaxy.

CHAPTER TWENTY-EIGHT

There's a new ship in the dock when we return. It's an unremarkable class of starship and would probably have gone completely unnoticed if it hadn't been for the excited servants clustered nearby.

I quickly discern the subject of their conversation: the ship belongs to a soothsayer. She arrived unexpectedly and wanted to speak to the king, and he agreed to pay her ten thousand silvers for the advice she gave him.

"Saw it with my own eyes!" says the servant at the center of the cluster. "He ordered the silvers sent to her account."

"But what did she tell him? It must have been *very* useful!"

"No one knows. They spoke in private."

My eyes widen. Ten thousand silvers for advice? I push the kiss to the back of my mind and give Max an incredulous look, one he returns.

"I don't like it," I say.

"I don't either."

"Well, she's still here. Why don't we go speak with her? If she's a true soothsayer, she can prove it."

"By all means," he says drily, "Go ahead and poke the beast."

"Poke it?" I hoot. "Who said anything about *poking* it? I'm going to skewer it."

Max doesn't reply, but when I look back at him there's a crooked, rueful smile on his face.

The soothsayer is alone in a visitor parlor upstairs, finishing a cup of spiced tea before her departure. The room has a magnificent view of one of the arched bridges that connects two of the palace towers. The soothsayer, however, has her back to the scene, unmoved by the view. The glow from the artificial fireplace flickers over her face. She's quite nondescript at first, with almost colorless gold hair and fast, slender hands, but then her eyes flash up to mine and I see mischief there.

She looks away and shuffles cards on the table in front of her. "You almost missed me," she says. "Which of you wants answers?"

"I do," I say.

She doesn't look up at Max but points in his direction. "And him?"

"He's not thrilled that his father gave you ten thousand silvers, so he's here to make sure you're not a fraud."

Her mouth twitches. "I think that's reasonable." She gestures to the seat on the other side of the little tea table. Shadows skitter across the wall. "What would you like to know?"

I sit. "Everything."

She gives me an amused look. When our eyes meet, an odd sensation creeps over me. I can't quite work out what it is. She shifts the cards some more. I try to read them myself, taking in pictures of horsemen and skeletons and broken hearts, but none of it makes any sense to me. I search the soothsayer's face. Her eyes don't feel right. She doesn't *fit*.

"You are Esmae Rey," she says. I'm understandably unimpressed, but what she says next throws me completely off balance. "You are a curse made out of flesh and blood. And cursed yourself."

No one outside the family knows my mother was cursed and almost nobody knows *I've* been cursed.

"You are the wielder of the Black Bow," she goes on. "The winner of warships, the one whose heart will always be cleaved in two. You want your brother to win back his throne and his home, but you know what defeat will mean for the ones here who you have come to love. You will always be torn."

"I—"

But she hasn't finished. "You have a fierce, roaring lion heart. It believes in hope and love today, but will it always? Will it in seven weeks' time?"

"Why?" I demand. "What will happen in seven weeks?"

"*Esmae*," she says, emphasizing the syllables, "which means *beloved*, but may as well also mean *betrayed*." She finally looks up at Max, a sharp direct stare like a knife, and his eyes go wide. She continued to look at him as she says, to me, "If you remember only one thing when I go, Esmae Rey, remember this: you are beloved by gods you don't trust and will be betrayed by mortals you do."

My spine prickles with cold. I look closely at her and suddenly I feel like I've seen her eyes somewhere before . . .

The chair falls over as I scramble to my feet. She doesn't flinch.

Amba once told me that a god's true celestial form is indescribable and a mortal couldn't look upon it without losing their sanity. As a result, gods have become accustomed to taking human or animal forms instead, and they usually have a favorite form that mortals tend to recognize. Amba's is the stern, beautiful woman I saw when I first met her. It's only when a god wants to deliberately hide themselves that they will assume a different avatar, that of a cow or an old woman or a child or a beefy bushy-browed man, all of which I've seen Amba embody. Only her ancient, fathomless, god-dark eyes always gave her away.

Eyes strikingly like the ones in front of me.

"Are *you* one of the gods who love me?" I ask sarcastically.

She smiles.

I cut a look at Max. A muscle jumps in his jaw, but he doesn't look surprised. He must have worked it out at the same time I did.

When I turn back, the soothsayer has vanished and in her place is a grinning boy god.

"Kirrin," says Max, more exasperated than angry, "Of course it's you. How appropriate for the god of tricks."

"Tricks *and* bargains," the god corrects him. "Never forget the *and bargains*. You may need one of those someday."

"I certainly wouldn't strike one with you," says Max.

"Not you, Max," Kirrin replies as his eyes flash in my direction. "That part was meant for Esmae."

Kirrin looks no older than I am. He's lithe, quick, with a tousled mess of blue hair and pale blue skin. His eyes are full of mischief.

I scowl at him. "Was any part of what you said to me true?"

"Every word I said to you was true. I never lie."

"I hardly think you were telling the truth when you entered the palace and introduced yourself as a soothsayer."

"I didn't do that," says Kirrin, offended. "The form I chose may have been described to Elvar and he may have come to his own conclusions about my identity, but my exact words, I believe, were 'I come to give you valuable advice, King Elvar, and ask only ten thousand silvers in return.' All of which," he says with glee, "is entirely truthful."

"Why did you bother?" I ask. "Does a god even need money?" Kirrin's grin widens. "It's not for you, is it? It's for Alexi. To help him gather and equip his army."

Kirrin doesn't look sorry. "I'm very attached to Alexi."

I can't help but admire the audacity of handing funds to Alexi supplied by the very person fighting against him.

"Don't make me remind you to leave my father alone," Max says severely.

"I never agreed to do that, Max," says the god, but his tone is fond. "I promised you I would leave him alone while you watched over him, but you were not watching over him today."

Max looks fed up, like he more or less expected to be confronted with tricks and loopholes. It's obvious he knows Kirrin well. At first, I assume this is because Max, like Alexi, got to know the god when they were children. Then, as I watch them and think of how easily Kirrin took on the guise of the soothsayer, I realize it goes far beyond that.

"It was you," I say.

Kirrin raises an eyebrow. "What was?"

"The woman on the balcony. The one talking to Max when I was on the training field with Sybilla. That was you."

"Indeed it was."

And the old man the other day? The one who was so interested in my blueflower jewel? Kirrin rules the Empty Moon. *It would be a travesty if I didn't know a blueflower when I saw one*, the old man had said. Of course he recognized it. Blueflowers come from his seas.

"They were *all* you. All those people. That's why no one's ever seen them before. And why we never see them again. You come here to meet Max and you take on a different form every time."

"I like you," Kirrin says. "Few mortals speak so boldly to gods they've never met before." He seems more amused than offended. "I suppose your relationship with Amba has made you quite comfortable with our glorious presence?"

I don't reply. A god comes to Kali to meet Max at least a few times a week. Why? Kirrin is supposedly determined to help Alexi, so why does he spend so much time in discussion with the other side? What do he and Max talk about?

I take them in, the silent prince and the smiling, mysterious god. "I don't understand."

"No, but you will when I'm finished."

"Kirrin," Max protests.

The god ignores him. "I assume you know of the fire that nearly killed your mother and brothers?"

"Yes," I say warily.

"Do you know why it *didn't* kill them?"

I repeat what Max told me: "They managed to get out in time."

Kirrin snorts. "That's only half the picture. It wasn't the kind of fire that starts with an overturned candle and allows you time to flee if you smell the smoke in time. It was an explosion. Your family escaped because they fled before it even started. I told them the house was about to burn. The house, you see, had been specifically built so that it would burn easily when the time came."

I recoil. "So it *wasn't* an accident! Elvar tried to kill them?"

"No," Max quickly interjects. "My father didn't give the order."

"But someone did."

There's no reply.

"Your uncle? Lord Selwyn?"

"Give the girl a prize," says Kirrin. "Of course Elvar and Guinne aren't blameless. I suspect they know what Selwyn is up to but won't acknowledge it. Elvar, you see, is more terrified of losing his throne to Alexi than he is of losing Alexi."

It's no wonder my mother resorted to poison. How else to put an end to these attempts to kill her children?

Max looks upset, but I have no room for sympathy for him. Does he want my brothers dead, too? Is that where his jealousy has led him? Why else hasn't he tried to stop this? How can he allow his uncle to remain on the war council and in such a position of power?

"I can't get rid of him," Max says, as if I spoke aloud. "My uncle was the one who convinced my father to lay claim to the throne he wanted so badly. My father now has that throne. He pays attention to my uncle's advice, trusts him. Selwyn wants what Mother and Father want. He wants Father on the throne."

"Not for Elvar's own sake! He just wants to be able to control the king."

"Yes. And he hates you and Alexi because if either of you were to rule Kali, you wouldn't let him control you. With my father dethroned, Selwyn would lose all he has."

"But you have power of your own. If you can't persuade the king and queen to send your uncle far from here, why don't you at least tell the war council what he's done? Grandmother and Rickard would happily see him imprisoned."

"If I do that, Selwyn will know he can't trust me. Right now, he thinks I'm on his side. I've never given him reason to think otherwise." Max looks more exhausted than angry. "As long as he trusts me, he shares his plans with me."

"And that means you're prepared for whatever he does," I say slowly. *Like Skylark.* He knew just how to persuade his uncle and the war council that an invasion would be a mistake. Would he have been able to cut off that plot so quickly if he hadn't known it was coming beforehand?

"The consequences of revealing his hand could be worse than that," Kirrin pipes up. "Selwyn has Elvar's ear. Who knows how deeply the rot has set in? If Max gives himself away, Elvar may take Selwyn's side, and Selwyn may be able to convince the king that his own son can't be trusted. They'd find a way to take what power Max holds at present. It would be the end of Kali as you know it."

I rock back on my heels, furious and frustrated. There's a frightened king on the throne and a sly, cruel man whispering in his ear. A man who almost killed my mother and brothers. And we can't even punish him for it.

"You haven't asked me the most important question of all," Kirrin says, grinning.

I tread cautiously. "And which one is that?"

"How did I find out about the flammable house? About the assassin who was supposed to stab Alexi when he was alone and unarmed at a temple? About the *raksha* demon that tried to drown Bear last year?"

Max glares at the trickster god. My fists clench at my sides and my nails press half moons into my palms. Have my brothers been hunted the entire time they've been exiled? I can wrap my head around my uncle and brother at war, but this is different. This is murder, as cold and sharp as winter.

"I assume you found out because you're a god," I say to Kirrin, but I know better. I know how little the gods sometimes see.

"I knew," Kirrin says, and Max looks away as if he's been defeated at last, "because Max told me."

The floor tilts, but there hasn't been a rock assault. I turn to Max. "Is that true?"

"Yes." He says the word so quietly, I barely hear it at all.

"You saved them all those times? You've been keeping my family safe for years?"

"*Safe*," says Max with some bitterness. "Alive, yes. Safe? No, I haven't been able to keep them safe."

"But why would you even try?"

"Because I can't stand the idea of them dead." He laughs, the sound sadder than anything I've heard in a long time. "We grew up together. They were my family."

"Wait. You're not jealous of them? You *love* them?"

"Of course I'm jealous of them, but that hasn't kept me from loving them."

"But," I protest, incredulous, "but that's not how you behave. You act like you don't care about them at all."

"And what would happen if I acted like I did? Would my father trust me with any control if he knew how much I want to keep his enemies alive? I can't protect them if I have no power."

My mind spins. It's obvious, of course, as soon as he explains it. *Give a little bit of the truth to make them believe the lie.* How many times have I used that lesson? It shouldn't surprise me that he has, too. He's used the jealousy to hide the love.

There's still one thing I have to know. "Why did you exile them if you knew they'd be hunted? How could you love them and still take their home away from them?"

"I hoped you'd ask him that," says Kirrin triumphantly. "Tell her, Max. Tell her why you came up with the idea to send them away."

He grits his teeth. "Leave it alone."

"I shall not." Kirrin pivots on his heel to look at me. "He sent them away because if they'd stayed, they would have been executed."

I shake my head. "No, Elvar wouldn't have—"

"Elvar is afraid, and Selwyn has trickled poison into his impressionable ear for a long, long time."

"But Rickard never said—"

"It never got beyond their immediate family. Selwyn suggested it to Elvar and Guinne. He claimed it was the only way to ensure the coup would be successful, the only way the boys would never be a threat to Elvar's claim to the throne. Selwyn, of course, didn't expect his own nephew to get in the way. Max refused to support the plot. He convinced his father that Alexi and Bear would be no trouble if they were exiled. He rather cleverly pointed out that it would win Elvar goodwill with the rest of the star system that he would undoubtedly lose if he executed his brother's children. Elvar didn't really *want* to kill the boys, you know. And thus"—Kirrin spreads his hands wide—"Alexi, Bear, and Kyra were sent away from their home, and the boy who saved them was reviled for it."

My eyes fill with tears. "I hated you for what you did. I refused to trust you because of it. Why didn't you tell me the truth?"

"Why does the truth matter?" Max asks. "It doesn't make me any better than I was ten minutes ago. I won't betray my father or mother, no matter what they've done or would have done if I hadn't stopped them. If there's war, I'll fight it for them until the end. I'll fight for them even if they allow my uncle to convince them that they have to destroy everyone else to keep themselves safe. So why, Esmae, does the truth matter? What difference does it make?"

"It makes a difference to me." *It makes all the difference.*

He swallows, but doesn't reply, instead turning to face the god. "Why couldn't you just leave it alone?"

"You know why," says Kirrin. He claps his hands. "Now, as much as I'd like to chat all day, I'd better go give Alexi a certain someone's ten thousand silvers."

"Kirrin," I say, before he can go.

He pauses. He already knows what I'm about to ask him.

What did he say when he was still playing the part of the soothsayer? *You have a fierce, roaring lion heart. It believes in hope and love today, but will it always? Will it in seven weeks' time?*

"The seven weeks you mentioned—"

For a brief moment, the mischief is gone from his eyes. "You already know the answer, Esmae."

And it's true, of course. I know.

The duel will be in seven weeks. The broken arrow. My blood on the grass.

I want to not be afraid, but I am. I'm afraid even as I refuse to believe it could happen. Even as I swear again and again that it will not come to pass.

"I'm sorry," says the god.

Puzzled, Max asks, "What exactly is supposed to be happening in seven weeks' time?"

Kirrin gives him a guilty look, then darts out of the room. It's odd that he's never told Max about the future he and Amba have seen. They seem to share so much else, so why not this?

Max stares at me. "You're going to ask me what he meant," I say. "And I'll tell you, but not today. I can't talk about it today."

He nods but says nothing more.

CHAPTER TWENTY-NINE

I confine myself to my suite for the rest of the day, pretending I'm unwell. I don't know how to face the king, queen, or their monstrous confidant so soon after finding out they almost murdered my brothers.

At some point that evening, while shut up in the bedroom of my suite, I realize I can hear sounds in the outer room. I open the door in a fit of temper, ready to confront the unwanted intruder—

—and find that the intruder is Rama.

The *real* one, not a face on a piece of tech.

"Rama!" I shriek. I throw myself at him, almost knocking him over. He hugs me back and laughs. "What are you doing here? How did you even get into my suite?"

"That bad-tempered friend of yours has your passcode," he tells me. "She let me in. We didn't think you'd mind the intrusion. As for why I'm here, what kind of question is that? You sent a goddess on an errand to speak to me. Let me repeat that: a *goddess*. On an *errand*. It struck me that we might never have a real conversation again if I didn't come here myself."

I scrub at my wet eyes. "I'm so, so glad you did."

"And I'm so glad you're glad, Ez," he says, throwing himself across the sofa. "Because I have every intention of abusing the king and queen's hospitality and planting myself in this realm for the foreseeable future, so you may find that you get fed up of me long before I can find the energy to return myself to Wychstar."

I curl up on the opposite end of the sofa, pushing his legs off to make room. "I saw your brother at Princess Katya's wedding. He said you couldn't be bothered to make the journey to Winter. And yet you came here."

"This may be news to you, Esmae, so brace yourself: You are not the wedding of a princess I've never met. I can muster a tiny bit more effort on your behalf."

"And I do appreciate that effort."

"You owe me exactly two hundred and twelve favors for this," he replies, eyes shut as he feigns indifference.

I reach across the sofa and curl my hand into his. "It's all a mess, Rama."

He opens his eyes. "Tell me."

The words spill out, big details and small, my position on the war council, how kind Elvar and Guinne have been to me and how they almost had my brothers executed, the kiss and the truth about Max, what Elvar told me about King Darshan and Rickard, Lord Selwyn and the simulation chamber, Rickard's curse, my new relationship with my brothers, and, finally, the blueflower.

"I've never heard of anyone who was protected by a blue-flower," he says. "Amba must care very much about you."

"I don't think gods care like that," I say, but even as I say it, I wonder if I'm wrong. *Beloved by gods.* They keep saying *gods*, not *god*. Amba could be one, but who are the others? Have I ever even met them?

"What would have happened to you if we'd both fallen, Esmae? That day you saved me?"

It was years ago. We'd stolen a small ship from King Darshan's dock. Rama, who had started flying lessons the month before, decided he'd become an expert and wanted to show off. We flew out to the shields, as close to the stars as we dared, and Rama tried every trick he knew. He flipped, he dove, he made the ship twirl in the air like a dancer.

He didn't know the ship had been so easy to steal because it had been set aside for repairs, pushed into a dusty corner of the dock where no one cared to keep an eye on it.

In the middle of a roll, the faulty hatch slammed open. We both fell, but Rama slid out of the open hatch while I hit the wall beside it. I grabbed his hand before he could slide away into space, but he was too heavy and I started to slip.

He cried then. Begged me to let him go before we both tumbled from the ship. I could see his face below me, tear-streaked and terrified. I could see the stars and the gas clouds swirling far below. My hands were sticky with sweat. I held on and refused to let him go.

In the end, I wedged my foot over the console and pulled a lever, spinning the ship around again. We tumbled back into the ship and slammed the emergency hatch closed, sobbing in terror and relief. We were so pathetically miserable when King Darshan's guards found us ten minutes later that the king didn't even have the heart to be angry.

"We were halfway out of the shield," I remind Rama now. "We would have both been sucked out into open space and ripped apart if we'd fallen. I don't know how a blueflower could have saved me from *that*."

He huffs. "I was hoping you'd say you risked your life because you knew you would have been fine. Why didn't you just let me go?"

"Would you have let me go?"

"In a heartbeat," he says, and I giggle.

With my news all spent, Rama finally tells me his: what he's been up to since the last time we spoke (not much); what his father has been doing ("stewing, mostly, and plotting . . ."); and all the small, pointless details about everyday life that I've missed dreadfully these past weeks ("there's a horrid cat in the palace who keeps trying to take naps on me," "the cook is trying to poison me, I swear it," "I've been told I sleep too much, and at inappropriate times. Is such a thing even possible?").

At the end of it all, only one thing remains unsaid, and I can't bring myself to mention it. *Titania* told me what he had said to her. *Don't let me lose her.* So how can I tell him what Amba and Kirrin have seen?

Seven weeks.

I'll tell him another time.

The sun lamps have turned dawn-pink by the time Rama finally gives in to his eternal lethargy and yawns. I yawn in sympathy and climb sluggishly to my feet, my dress crumpled and creased, and help Rama find his way back to the guest suite he's been given while he's here.

A few of the guards eye me askance. Jemsy from the Hundred and One, who is on duty tonight, grins mischievously as I pass. Rama almost splits himself open when I tell him their reactions are probably because they can think of only one reason why the rumored lover of their future king is roaming the palace with a visiting prince at such an hour.

"Oh gods," he says, wiping tears from his eyes. "I'm so happy I came."

If he comes to feel differently in the days that follow, when he starts to see for himself just how matters stand on Kali, he doesn't let on. As a prince of Wychstar and my oldest friend, he has an open invitation to stay as long as he likes, and Elvar and Guinne go out of their way to make him feel welcome.

I try to appreciate that, but I find it difficult now that I know the truth. I can't forgive it. I avoid my aunt and uncle as much as possible and keep myself busy where I can.

Rama, meanwhile, does the same. He adapts to Kali so beautifully that anyone would be forgiven for thinking he's lived here for years. He earns an invitation to family meals. He visits *Titania*. He puts on a brave face and actually attends the state events when he's invited. He doesn't fall asleep in public. He explores Erys with Max. He watches me train the Hundred and One. He helps me keep hold of my temper every time I set eyes on Lord Selwyn. He draws me out of the miseries I fall into, even when he doesn't understand them.

I fly *Titania* to Arcadia a few times, even taking Rama with me once or twice. Bear tries to teach me how to use a mace, which is something Rickard never achieved, then gives up and teaches me how to play dice instead. Alexi teaches me how to fish. I teach them the games the children play on Wychstar. We spend hours under the weeping trees. I start to call my brother *Alex* and don't even notice until days later.

My brothers and I quickly learn what we can and can't talk about. We can share our frustrations about the gods who meddle in our lives; we avoid talking about my mother, who refuses to see me, no matter how many times I ask. (Why do I still ask? I should stop. I wish I could stop.) We share stories of *Titania*; we avoid all discussion of Kali.

Except for one time, when I say something innocuous about the markets of Erys and Alexi looks up at the sky like he can see Kali there.

"We rebuilt the streets of Arcadia when we came here and made it our home," he says. "We built the city. We chose where the markets would go, where the weapons would be built, where the livestock would live. We chose what we grew in the orchards, which of the rolling hills to convert to training fields. We chose every piece of our castle. And it was only when it was finished and we stepped back to look at it that I noticed—we'd tried to recreate Kali." His voice cracks, and he looks away from the faraway point in the sky. "But you can't recreate Kali."

I never mention Kali to either of them again.

"Do you wish you'd stayed on Wychstar?" Rama asks me one day.

"No."

"Answer a little faster, why don't you," he grumbles.

It's that lull after dinner again. Everyone is chatting or reading or dozing by the artificial fire. A servant pours drinks. Max tests the wine before he allows it to be served. Grandmother says something deliberately inflammatory, and Rickard deflects it. Rama tells a popular Wych folk tale to entertain everyone. Elvar takes his second cup of wine, then asks if I'd like to stroll around the gardens with him. We sit on our usual bench. I can hear Rickard's laughter from inside. Elvar drinks from his cup.

And then his face turns purple.

CHAPTER THIRTY

It's the sound that gets my attention. I'm counting the stars when I hear the terrible rattle of his breath. I look over and see he has his hands pressed to his throat. It's such an unexpected and appalling sight that for half a second, I can't even think.

So my mother's poison finally slipped through the cracks.

And then there's a moment—just a fragment of a moment—where I see it all unfolding: Elvar will die; Max won't want the throne; the war council will take the easy way out and declare an end to Alexi's exile; and my brothers will return home. The crown will return to where it should always have been. No war, no battle, no bloodshed. No death except that of the usurper king. Just one man. An easy, quick end. Just the simple solution I came here for.

And all I need to do to achieve it is do absolutely nothing.

So it comes as a shock to me that I can't. The brief glimpse of the future blinks away, replaced with a terrible horror.

The usurper king was once a boy who just wanted to be worthy.

The usurper king gave me a home.

The usurper king cried when he touched my face.

He was a monster, but now he's just my uncle.

The pieces in my game of Warlords are all jumbled up, and I don't know which side is which anymore.

And so, I scream for help.

In the immediate chaos that follows, the world is just snapshots. Max slams a needle into his father's chest. Voices rise in panic. Guinne pleads with someone to tell her what's happened. Lord Selwyn tries to soothe her. Max and Rickard crouch on the ground beside the fallen king. Elvar's hand grabs Max's wrist and then he goes gray and still.

I snap to life, spinning away from Elvar, and look across the gardens and into the family parlor. Max tested the wine, which means the poison was added to Elvar's glass afterward. No one has left the room since the servant who poured the wine left, and that was before the test. The person who put the poison into Elvar's cup is still here.

I dismiss possibilities one by one, until I'm left with only the three guards. Henry and Juniper—they're loyal to Max and I can't see any possible way either of them could even know my mother.

But the third guard, oh yes, he's older. A grizzled bear of a soldier who probably served for years while my father and mother ruled.

His eyes meet mine, and he sees the accusation there. He blanches, his guilt plain, and then he makes for the door.

I pounce. The force sends him to the ground. He grabs a knife from his belt and lashes out. I dodge, but the blow slices my arm open. The pain makes me hiss, but the wound quickly closes up. I spring onto his chest and slam my foot down on his knife hand. He grabs hold of me and throws me down again so hard my head spins. His knife slashes at my throat, but only nicks it.

Then Sybilla is there, a hurricane of rage. She wrenches him away, pushing him against the wall as she draws her sword. He dives at her, but she's already jumped out of his reach. She spins the sword around and breaks his nose with the hilt. He howls. From the floor, I kick the back of his knee and he buckles. Once he's down, I twist his knife away and knock him unconscious with the handle. He goes still.

It all happened so quickly that no one else has had a chance to react. Rickard rushes across the room. When he reaches my side, he looks grimly down at the guard and then points at the door. "Henry, Juniper, get rid of him. Allow no one to see him until I've dealt with him."

They obey, faces drawn. I wonder how long it will take before the guard gives up the name of the person who convinced him to try and assassinate the king.

Rickard crouches down next to me, lines of concern scored across his forehead. Rama joins us. "Esmae, are you hurt?"

They both know I can't stay injured, but there's admittedly a lot of blood on my sleeve and throat. "I'm fine." Rama helps me up. I sway unsteadily on my feet. "What happened to Elvar?"

"We're lucky Max had the stasis serum on hand," says Rickard. "It only works within the first few moments of an incident like this. He's frozen Elvar so the poison can't spread to his heart. Stasis will give the doctors time to identify the toxin and either find or make the antidote."

I nod, relieved, then look for my uncle. Elvar is cold and gray, a sad, crumpled figure. He doesn't look like a monster.

I hated him for years. How many times did I picture this? How many times did I wish for it? I could have let him die. I could have let my mother end this conflict.

I didn't.

I pick my way across the chaos to Max's side. He's still with Elvar, his father's hand still locked in place around his wrist.

"Are you okay?"

He looks pale, shaken, incredulous. He reaches up with his free hand and runs his thumb down my cheek, uncaring of what anyone else might think of the gesture. "Are *you*?"

I have no idea why he's so worried. He, too, knows perfectly well I'm protected by the blueflower. "You saved his life, Max."

"You did, actually. Twice. You saved him the day you warned me about your mother's plan, and you saved him again today. And you still haven't answered my question."

Honestly, why is everyone fussing?

"I'm fine," I insist.

Even as I say the words, the room tilts. What an inconvenient time for a rock assault.

Only, this time, it's not a rock assault.

Oh, I think before the room goes black. *Damn it.*

CHAPTER THIRTY-ONE

I wake in my own bed, connected to machines, with a nurse sitting beside me. It's a novel experience. I've had colds and fevers and various other minor illnesses in my lifetime, but I have never been in an infirmary bed of any sort, and it seems especially absurd that they've made me one in my own suite when I feel completely and absolutely normal.

Of course, the palace doctors don't know that, and I suppose some overreaction is inevitable when royal princesses are thrown to the floor like dolls.

The blueflower jewel obviously did its job a long time ago, healed the cut on my arm and throat and whatever happened to my bones when the guard threw me down, but my brain may be a different matter. My head was badly rattled. Maybe I needed to black out before the flower could get to the wounds inside.

"Welcome back, Princess," says the nurse. "I'll fetch you some water and summon the doctor."

She trots off before I can thank her. I check my watch and see that it's past one o'clock, so I've been unconscious for a good few hours. Long enough to acquire a display on the table by my bedroom window. Flowers. A card from Rama that has the words *I know you're not really hurt, so don't expect any sympathy from me* looped across the front. A cake shaped like a dagger from the Hundred and One. I push myself up onto my elbows to see more clearly. And there, in the middle, a little robin made of feathers and twine, with bright curious eyes, its wings slightly open as if poised to fly.

I jerk my eyes away as the doctor enters my chamber. "Good evening, Princess," she says, glancing at the nearest machine to check my heart rate. "Or perhaps I should say *morning*. You look well. How much pain are you in?"

I'm about to tell her none at all, then remember that such a recovery isn't normal, and so I fib. "I feel bruised."

"That will pass. You don't have any fractures. Your brain scan also shows no swelling or injury. You may ache for a few days, but I'll leave you some pain medication for that. I think we can clear our machines out of your suite and let you get on with your life." She smiles. "You've been very lucky."

I thank her. "I can't believe I've been out of it for so long."

"It wasn't without help. We kept you under because we weren't sure how badly you'd hit your head. We didn't want you awake before we had a chance to assess and address any trauma."

"Have you seen my uncle? How is he?"

"Stable," the doctor replies. "We've identified the poison and are in the process of making the antidote. We expect him to make a full recovery. He should be ready for visitors later today, but it'll take him a week or two to regain his strength."

I fiddle with the bedcovers and ask, in a suitably innocent voice, "And have they determined why the guard poisoned him?"

"I'm afraid not, Princess. Master Rickard has interrogated the guard, but I don't believe he said much." She pauses, then adds, "I hear that Lord Selwyn would like him executed immediately, but the elders haven't yet come to a decision on the matter. They wish to consult the king first."

"As they should," I mutter under my breath. It's time Lord Selwyn remembered who really rules Kali.

Once my suite returns to normal, I shower off whatever dried blood is left on my skin. By the time I return to my bed, the sheets have been changed and Max is asleep in the chair the nurse vacated. The sight makes me smile, and for the first time, I don't feel guilty for feeling that way.

I don't wake him. I get back into bed, prop the robin on my shelf beside the metal model of *Titania*, and close my eyes.

Almost an hour passes and I still can't shut off my brain. I hadn't realized how shaken I am. Parts of the evening flash in my mind: poison; the purple of Elvar's face; the pain that seized my entire body as I was thrown to the floor; the blood; the terrified faces; the chaos.

I curl my hand into my pillow and think of the stars and the moon rocks hurtling past *Titania* on our way to the Empty Moon. It calms me. I activate the portable music system Rama gave me years ago, then close my eyes, swallowed up by music and memories of rocks and—

—*will be addressed as soon as possible.*

My eyes fly open.

It's just after dawn, if the glow of the sun lamps outside is any indication. Max's chair is empty. I squint at my clock for confirmation. I must have dozed off after all.

The ship's electronic voice doesn't normally wake me, but it's louder than usual. I sit up abruptly as the voice broadcasts across the realm again.

External communication systems are down. There is no need to be alarmed. The situation will be addressed as soon as possible.

This is bad. It's never ideal for a spaceship kingdom's communications to go down, but there normally *isn't* any need to be alarmed.

External communication systems are down, the voice repeats for the third and final time. *There is no need to be alarmed.*

"I am alarmed!" I snap back.

It can be no coincidence that the communications systems have gone down mere hours after the king was poisoned.

Someone hammers on my suite door. I startle, but I'm not really surprised. "Esmae!" Rama calls. "Hurry up, we need to talk!"

I dash forward and open the door. Rama practically tumbles in, followed by Max and Sybilla.

"What—"

"They went to Skylark," Rama blurts.

I recoil. "Who?"

"Twelve ships," says Max, "Three generals, at least a hundred soldiers. It wouldn't matter if that was the extent of it, but it wasn't."

Of course not. "They've taken *Titania*."

He nods.

"How? She's *my* ship!"

"Trickery, I believe. There was a recording of your voice on my uncle's tech, different words in your voice spliced together to create a message for *Titania* giving her your permission to follow his orders. I assume the fact that he could prove you couldn't go to her yourself because you were unconscious and wounded in bed helped his case."

I swear bitterly. I should have been more careful. I should have expected this and put more safeguards in place to make sure no one could trick *Titania* this way. The generals won't need more than twelve ships and a hundred soldiers to invade a small realm if they have *Titania* with them. I remember only too vividly what she did to the three warships out in deep space. There one minute, gone the next. That could be Skylark's fate in just a few hours.

"Father woke about forty minutes ago," says Max. "He was only conscious for a few minutes, and I wasn't with him, but Mother was. Selwyn joined her and convinced Father that no one would ever try to kill him again if they feared his wrath." Max looks every bit as angry as I feel, but his is a colder, harder fury. "My uncle's planned this for a long time, Esmae. This is why he wanted you to do more interviews about *Titania*, and get more footage of you, so he would have access to more words in your voice. He may not have expected an opportunity quite like this, but he certainly wasn't about to pass it up when it arrived. He must have used what little footage he could find to construct the message for *Titania*. He had three generals and their warriors primed by the time Father woke. And if Father hadn't woken, he probably would have pretended to have received his permission and Mother would have backed him."

"Why didn't Rickard stop him?"

"He would have if he'd been here," says Max grimly. "He's in Arcadia. I assume he went to confront your mother."

I press the heels of my hands to my eyes, trying to think. "What about you? Couldn't you have stopped it? What about the other elders?"

"I didn't know about it until external communications went down about twenty minutes ago. We haven't been able to get the system back up yet."

"He jammed the system to make sure you can't call the fleet back, I assume?"

"We tried to get around it by flying outside the shields and calling the fleet," says Sybilla, "but the bastard must have given the generals orders to keep the fleet's systems down so that they can't receive overriding commands to return."

Rama looks angry. "So the generals know this is all very sketchy?"

"My uncle recruited all three of them years ago," says Max. "They all have excellent records, but it's obvious now that he always intended for them to be more loyal to him than to Kali."

My fists open and close, my knuckles turning white. How could we have been so careless?

"What about the Wych ships?" I ask. "Rama? Aren't they still with Princess Shay?"

"Yes," he says, "My father, however, is not. *Titania* will only be neutralized if she goes up against Father or Wychstar itself. Our ships were only supposed to be a deterrent. Lord Selwyn must have made sure Father himself was nowhere near Skylark today. Even if I could warn him now, he won't be able to fly there before your fleet arrives."

SANGU MANDANNA

I spin around to face Max. "Can't you warn Princess Shay?"

"I already have. I reached out to her when we flew outside the shields. I told her it was a mistake, that communications had been scrambled somewhere. I told her I'd fix it. I'm going there now."

"*Titania*'s much faster than any other ship in the star system," I remind him. "We'll be too far behind to stop an invasion."

"They won't send her ahead of the rest of the fleet," says Max, "so we shouldn't be more than an hour behind them if we can get out of here in the next few minutes. I have a pilot in the dock getting a ship ready. I tried to reach Rickard while we were outside the shields, but my uncle must have jammed his communications, too. He can't have Rickard coming back too early, of course."

I nod, then march back to my bedroom to get dressed.

"What do you think you're doing?" Rama lets out a groan of defeat. "You're planning to go with them, aren't you?"

"Of course I am," I snap.

Max protests. "Esmae—"

I go back to the door, a pair of leggings in my hands. "Tell me why *Titania* is about to attack a realm that doesn't stand a chance against her, Max."

He grits his teeth. "My uncle sent her there."

"And how was he able to do that? Because I flew her to this kingdom and left her unattended in the palace dock."

"This is not your fault," he growls.

I want to cry. "It really is. I could have let Alexi have her. I could have refused to accept her. I could have given her to him. But I didn't do any of those things, and now look where we are."

244

I slam the door, throw off my sleepshirt and fumble with my leggings. My hands are so unsteady that I can't even get a foot in. I almost break down in tears. I did this. *Titania* will be in Skylark in four or five hours. *Titania*, who hates battle. I have no illusions about her power. I've seen what she can do with my own eyes. People will die. And it will be because I fired an arrow and won a competition.

The door cracks open. "Let me help," Sybilla says.

I look up. Her face is uncharacteristically gentle. She helps me until my hands grow steadier. I find a tunic, then put on my chain mail vest and vambraces. I hesitate, then retrieve the Black Bow from under my bed. If ever there was a time to use it, now is that time. I slot it into place across my back.

"I didn't know you had a divine bow stashed under your bed," Sybilla says, with an awed, lustful look on her face that she only seems to assume when she's faced with a beautiful weapon. She traces the celestial symbols carved into the black wood. "Maybe it'll bring us luck."

"We could certainly use some."

When we return to the parlor, Max is alone. I catch a glimpse of a dozen messy emotions crowding his face before he hides them.

"Where's Rama?"

"He went to fetch his sword."

"Why? He's not coming with us!"

"You're welcome to try and stop him, Esmae."

Max is too kind to say what he should: Rama's doing this because I am. I swallow and try not to think about that truth. Maybe it won't matter who goes. The point of this trip is to *stop* a battle, not to fight one.

Definitely, absolutely, not to fight one.

CHAPTER THIRTY-TWO

I watch as Panchal approaches in the distance. It's a blue and brown planet surrounded by nine tiny moons and shared by four realms. Skylark is one of those realms.

The pilot flies us closer. My nerves feel shredded. I stay very still, keeping my eyes fixed on the glass panels ahead. I'm afraid. I shouldn't be because all we need to do is reach our fleet; the generals will have to listen to Max once they see him, and *Titania* will stop when she sees me.

Except there's this horrid, scratchy voice in the back of my mind telling me events won't unfold that way. That Lord Selwyn will have told his generals not to stop no matter what happens.

Rama, Sybilla, and the pilot have talked most of the journey, overly cheerful conversation to hide the fact that they're all uneasy, but Max and I have scarcely said a word. I know he's more than uneasy. He's afraid too. His sword is on the floor beneath his seat.

I get up abruptly and cross to the back of the ship where the weapons are shelved. I strap a quiver of arrows to my back beside the Black Bow, slide two short swords into loops at my hips, and hide a knife in my boot. The movements feel easy and familiar after thousands of hours in simulations. I twitch my foot, feel the knife pull down on my boot. I can almost hear Rickard's voice in my ear. *Count your weapons, Esmae. How many have you got? Good. Now put one back. Weapons weigh you down, and speed is worth a dozen weapons.* I put the knife back.

When I turn back, the others are all staring at me.

"Shouldn't you be concentrating on where the ship's going?" I ask the pilot.

He pays my question no attention. "Why did you just do all that?" he asks.

"I was getting ready."

"For what?" Rama asks. "An invasion of your own? You look like you're about to storm a fortress, Ez." He grins, delighted with the picture he's painted. "I think you'd make a fine stormer of fortresses. I can see you plotting whole wars with just a handful of soldiers. Esmae Rey, the winner of warships. In command of Kali's forces, you'll conquer the enemies who won't bow and set fire to the entire world."

Sybilla and the pilot fall about in fits of giggles. I ignore them. "You should write a book."

"I will," Rama assures me. "I'll call it *The Grumpy Princess.*"

I yank a handful of his hair and he yelps.

Then the pilot, abruptly sober, speaks up. "We're almost there."

Max stands and approaches the console, looking out on our quickly approaching target. His shoulders are tense. Sybilla takes a few weapons off the shelf for herself.

As we enter the planet's orbit, outer space gives way to sky. We dive toward Skylark. The light is soft, a pale gold streaked with pink. It's only just morning here.

There's so much smoke in the air that it's difficult to see much of the realm itself, just glimpses of glass domes and temple spires and fields dotted here and there. By the time we get close to the Sky sentries and defenses, it's clear Lord Selwyn's generals have already used *Titania* to wreak havoc. Two sentry towers are ablaze. The ruins of three patrol ships lie on the ground far below us. I have no idea if their occupants escaped alive. Kali's fleet is poised behind *Titania*, who faces a much, much larger and much, much weaker fleet of Sky ships. I see soldiers balanced on their ships' wings, tense, waiting. Everything is smoke. Everything is chaos.

That's when it really hits me: this is a battle. I've never done this before. This isn't a lesson. It's not a carefully controlled simulation. This is real. My heart rattles in my chest, panicked.

"We need to get between them," Max says.

The pilot gulps and swoops down between the two fleets and spins our ship around to face *Titania*. Princess Shay must have told her ships what to look for; the Sky fleet makes no move to attack us.

Our own fleet, however, does.

The pilot wrenches the ship upward as soon as the first launcher fires, and the shot nicks the corner of our tail. I crash back into a wall, but it doesn't hurt. All I can think is that people I love would have died if that shot hadn't missed.

My rage swells. There are lions in my heart, and bears and wolves, and they roar and growl and break free of the chains that have kept them at bay all this time.

"Get me close," I say, teeth gritted.

"What?"

"Get me close to *Titania*," I tell the pilot. "The only way to stop this is to make *her* stop. She won't do that if she thinks I asked her to invade. I need to get inside her control room and speak to her."

I open the hatch and climb up onto the left wing. Wind buffets me and the smoke in the air makes it difficult to breathe. I stay balanced, steady, as the ship flies closer.

Someone slams into me, and we both crash down onto the hard metal of the wing. It takes me half a second to realize a warrior from a Kalian ship has leapt aboard as we passed. He pins me to the wing and drives his sword down.

But his steel clangs against another. I look up and see Max. He pulls the warrior off me and pushes him away so fast that I don't even have time to blink.

"Listen to me," Max growls at him. "*Listen.*"

The soldier strikes back. "Wear your own face, imposter."

"What?" Max says, startled.

"We know what you're doing," the soldier scoffs. "The generals told us. Do you think we're stupid? We know you've been cloaked to look like Prince Max and Princess Esmae. You want to trick us into letting you steal *Titania* for Alexi. It's not going to work."

"Don't be ridiculous," I snap. "The gods haven't cloaked humans in years!"

"I guess they made an exception for precious, perfect Alexi," the soldier shouts over the sound of the wind.

There's no time to argue anymore; more of them arrive, a swarm on the ship. I see flashes of Max, Rama, and Sybilla in the smoke—Max's sword spinning through the air, Sybilla's hair whisking out of sight, Rama trying futilely to match the skill of soldiers who have trained all their lives.

I snatch the Black Bow off my back and reach for an arrow, shooting two soldiers in their sword arms, and then shoot a third who was about to stick a knife in Rama's throat. Rama spins around as the soldier falls behind him and gapes at me in shock.

I fight past another soldier to get to his side and grab his arm. "Get back inside the ship. You can't fight these people!"

"I'm not leaving you, Ez," he says.

"And I'm not letting you die. Now get back inside the ship and lock the hatch!"

He shakes his head. Almost on cue, the ship veers to the side and we all have to scramble not to fall off. I use the opportunity to push Rama into the hatch and slam it shut.

My hand clenches on the Black Bow. The day Rickard gave it to me, he whispered an incantation in my ear and told me it would transform the Bow into the true celestial weapon it was meant to be should I repeat it. The incantation hovers on my lips. I could use it now. I could transform the Bow—

No. My priority is *Titania*. I have to get to my ship.

I slam the Black Bow onto my back and run.

Launchers fire, arrows fly. Faces and obstacles whisk past. As a child, when the blueflower was still new to me, I used to think it would make me unafraid. What did I have to fear if I couldn't be hurt? Then I discovered that *staying* hurt and *feeling* hurt were two different things.

I take blows as I run across the ship and they slow me down. They almost break me. Blood, pain, smoke, fear, all cycling in a loop. I bleed and I heal and I run.

I don't dare stop or look back at Max and Sybilla. I don't dare look back to find out what's become of them, because I'll stop if I do and I can't stop.

Just get me a little closer.

There's too much crossfire. If the pilot gets any closer, there's a good chance the entire ship will go up in flames. We've already skimmed death a dozen times. Every time one of *Titania*'s five deadly launchers has fired and nearly hit us, we've almost become ash, as completely gone as the three warships in deep space. The terror I feel every time I see a flash from her launchers is almost crippling.

We can't get any closer, so I'm going to have to try to reach *Titania* from here. I move faster.

"Don't!" I hear Max shout behind me. "Esmae! Stop! We're still too far away—"

I leap.

For a moment, I soar, a bird taking flight against the backdrop of smoke and ruin. I fly.

And then I plummet.

My hands grab the edge of *Titania*'s wing before I can fall too far. I glance back, just once, just to make sure Max and Sybilla are okay. Sybilla is armed with a spear and smiling her angriest, deadliest smile. And Max has a knife at his throat. I see a flash of red, but I can't help him, I'm barely hanging on—

He ducks out of the soldier's hold. He's alive.

I've lost too much time. As I try to pull myself up onto *Titania*'s wing, a warrior appears above me. His face is grim as he stomps down hard on my hand.

I fall.

And land on a ship's wing.

The breath is knocked clean out of me. I gasp, hands gripping the metal loops beneath me. I need to get up. I don't know whose ship this is. It may not be a friendly one.

A hand appears in front of me, to help me up. I look up into my twin brother's face.

"Alex?"

"Fancy seeing you here," he says. He gestures behind him, where Bear and Rickard are trying to make a Kalian soldier see reason. "Princess Shay reached out to me. We came to help."

"Of course you did. Always the hero."

"So what do you think?" he asks, a grin spreading across his face. He's in his element, sunlight glinting off his armor. "Shall we show them what we can do together?"

I reach for the twin swords and grip them tightly. We spin, back to back, and fight. Swords catch the light; metal echoes like thunder; the wind roars past us. For just one moment, I forget how much I despise battle and it's glorious.

"Get back onto *Titania* if you can," Alexi calls over his shoulder. "I'll cover you."

His pilot steers us closer to *Titania*. This time I make the jump easily. Alexi fires arrows at the soldiers who try to stop me. Others emerge from inside *Titania* when they see me on the wing. I dart out of the way of the first warrior and disarm the second before leaping into *Titania*'s open hatch.

I scramble inside and slam the door shut. Two of the three generals stand inside the control room. They're frightened but also determined. One snatches up a sword, but the other has more sense and gestures for his companion to put it back down.

"Excellent decision," I say. "Now back away."

They obey.

"Esmae?" It's *Titania*.

"It's time to stop," I tell her.

"I saw you," she says. "I saw Max. I wanted to stop, but they told me you were imposters. That your real orders were to invade."

"It's me, I swear."

"Prove it."

"Would an impostor know you took me to the Empty Moon?" I ask. "Would they know that you told me our hearts are the same?"

There's a soft *whoosh*, as if *Titania* has just let out a breath in relief. The launchers abruptly stop firing. She pulls back, away from the Sky fleet, farther and farther, until the rest of Kali's fleet has no choice but to do the same.

"I'm glad you came," *Titania* hums softly in my ear. "I'm not a very bloodthirsty warship."

I start to laugh, but it comes out sounding more like a sob.

CHAPTER THIRTY-THREE

Afterward, it's the numbers I think about: thirty-seven dead, more than a hundred wounded. Some of the casualties were innocent bystanders who happened to be below when *Titania* shot the three Sky ships from the skies.

Everyone maintains the numbers could have been far worse, but I can't shake the terrible, painful awareness that each number represents a real person. A person other people loved, who perhaps liked vegetables or didn't think they looked good in the color red, an arrogant person or a kind person or, perhaps, a bit of both. Each number represents someone unique and individual and *real*. And it never stops—the little voice in my head that keeps reminding me that this is not a simulation.

Max promises to make amends for what's happened, but Princess Shay isn't interested. She asks us to leave. Rickard, who came here with Alexi, joins us for the journey home. As we fly away, I look back down and see her hugging Alexi. He came to her kingdom's rescue in spite of having no stake in the battle; she'll be grateful to him forever now.

When we return to Kali, the rest of the mess must be cleaned up. The three generals are exiled to off-ship prisons for treason, and the soldiers under their command are suspended for a year.

Holding Lord Selwyn accountable is far less successful. Elvar, weak but awake, insists that he gave Lord Selwyn permission to carry out the invasion. Lord Selwyn maintains that he did not give his generals orders to attack us and there's no real proof to the contrary. "Why would I tell my men that you were cloaked imposters?" he says with exaggerated surprise. "Everyone knows the gods haven't cloaked anyone in a hundred years!" I want to throttle him. And my spliced voice, used to trick *Titania*? That, he tells the king and queen, was a necessary measure to protect the throne. Could we really begrudge him that?

His false contrition is all Elvar and Guinne need to declare the matter at an end.

Rickard is furious with us. "How dare you?" he barks, as soon as he gets us alone. "How *dare* you go there by yourselves? How dare you put yourselves at risk that way?"

Max tries to explain. "But you weren't here—"

"I'll thank you to keep your objections to yourself, Max! I don't care that you couldn't reach me. Do you know how terrified I was when I found out? You shouldn't have gone!"

And then, before any of us can reply, he walks away. I catch the glint of tears in his eyes.

When the dust finally settles, after endless questions from the war council and a series of doctors' examinations, I escape to my suite and allow my composure to crumble at last.

I frantically scrub blood and smoke from my body. I stuff my clothes down the incinerator chute, and I scrub determinedly at my nails. Even after that, even with freshly washed skin and hair, and with all physical traces of the battle gone, I feel like I can still smell smoke and feel the heat and sharp edges of metal when I so much as press my palms against any surface.

—catching hold of the edge of Titania's *wing, the hot bite of the metal in my hands—*

There's a knock at the door. It isn't loud and urgent, but my heart quickens anyway.

Max's hair is damp and his clothes are clean, like he's tried to scrub the battle off, too, but he couldn't wash away the mark on his throat and the cuts and bruises on his skin.

—She had the knife at his throat, and would have sliced it open from ear-to-ear if he hadn't twisted away in time—

It's a terrible memory.

—I couldn't help him, couldn't help any of them, because I was hanging on—

And then one corner of Max's mouth turns up and the memory vanishes into nothing. The smile grows in his eyes like the sun rising, at first a sliver and then a little more and then a final burst of light. "Hello."

I step away so he can enter. He pushes the door shut behind him, then hesitates, uncertain.

I'm not. This time, I know the truth of him, the good and the bad and there's no part of it I can't live with. This time, I'm certain.

I kiss him. It tastes of desperation and sweetness, but then there's also smoke and metal, and it makes me cry because I wonder if the darkness can ever be scrubbed away. Max crushes me to him and I bury my face in the side of his neck and breathe him in.

"It was so *ugly*," I say at last.

I feel his jaw working. "Yes."

I pull back so that I can take in his face. "Do you think that's what it'll be like if there's a real war between Alex and Elvar?"

Max doesn't have to answer. I already know. It isn't *yes* or *no*. It's *It'll be worse than that. So much worse.*

"We can't let that happen."

"It hasn't happened yet," he says. And then, after a moment, he adds, "Today *was* ugly, but it's over. Battles explode and then they end. Wars are always temporary. And the smoke and ashes they leave behind will blow away eventually."

I know that, of course, but I still think I needed to hear it from someone else, because it's only after I wrap the words inside layers of myself that I realize the smell of the smoke on the air has finally gone. And when Max brushes his thumb over my bottom lip and kisses me again, the only taste left is the sharp, sweet *wanting*.

I ask him to stay, and so he does. We talk about books and stories and birds made of feathers and twine. And when we have no more words, we still don't let go. I want his hands on me; I want to touch him. I kiss the cut on his throat. He runs his thumb over the blueflower jewel in my hair, almost like he's saying *thank you*. My whole body feels alive and taut, strung like a bow ready to snap, but even this can't keep the exhaustion at bay forever.

"How long before Alex will be ready to start his war?" I ask, stifling a yawn.

"Kirrin says he isn't far away." Max's eyes are full of shadows, as though he can already see the chaos of the war unfolding. "My uncle still wants to unleash *Titania* on your brother before he can come after us, but she won't be tricked again. Alex is far likelier to start this war than we are."

I swallow. I don't know how I should feel. I want Lord Selwyn gone. I want my brothers to be able to return to their home. I want Alexi to take back the crown that should have been his. And yet—

And yet I'm full of dread, full of a terrible inevitability that I'll lose no matter who wins.

"I didn't know Alexi's army had grown so quickly," I say.

"Kali is a formidable enemy, but Alexi has an equally formidable reputation, and he's won a lot of sympathy from the rest of the star system." Max grimaces. "Skylark's a small realm, but we were better off when Princess Shay wanted to stay out of the war. We made an enemy today. Or was it yesterday? I don't even know anymore."

"Yesterday," I say, checking the date on my watch. I take a moment to absorb what it means.

Three weeks left.

My conflicted feelings don't matter. Unless war breaks out in less than three weeks, unless I make the impossible words I swore to the gods come true, it won't matter which side I'm on, because I won't be here to choose.

I startle when I hear Max's voice. "Three weeks," he says, and at first I think I must have said it out loud. And then I realize he's remembered Kirrin's words the day he pretended to be a soothsayer. "What's supposed to happen in three weeks, Esmae?"

I tell him.

And watch as the smile in his eyes dies.

"They can't have seen that," he says. "Why would you and Alexi ever duel? Duels are formal, planned in advance. You'd have to both agree to it. A duel is such an easy situation to avoid, so how could the gods have seen him kill you that way?"

"It's inexplicable, but that's what they say they saw."

Max stares at me. "Is this what you were really talking about that day you told me the story of Ness and Amba?"

I nod. I watch as he revisits everything he's said to me, including that he doesn't believe such things can be avoided forever. "Oh, Esmae."

"It's okay."

"No, it's not. And I can't understand it—"

"You could ask Kirrin."

"He won't come if I call," Max says wryly. "He'll know I'm angry and he'll hide from me until it blows over." This seems such an absurd thing to say about a god, and I open my mouth to say as much, but then Max says, "Amba?"

And there she is, standing a few yards away from us in her favored form, stern and beautiful, one eyebrow raised. "You summoned?"

"Is it possible to summon you?" Max counters.

She ignores the jibe and gives me a severe look. "Couldn't *you* furnish him with all the facts?"

Max gives her an equally severe look. I would remind him that this is a goddess and he should probably be more polite, but it's actually rather nice to have someone other than me refusing to be cowed by Amba's ire. "You haven't visited in some time. Have you been avoiding me?"

"You know each other?" I ask, surprised.

"Indeed," says Amba. I notice that while she seems annoyed, she has neither pushed Max into the wall with the force of her annoyance, nor has she simply left.

"Is it true?" Max asks her.

"Of course it's true." Her eyes cut briefly to me and I see that same flash of sorrow that's been there for weeks now.

He growls low in his throat. "It just doesn't make any sense."

"It isn't up to me to make sense of it," Amba snaps. "It is what it is. And it will happen."

"You could stop it," Max says.

She scoffs. "How? By taking hold of Alexi's sword hand before can strike?"

Max doesn't look away. "That's one option."

Amba's eyes ignite like firecrackers. I tense as she advances on Max. She must make herself grow a little taller as she strides across the room, because by the time she stops in front of him, they are exactly eye to eye. He doesn't even flinch.

Her voice is full of wrath. "How dare you."

He doesn't reply, doesn't look away.

Amba abruptly spins on her heel to face me. "Have I ever told you the story of my brother Valin?"

"Is that important now?" Max snaps.

She ignores him and addresses me. "He was a god of wisdom and choices, proud and clever, until the day he made the choice that cost him his life. And gods are not supposed to lose their lives." Her mouth presses into a sad, bitter line. "A hundred years ago, when Winter cut off trade with Kali and refused to supply this realm with goods or fuel, there was a war. It started to turn ugly. Valin intervened."

"Why?"

"He always had a soft spot for Kali." Amba lifts a shoulder in a shrug. "He stepped in. He planned battles and strategized and minimized the loss of life. He was able to achieve all this with his godhood intact because he never actually involved himself *physically* in the battle. And then he did."

"How?"

"One of the other goddesses had been helping Winter. Loussa, goddess of the arts. She was in love with a Winter princess. She transformed one of their archers into a likeness of a royal cousin of the Reys so that he could sneak past the king's guards. Once inside, he tried to shoot the king of Kali. Valin reached out and plucked the arrow out of the air. And became mortal for his pains."

A god did an act of good and lost his entire world for his troubles. "What happened to him?"

"The battle ended shortly thereafter, in large part due to Valin's help. Valin himself would have aged and died eventually, in constant agony, cut off from the celestial realms, with no mortal family or friends to spend the remainder of his life with, but then Kirrin stepped in. They *both* ruled the Empty Moon once, you know. Valin and Kirrin. My brothers. They were devoted to each other. When Valin lost his godhood, Kirrin gave him a blessed dagger and asked him to put it in his own heart."

"He asked the brother he loved to kill himself?"

"The knife was blessed," Amba repeats. "It was Kirrin's boon. It ended Valin's life but gave him another. One where he could be born mortal, to a mortal mother, and grow up surrounded by mortal family and mortal friends. Kirrin gave him a chance to be happy. A reward for the sacrifice he had made."

"So Valin died, was reborn somewhere else, and had a happy mortal life until he eventually died again?"

"Not quite," Amba says, and then she stops, releasing a breath like all the anger has gone out of her. "Never mind. It isn't relevant. What *is* relevant is the fact that I would be making the same mistake Valin did if I were to physically intervene in your duel." Her eyes flash back to Max. "You have no business asking it of me. I am not inclined to throw away my immortality like my brother did."

"You sound angry with him," I say tentatively.

"I killed our father to save him," Amba says. "I raised him. I raised all five of them. I loved them all and then he left. He *left* me. Of course I'm angry."

Max's jaw unclenches, his eyes softening with regret. He doesn't mention Amba's immortality again.

She turns back to me. "Have you told Rama about the vision?"

"Not yet," I admit.

She tuts, and I don't blame her; I've put it off too long. I promise myself I'll tell him when I see him tomorrow, and Sybilla too. Imagining it fills me with dread. *Don't let me lose her*, Rama had said to *Titania*. But there's nothing *Titania* can do about this.

"At any rate," Amba says, addressing Max again, "I fail to see what you're so worried about. Don't you know Esmae has sworn she won't fall prey to that fate?"

Max looks startled. "You swore?"

I nod. And I'm no less determined to hold to it than I was when I said it. "Vows are sealed in stone the moment the gods and the universe hear them, aren't they? I said it. I swore I wouldn't die that way."

I sound fierce, and I wonder if I sound completely mad, too. How can I possibly deflect something two gods have seen?

And yet, when Max's eyes meet mine, I see that the smile there has flickered back to life.

"You think I can do it," I say in wonder.

"I believed in you the day I met you, Esmae. I believe in you now."

It's a beautiful thing to hear him say, but it isn't necessary. There's already a voice inside my head, and it's been there for some time now. It says, *I believe in me too*.

CHAPTER THIRTY-FOUR

Bereft of a victory in Skylark, Lord Selwyn's contrition rapidly fades away. I know it's only a matter of time before he suggests a new plan of aggression and finds a way to manipulate Elvar into giving him permission to put it into effect. Anyone could be his new target. Tamini or Winter, for supporting Alexi. Some other poor territory that he feels must be made an example of. Alexi himself.

It's unbearable to sit here and wait. Wait to die. Wait for someone to set loose the warship I won for them. Watch as the people I love wait for the days to run out. Max, Rama, and Sybilla all look afraid when they think I'm not watching, and they spend far too much time looking at the clock. I hoped it would help to tell them all the truth, but I just feel worse, because now they have to share my fear. Now they wait for the inevitable with me.

There is not much I can do about the gods' vision, so I put my mind to the problem of the war. Lord Selwyn has to be stopped.

Unfortunately, I don't know how to remove him from the equation. Elvar and Guinne would never agree to imprison him or exile him from Kali. And I'm not sure I can bring myself to murder him in cold blood. So what other options are there? What can I possibly do to end this war?

I should have let Elvar die, I tell myself, but there's no ring of truth to the words anymore. I don't believe them.

And as it happens, there's really no better way to gain someone's trust than to save them.

I sit with Elvar in his private rooms every afternoon as he recovers from the effects of the poison, helping him complete his daily paperwork. He talks to me while we work, telling me more of his fears and hopes than he's ever shared before.

"He's coming for me," he tells me one afternoon. His blindfold twitches. "Alexi. He'll come sooner or later. And he *will* kill me. You know about his Golden Bow? It can destroy any enemy. He doesn't need to touch them. He doesn't even need to be close. He merely needs to be able to see them."

"Alexi has far too much honor to use it on you," I assure him. "He would fight you properly—"

"You haven't seen the monsters people become when they want something so badly they'll do whatever it takes to get it. Even Alexi, our brave, honorable Alexi, will lose his better self when what he wants is almost within reach." Something terribly tired and terribly sad crosses Elvar's face. "We all do."

He's ashamed. He sincerely believes he was unjustly deprived of the crown that should have been his by virtue of his birth, but he's nevertheless ashamed of what he's done. His guilt softens the hard edges of my anger.

"Uncle," I say, "do you remember the soothsayer?"

He looks surprised. "Of course."

"What did she tell you? What advice could she possibly have given that was worth ten thousand silvers?"

Elvar's smile is rueful. "I didn't want to tell anyone. It's not unusual to hear of a future you want and find yourself terrified you'll shatter it if you speak it out loud."

"I understand. Probably better than you know."

"I'll make an exception for you, my dear," he says. "I think you'll find it interesting. She painted me a picture of my army spread across the galaxy, dismantling my enemies and shattering Alexi. She told me that future wasn't certain, but it was there. A very real possibility just ahead."

My fingers clutch the papers in my hand, but I don't dare breathe lest he hear my horror. Was Kirrin being truthful? He said he never lies. Does that mean Elvar's victory is really that likely?

"I don't see how that's worth ten thousand silvers," I say when I can finally trust that my voice won't give me away.

Elvar shakes his head. "It isn't. She didn't stop there. She told me that if I wanted to keep the crown and claim that future, I needed to trust you."

I freeze. "Me?"

"You," he repeats. "She said, 'Trust Esmae, and Alexi will break. Trust her even when you fear she's gone astray. Trust your niece, and she will shatter your enemy for you.'"

I stare at him in stunned silence. *Trust your niece, and she will shatter your enemy for you.*

"You're shocked," he says.

"Yes."

"I must admit I was, too." He gives me a fond smile. "I'm sorry, my dear, but I didn't trust you at first. Selwyn, you see, rightfully pointed out how easy it would be for you to take *Titania* and leave us for your brother. And you always seemed so suspiciously eager to vote against aggression in the council. I love you dearly, but trust doesn't come easily to me."

"I'm not offended, Uncle. I don't blame you."

"But then you saved my life and risked your own to pin down that treacherous guard. I can't fathom why you would do that if not out of loyalty, and I believe now that the soothsayer was right. I trust you. And I believe that if I trust you, you will win this war for me."

"I can't promise that."

"Of course not, but a future was seen and I believe I know how to claim that future. You could be an unstoppable force on my side, Esmae. You could even be queen of Kali after I'm gone."

I wince. "No, I could not. If you love Max at all, Uncle, don't ever repeat what you just said. I don't think he wants to be a king, but it would break his heart if you cast him aside. He deserves more than that."

"Then I will simply put my trust in you," Elvar says, "and let you play any part you wish."

I always knew, of course, that Kirrin was a trickster, but I never appreciated just how devious he could be.

Oh, Elvar. You never stood a chance against the god of tricks.

"Thank you for trusting me, Uncle," I say softly. "I'll always try to do what's best for Kali."

Power is a funny thing. I always imagined it would feel good to have it, since I'd grown up with none, but the power I've held by possessing *Titania* has only made me afraid, and the power I hold in my hands now is jagged with guilt.

I only ever wanted to be master of my own fate, and that's the one kind of power I don't seem to have at the moment.

When I leave Elvar's suite, I go to the gods' altar in the conservatory and lock the door behind me.

"Kirrin," I say.

I blink, and he's there, eyes brimming with mischief. "Hello, Esmae."

"Funny bit of advice," I reply. "'Trust your niece,' was it? I imagine he'll find it difficult to do that if I'm dead in a week or so."

"True. But if you live, you will do exactly what I told him."

I show my teeth. "Irrelevant if you and Amba have seen my death set in stone."

"Also true," he says. His unrepentant grin fades. "Let me be clear, Esmae, I do not take any pleasure in the sad future ahead of you. I'm sorry for my glee. I'm pleased with the trick I played on your uncle, that's all. I do not rejoice in the idea of your death."

"You knew I'd find out about this. You knew I would ask him about your advice sooner or later. You knew he would tell me. You must know, then, that I will find a way to use his trust in me in the little time I have left."

"I had a feeling you were extremely resourceful when I first met you," says the god smugly. "I'm relying on it."

I study him, profoundly mistrustful. "What do you hope to gain from this? Why do you want me to have power over Elvar, however briefly? I assume you want me to help Alexi."

"Isn't that what you've wanted to do the whole time?"

"Yes, but I have no intention of letting you dictate the terms. Elvar ignored your advice until I saved him. *I* did that, not you."

Kirrin grins. "Let me reassure you. You are free to do as you wish with this power you have over your uncle. Make the most of it in the little time you have left. All I want from you in return for helping you is a favor."

"A favor," I repeat.

"A favor that I will claim from you at some point before you die. One favor. That's all."

I consider. "You can't ask me to hurt anyone." He nods. "And," I add, pointedly, "I won't lose a battle or duel on purpose."

He looks offended. "I would never ask that of anyone. I don't hold with cheating."

"You're the god of tricks!"

"A trick is fair," he replies. "Tricks have rules. You can avoid being tricked if you see the trick in time. Cheating *breaks* rules. As for the matter at hand, I will gladly abide by your conditions. Do you agree to owe me a favor?"

I hesitate, then say, "Yes."

"Thank you," says Kirrin. He pauses. "You know, you didn't have to agree. You could have refused me."

"I could have, but that wouldn't have been fair. You've helped me, whatever your motives are, so I owe you."

He smiles and says gently, "Never let anyone make you feel like you are less than Alexi, Esmae. He's not the only Rey with honor."

Then he's gone, and I'm left with the inevitable question. What do I do with this power I have?

CHAPTER THIRTY-FIVE

Two days later, at the next meeting of the war council, I'm prepared. I've charted a new game of Warlords and I intend to win.

Grandmother squints at the agenda. "It would appear you have something you wish to discuss with us, Ez-may."

All heads turn toward me. Elvar's blindfold twitches as he frowns, Lord Selwyn looks irritated, and my great-grandmother is almost bouncing with curiosity. Most of the others just seem puzzled.

I don't dare look at Max or Rickard. I feel awful about the way I'm about to blindside them.

I press my hands flat on the table in front of me. "I think we should negotiate with Alexi."

"We tried that years ago," says one of the advisers. "He will not discuss terms with us."

"Come, come, we must forgive the princess for her ignorance," says Lord Selwyn, the points of his teeth glittering in a smile. "She is still new to our world and does not yet realize that there are matters here beyond her very limited understanding."

I smile sweetly at him. "I'd like to believe that while we don't always see eye to eye on the issues we discuss here, we all want what's best for Kali. Is that not so, Lord Selwyn?"

His eyes narrow. "Of course."

Liar.

"Letting our armies rip this realm apart is not what's best for Kali," I go on. "The best thing we could possibly do for this kingdom is to end this war before anyone else dies."

"I agree, wholeheartedly," says Rickard, his voice deep and warm. "Unfortunately, the point about negotiation stands. We've tried. I am Alexi's teacher and I have tried to talk to him about this more times than I can count, but he is not interested in coming to mutually agreeable terms."

"He's not interested in the terms you've offered so far," I reply. "What if we offered him something he actually wants?"

"He wants the crown," Lord Selwyn snaps. "Do you intend to offer him *that*?"

"Yes."

Everyone stares at me.

"Sort of." I steady my breath. I've spent the past two days hammering this plan out in my mind. It's an outrageous idea, but I don't have the luxury of time. And while this may never work, it's all I can think of that might end this war now before we all pay a terrible price. "I think my brother and uncle could share the crown."

Lord Selwyn snorts. "*Share* the crown? They are not children fighting over a toy!"

"A thousand years ago, in the old kingdom of Kuru, there was a dispute over who would rule," I explain. "I read about it just a couple days ago. Two sisters wished to claim the throne of Kuru, and no one wanted war. They agreed that the sisters would share the crown. One would have five years on the throne, then the other would take over, back and forth, back and forth. It worked well for them and I don't see why it can't work for us."

For a moment, the room is completely silent, and then the old queen roars with laughter. No one else seems to know how to react.

"I love it," she says between cackles of laughter.

Rickard sits back in his chair, stunned. "Could that even work?"

"I don't know," I say. "Uncle Elvar and Alexi would have to agree. I know it's not what either side wants, but I don't see any other way around a war. And is there a fairer alternative? Who really deserves the crown? Elvar is a rightful heir who was stripped of his birthright for no crime of his own, and Alexi is a rightful heir who had his birthright taken from him for no crime of his own. Which of them has a greater claim to the throne? There's been a great deal of betrayal and pain on both sides, but maybe that can be put aside for the sake of a better future."

"Madness," Lord Selwyn hisses, his face livid. "Absolute madness. This is a trick to get her brothers back on Kali. They will murder us all as soon as we let them set foot here. I told you she was on his side, my king."

"Alexi has far too much honor to break a vow," Rickard says. "*If* he agrees to this, he will respect it."

Lord Selwyn turns sharply. "Nephew, you've been very quiet. I think it's time you reminded the princess that it is not she who rules this kingdom and makes the decisions here."

Max has indeed been very quiet. I finally dare to look at him and see that his eyes are dark and furious. His jaw is set, but his voice is almost too calm as he says, "I don't intend to remind the princess of any such thing, Uncle. What I will do is suggest that we give the king a chance to speak. Father?"

Elvar's face is very pale, but his forehead is creased as if he's actually considering the idea. "Esmae," he says softly, "how can this possibly be the victory I was promised?"

I get up and cross the room, around the table, crouching down in front of his chair and holding his hands very tightly. "You were asked to trust me, Uncle, even when you fear I'm going astray," I remind him quietly. "Trust me now. If you want to keep your crown, I believe this is the best way to make sure that happens."

"How can I share the crown with him? How can I allow the world think I'm weak?"

"They'll think you're strong," I say. "They'll cheer you for your generosity. Rickard once told me it takes more strength and courage to stop a war than it does to start one."

"He told me that, too," Elvar says. "When I was a boy. Do you truly believe this is the best way forward?"

"I don't know everything," I reply. I'm a pawn who became a queen, but queens and princesses and kings and knights are human, too. And more than capable of making terrible mistakes. "I could be wrong, but I do believe this is the best course."

"Then I will trust you," he says, the words coming out on a shaky breath. I know what he's thinking. That there's a trick here he hasn't yet seen, a twist of fate that will get him what he wants. He's sure this path is the one that will lead him to that future of shattered armies and a broken Alexi. He will agree to share the crown now because he believes that somewhere down the line he will not have to share the crown anymore.

That is a problem for another day.

I am not crafting a trick. There is no trap. I wanted and will always want Alexi to have his crown, but my idea of justice isn't what it was. Two rightful heirs had their futures stolen from them. Can't we put that right for both of them? Is that really such a naïve and impossible desire? There are people I love on both sides of this battleground and the world is grayer than it used to be. I can settle for a shared crown. A crown is less important than my mother and brothers getting their home back.

Lord Selwyn is beside himself. "This is a farce. You cannot all seriously be considering this madness!"

"I am willing to consider it," says Elvar, and Selwyn blanches. He bows deferentially, teeth clenched, and I can feel his hatred.

And I'm glad. I want him to be enraged. When you approach your enemy in Warlords, you have to make sure there's at least one move he can make at all times. Leave him nowhere to go, and the game ends in a stalemate. Give him only one move, however, and you can nudge him into your trap. You can put him in a Warlord lock and win.

I've given Lord Selwyn exactly one move. I can't force him to take his turn. I can only hope he does.

The war council agrees to nail down the terms of this proposal so that we can take it to Alexi. Perhaps sensing my urgency, even if he doesn't understand the reason for it, Rickard promises that the proposal will be ready in two days.

As advisers leave the room, he approaches me. "Well," he says. His lips twitch like he can't quite quash his smile. "*Well.*"

For just one moment, I feel like the hopeful, wide-eyed child I used to be. "What do you think?"

"I think," he says, before the smile finally breaks across his face. "I think I'm very proud of you today, Esmae."

I've waited so long to hear those words.

The room empties until it's just Max and I left. I face him. "You're angry."

"Yes."

"I shouldn't have planned it behind your back. I'm sorry."

"I assume you planned it behind my back because you didn't want me to fight you. And you're right. I would have raised hell. Just not for the reason you expected. It's a brilliant way around the problem, Esmae. I don't know if it can work, but it's the fairest and the kindest solution anyone has offered. I would have jumped at it a few weeks ago."

"So why aren't you jumping at it now? Are you worried about what your uncle will do to me now that I've made him angry? You don't have to worry about him. You know I can handle whatever Lord Selwyn throws my way."

Max shakes his head, all the anger gone. He just looks sad. "You don't see, do you?"

"See what?"

"I don't know how to say it," he says. "I don't know how to be the one to break your heart. I'm sorry. I can't."

He walks away and I'm left behind, trying in vain to understand.

CHAPTER THIRTY-SIX

Lord Selwyn will move quickly.

It's not entirely unexpected, then, when he offers to serve drinks at dinner and spends a little more time than necessary with my glass.

It's not entirely unexpected when he overrides the passcode to my suite and slips inside a few hours later.

The knob turns almost soundlessly, but it would have woken me if I'd been asleep. He looks around, making sure I'm alone, checking the time on the tech screen by the door. The lamps are on, but they're dim. He crosses the room to my bed. I'm mostly buried in blankets, but he can see my hair across the pillow and the shape of me underneath, so he knows where to aim.

He has rope in his hands. He ties it to the curtain rail, constructing a clumsy noose. He picks up a spare pillow.

Hesitates. He doesn't look happy. I didn't expect that, this last flicker of mercy.

And then he presses the pillow over my face.

It's not *really* my face, of course.

I open my wardrobe door and step out into my room. Selwyn's face goes deathly white. It's hugely satisfying.

"It's a dummy," I say and walk forward to pull back my blankets, revealing the wig and the synthetic, humanoid shape underneath. "The Hundred and One use them when they train."

Lord Selwyn opens his mouth and a choked sound comes out. "It was a mistake."

"Yes, it was." He's a reptile without teeth now. He wouldn't have come here if he hadn't been certain I wouldn't wake. He's immersed in politics and deceit, but he's not an especially talented warrior and he knows I'll win if he tries to attack. "A mistake, but not an accident. You murdered me. Or tried to." I point to the tech screen on the table by the door. "And I recorded every second of it."

"The drink—"

"I didn't even taste it. But I did send a sample to the lab at the university and they should have the results for me tomorrow. Some kind of tonic to make me sleep, I expect? And then you meant to come here, smother me, and hang me from my curtain rail to make it look like I did it to myself? Did you really think anyone would believe that?"

"What do you want?"

"You know, you could have avoided this trap. You could have accepted the end of this war, but a shared crown was never what you wanted, was it? You wanted to control the one and only king. I expected you to be so angry you would feel you had no option but to get rid of me once and for all. You didn't disappoint."

"What do you want?" he rasps again.

I've struggled with that question. "I planned to present the video and the lab results to the war council tomorrow," I say. "They wouldn't have been impressed with the attempted assassination of a royal princess. You would have been tried for treason and possibly executed. At best, you'd have spent the rest of your life in prison."

Lord Selwyn licks his lips nervously. "You said you *planned* to do that. You've decided otherwise."

"I've decided to let you go." I wonder if I'll regret this. "I want you to leave. Tell the king and queen you wish to retire immediately. Do whatever you must to convince them it's what you truly want. You have three days to retire from the war council and to leave Kali for good. I don't care where you go, as long as you never try to hurt my brothers again. If any more attempts are made on their lives, I'll show the war council what you tried to do to me. If you try to communicate any kind of advice to Elvar from wherever you are, I'll show the war council what you did. Are we understood?"

He spits the words out like they're poison. "Yes. I'll go."

"Oh," I add, "and if I die before you do, don't come back. I'll make sure that you're exposed even if I'm not here to see it."

"That isn't an *if*, Princess," Lord Selwyn says softly. "If you continue to collect enemies at this rate, I am entirely certain you will die before I do."

"Get out."

He slinks away.

"Very nice," Amba says from behind me. I swivel around, startled. Her eyes are bright. I think it's the most impressed

I've ever seen her. "Tricking him with a false you? Very nice indeed."

"Did you see it all?" I ask indignantly. "Did you know I wasn't in the bed? Because if you just stood by and let him smother me—"

"Don't get worked up, Esmae," she says. "Of course I knew that wasn't really you. I know you better than that."

I give her a somewhat bewildered look. "Thank you?"

"You're welcome."

"You've been around an awful lot lately."

"Why wouldn't I hover?" she asks. "You are on the cusp of a fatal duel, you know."

I turn away. "There won't be a duel. Did you not see what happened today? The war is over."

"The war hasn't started yet," she says, and is gone.

CHAPTER THIRTY-SEVEN

Titania and I talk about the gods' vision. I will not allow it to come to pass, but I have to take measures just in case. She promises she'll keep my promises, even if I can't anymore.

"If you die," she says, "I'll travel. The galaxy is a vast place, and I haven't seen the half of it. I'll stay away from wars and battles. I'll visit the gods. I'll vanish into space and stars."

"Sometimes I wish I could vanish into space and stars," I tell her. "Maybe we can both go someday."

"There are many, many beautiful places to see out there, Esmae," she says. "There are worse things we could do."

That night, Rama persuades Max, Sybilla, and me to go down to the fayre by the river. There are pockets of the Hundred and One already there, scattered throughout the crowd. There are ladders propped against rooftops so that people can climb up and enjoy the view. We find a spot on one of the rooftops. Below us, there's music and puppets and spices on the air. Above, the Scarlet Nebula is especially vivid, the reds and golds sharp against the black of the void.

Kali is currently at 71 percent human capacity, says the ship's electronic voice. *Airflow and water pressure will be increased by 2 percent for the next two hours.*

It's a subtle shift—hardly noticeable—but the air feels crisper, cooler. I breathe it in.

Rama passes a bottle of Kali's signature gooseberry wine around, then makes a disgusted face at me as if he can't understand how this is what passes for a drink on this realm. I prop my chin on my knees and look out over Erys. It's funny how the sight makes my heart twist in pain and with love. I hope I've been able to save this kingdom from the destruction of war.

Max's hand traces circles on my knee. I smile at him, at the others beside us. *Titania* is safe, Lord Selwyn will leave Kali at the end of the week, and there are people here that I love. And all of that is good. I want to hold the good close.

"Is this what it feels like to be happy?" I ask.

"Yes," says Max, but he looks more afraid than happy.

I turn back to the view and look at Winter. It's pale and ghostly. "Did Rickard take the proposal to Alexi?"

"Yes," Max says quietly.

"Alex hasn't replied?"

"Not yet."

Rama nudges me with his elbow. "Hey," he says, "if the war isn't stopped after all and I decide to fight in Kali's armies, can I be wherever you are? It seems wise to hide behind the one with the blueflower jewel in her hair."

"You're a horrid creature. And no, you cannot be wherever I am. I've already told Max you're not permitted in Kali's armies."

"Max!"

"Don't *Max* me," says Max, "I'm not getting involved in a spat between the two of you."

"Why do you want to follow me around battlefields anyway?" I ask Rama. "You know combat requires actual movement and energy, don't you? You can't just sleep on a palanquin while others tote you around."

Rama's tone stays light, but his teeth seem far too tightly clenched. "I don't want to let you out of my sight, Ez. Who knows what kind of trouble you'll get yourself into?"

The rooftop has suddenly gone quiet. Out of the corner of my eye, I see that Max and Sybilla have stopped smiling. *Don't look like that,* I want to tell them. *Don't be afraid for me. No one can hurt me.*

I squeeze Rama's arm. "I'll tell you what," I say. "I'm not letting you follow me onto battlefields, but I promise to take you on a trip into the stars with *Titania* in a couple of weeks."

"You can't promise that," he says.

"I promise it anyway," I say, brave and certain and *happy*, "And you know I always keep my promises."

Except, of course, being certain doesn't always last. It can change in the space of a breath.

Alexi sends his response to the proposal: *Let's talk. For our safety, we'll only meet with Esmae and one other person.*

The coordinates are those of the yellow weeping trees of Arcadia. Max decides he'll go with me. The entire journey there, *Titania* grumbles about how there's a serious dearth of sentient ships in the galaxy for her to make friends with. Max, most uncharacteristically, barely pays her any attention. I can feel tension radiating off him. He looks out at the stars, jaw clenched tight like he's trying to force himself to remain quiet.

When I point this out to him, his only reply is, "This trip is a bad idea."

"Don't you want this war to end?"

He stares at me for a minute, then says, "I suppose I just expect the worst." He tries to crack a smile. "Maybe my parents have rubbed off on me."

Max has never been to Alexi's Arcadia before, but he remembers it when it was just a cluster of towns and forests in Winter. "It looks like Kali now," he says quietly. He ignores the farms on the edges and gazes, instead, at the heart of the city, at the spiky towers of the palace, the snowy forests, the almost fairy-tale look of the streets and rooftops. "He made his perfect city, and he made it look like Erys."

"It creeps into your bones," I say. "Kali does, I mean. It creeps in and becomes a part of you."

"You'd make a good queen," Max tells me.

That amuses me. "I doubt that. And far too many people would have to die for that to happen anyway."

"You have a blueflower." He touches it, tracing the outline in my hair. "You may be the only one of us to survive a war."

"In which case, I will gladly take the opportunity to prove that I'd make a far better ruler than any of you," I tease. "I'll be Queen Esmae the Merciful. Queen Esmae the Just. Queen Esmae the Grand and Glorious. Queen—"

"I will crash into the nearest rock if I have to hear another word of that," says *Titania*.

"What would be the point of that?" I ask. "You're indestructible. Wouldn't you just bounce off?"

Max grins, but it slips away much too quickly.

Titania lands in her usual spot in the woods. We climb out. Leaves crunch farther ahead, in the direction of the hot spring. Alexi and Bear are already here.

As Max and I approach, it's obvious immediately that the atmosphere is all wrong. Alexi looks pale and strained. Bear looks miserable.

"Hello, Max," Alexi says. Max just nods. He's sensed the strain, too. His shoulders tense.

"You said you wanted to talk," I say, confused.

"I do," Alexi replies. "Just not about the proposal you sent."

I don't like his tone. "What's the matter? I know it's not ideal—"

"Not ideal," he repeats incredulously. "Seriously? What have they done to your mind up there?"

"What—"

"You said you wanted me to win," he says, quiet and intense. There's a current of pain in his voice. "Our mother warned me, but I trusted you. I believed you. You said you'd help us. But it turns out you're just as bad as the rest of them. A *shared* crown? You want me to forgive them for what they've done to me? What they took from me? You want me to share the crown with him?" He points at Max. "With my backstabbing uncle?"

"Alex," I say softly, "you weren't wrong to trust me. Of course I'm on your side. Max knows that. I want you home. I just don't want any of us to pay the price of a war."

"It's a price we have to pay for justice," he says.

I shake my head. "This is about avoiding thousands upon thousands of deaths."

"I don't *want* thousands upon thousands of deaths, Esmae! I will do every single thing in my power to avoid it, but I can't avoid a war altogether. I won't. Our lives were taken from us. Our futures were taken. I'm not going to just let that go."

I look at Max, but there's not even a hint of surprise on his face. He expected this. He knew all along that Alexi would never agree to my plan.

"Then why are we here?" I demand. "Why did you say you'd meet me? Why did you want me to bring someone with me?"

"So you'd have a witness," Alexi says. "I have Bear, you have Max."

"A witness? To what?"

Max swallows. "Don't do this, Alex. Please."

Alexi's cheekbones flush red. "I don't have a choice."

"Alex—" Bear tries.

"Don't *what*?" I ask.

Alexi looks me in the eye, and in the split second before he speaks, I suddenly understand what he's about to say.

I challenge you to a duel.

And he does.

I can't speak. I can't breathe. Time winds back to Max, his eyes dark and furious. *You don't see*, he said. *It's going to break your heart.*

And it does. My heart breaks.

"Why?" I croak, eventually. "You said you wouldn't do this."

"I'm proposing a formal duel," Alexi says softly. "Swords. Whoever draws first blood wins. If I win, you give me *Titania*."

Max knew. He knew Alexi would feel betrayed the moment he found out I'd suggested the truce. Max knew what betrayal would make my brother do. I believed nothing in the world would make my brother put any part of the gods' vision into play, but Max knew better. He knew Alexi better.

"How can you even suggest this?" The words burst from my lips. "How can you risk what Amba and Kirrin saw?"

"First blood," he says more gently. "Just a scratch. I can't trust you to fight for me, Esmae, but I love you and I would never let that vision play out. I just want the ship you took from me."

"I didn't take her from you. I *won* her. I was better than you." Rage floods my body. "I don't accept your terms. There will be no duel."

"If you win, our mother will see you," he says.

I stagger back. The betrayal is so painful that I bite the inside of my cheek and taste blood. "How could you? How could you take the thing you know I want most and use it against me?"

"I'm sorry. I have no other choice. I have to go home. I have to take back my crown."

Max is right behind me, so close I can feel the rise and fall of his chest, the rush of his heartbeat. "Just say no, Esmae."

But that's the problem, isn't it?

"I can't," I say softly. "I need to see her. I have to, or I'll never be free."

"You can choose to be free of her. You can choose to put her behind you. Facing her isn't the only way to leave the memory of the baby in the boat behind."

"If you're worried about *Titania*, you needn't be. I won't lose her. I'll win this duel."

"It's not *Titania* I'm worried about!"

I look up at him. "I will win, Max. You said you believe in me. Believe in me now."

"Then you accept?" Alexi asks.

"I accept," I say.

Then I turn and walk away, past the water and back into the yellow woods, faster and faster so that they never see the tears on my cheeks.

CHAPTER THIRTY-EIGHT

A duel. A broken arrow. Blood on the grass.

The duel is to be held in Gray Vale, neutral territory on Winter—a valley with harsh cliffs and grassy, snowy hills. It will take place just after dawn. We will each choose a sword from an identical set presented to us. No one else will be permitted to enter the marked area until the duel is completed, and that will only be when one of us draws the other's blood.

This is what Max tells me when he returns to the ship. Then he hands me a honey cake from Bear. I can't hold back my tears a moment longer.

The duel will be in four days, ample time for word to get around. By the day before, it's as though half the star system is on its way to Gray Vale to watch someone win the world's greatest warship. Again. We've come full circle; an endless, bitter cycle.

"Your mother will never be the person you want her to be," Rickard tells me. "Kyra will always put your brothers first. She wants Alexi to win *Titania*. Offering to see you was the only lure she could use on you, so she used it without hesitation. She doesn't think she'll have to keep her promise. She's sure Alexi will win."

"That's an assumption everyone seems to have made," I say. "They will find themselves mistaken."

Rickard doesn't respond. Maybe he doesn't believe I can win either. Or maybe he just doesn't want to choose between Alexi and me. "Even if you win," he says instead, "what good will it do to see her?"

"I still wonder if she cares. I still wonder if she hesitated before she threw me away. And if she wept. Truthfully, sometimes I don't even wonder. I convince myself that she put me in that boat and cried bitterly until she worked up the nerve to send it out into space." I swallow. "It's a myth, I know, the dream of her love. It's a lie I tell myself. But I won't stop telling it until I see the truth in her face. *That's* why I have to see her. I have to put the myth to rest for good."

"Then I wish you luck," he says softly.

I hesitate, then ask, "If there's war, who do you hope will win? Alexi or Elvar? You've never told me."

"I don't know," says Rickard. "I love them both. And I will protect Kali. That's all I know."

Sometimes I wonder if that's all I know, too.

We fly *Titania* out to Gray Vale the day before the duel, taking rooms at an inn built into the snowy hillside. The town is cold, rustic, and quiet. Twinkly. Utterly beautiful in the snow and the ice.

I can't stand the way everyone I pass stops to stare, so I leave the inn and return to *Titania*, tucking myself in next to her glass wall. I look out over the snow and grass, shivering until she increases the interior temperature to warm me.

I'm not the only one who can't escape the shadow of the duel:

Alexi sits at dinner in Arcadia. Bear is silent, furious with him despite the fact that he doesn't want our brother to share the crown with Elvar either. Our mother says something to Alexi, her eyes anxious and her mouth flattened by tension, but he doesn't hear a word. He's far away, in a universe where he teaches his sister to fish by a river, and they stay that way, suspended in time, in a moment where they can never grow old and will never be broken apart.

Guinne shuts herself in the conservatory and prays I don't lose *Titania* to Alexi. She doesn't know about the vision, but if she did, she would pray for me to live and to return to them.

Elvar sleeps, sedated after he worked himself into a panic. Rickard sits at his side, keeping watch over him, but his eyes drift to the window. He looks at Winter and winds back the clock, wishing he could take back the curse he placed on me.

Alone in her room at the inn, Sybilla paces like a tiger. Her face crumples, and she picks up her cup of tea and smashes it against a wall.

Rama is unnaturally quiet. He's outside, perched on a rock that looks out over the valley, ice chips sparkling in his hair. He stares into the darkness for a while, thinking about a day when he almost fell into the sky and someone grabbed hold of his hand and refused to let go. He gets up and dusts himself off before nodding to himself like he's ready to face whatever is coming.

Max cradles a paper hound in his hands—*my* paper hound, from the altar on Kali. He stares at it for a long time until he can't bear it anymore and crushes it into his pocket before walking away.

How do I know all this?

A god tells me.

I see Kirrin's reflection in the glass, but I don't turn my head, staring at him in silence.

"You could ask permission before just turning up, you know," *Titania* says tartly. "I'm not a hotel."

Kirrin grins, and *Titania* huffs like she's not really cross at all.

He approaches me. "You are loved, you know. Your friends and family are all thinking of you right now."

And that's when he tells me about them, about where they are and how they feel about what my brother and I are about to do.

"Why are you telling me all this?" I ask.

"Because I want you to know that you have made a mark on this world and that mark will not fade, even after you're gone."

"And you came here just to share that with me?"

"No," says Kirrin, "I came here to ask you for that favor you owe me."

I stand and turn to face him. The smile has left his boy's face, the twinkle vanished from his dark eyes. Now they're just as full of calamity as Amba's have been lately.

I reach into my hair and let my hand close over the blue-flower jewel. I pull it away and hold it out. It sits on my palm, deep and beautiful, as much a part of me as my foot or hand, and parting with it hurts as much as if I'd cut off one of those.

Kirrin stares at me, shocked.

"I knew when I saw you appear in the glass. I knew this would be the favor you'd ask of me. *I want your blueflower, Esmae,* you'd say. After all, Alexi can't kill me if I have it, can he?"

"And you're actually *giving* it to me? You're not going to refuse or try to persuade me to ask for something else?"

"I made you a promise."

The god looks deeply ashamed as he takes the jewel from my palm. My hand feels cold and empty when it's gone. "It's more generosity than I deserve."

"Maybe. May I ask why? Why do you want me to die?"

"I don't want it," he says emphatically. "Not in the least. But you must. For Alexi's sake." Kirrin is silent for a moment. "If you live, you see, you will destroy him. That future I tempted Elvar with? It will come to pass. Ash and fire and destruction and, at the end of it all, Alexi dead or broken. If you live, you will shatter your brother."

"I would never do that to him!"

"You will, Esmae. I don't know why, but you will. That's why, for his sake, you must die first. And I am truly sorry that it has to be this way."

"I'm not going to die tomorrow. I swore it."

The jewel has vanished. Kirrin looks at me for several moments, then says, "For your generosity, let me give you a gift. Close your eyes."

I obey. He presses the palm of his hand to my forehead like he's about to bless me, and my mind floods with color.

I see a galaxy of possibilities, a wheel of alternate futures, thousands of pieces of maybes: starships and books, fossils and gods and dreams, weddings and babies, and sometimes neither; Rama in his late thirties and Max at sixty and Sybilla refusing point-blank to die at the age of a hundred and sixteen; stories in firelit rooms and Rickard's forgiveness and my brothers beside me; birds with buttons for eyes and terrible gooseberry wine and a kiss on the base of my throat; children running wild up tower staircases and swords that aren't used very much.

There must be a million terrible possibilities too, somewhere out there, but Kirrin only shows me the good. By the time he's finished, my eyes have filled with tears.

"I didn't want to upset you," he says.

"They're happy tears," I tell him.

He smiles. "I'm glad."

I shake my head. "You don't understand. You think you showed me what could have been, but you didn't. You showed me what will be. I *will* have one of those futures. Maybe many of them. You showed me what to look forward to, Kirrin. Thank you. You showed me what will be waiting for me when all the ugliness is finally over."

CHAPTER THIRTY-NINE

"Esmae, wake up," says Max.

I open my eyes. I'm confused at first, disoriented, because I seem to be reclined in one of *Titania*'s seats with a blanket draped over me. Why am I here?

And then I remember. I must have fallen asleep at some point after Kirrin vanished.

It's morning now, the sun gleaming hard and gold into the ship and across the icy valley, and I have to go duel my brother.

"I've been looking everywhere for you," Max says, and the shadows under his eyes tell me he hasn't slept. "It didn't even occur to me that you'd be here in the dock with *Titania* until a minute ago. I looked in the woods, in the library, all over. You're late. You know that, don't you?"

I bolt up out of the seat and the blanket tumbles to the floor. "What?"

"The duel was supposed to start five minutes ago."

Horrified, I rush to find proper clothes. "*Titania*, how could you not wake me? Didn't I tell you what time the duel was?"

"Yes, but you didn't specifically ask me to wake you," she says. Her tone is prim and—

Guilty?

I stop, cocking my head to one side. "Why didn't you wake me, *Titania*?"

"I'd rather not say."

"*Titania*."

"Rama asked me not to wake you," she says. "He told me Amba came to him with a way to stop the duel, but she needed his help to make sure you didn't get there on time. He asked me to keep you here for a little while."

I grab a coat, furious. "How could they scheme behind my back? Why couldn't they just speak to me?"

"I don't know."

I turn on Max. "Did *you* know about this?"

"Of course not. If I'd hatched some sort of plot to stop the duel, you'd have known about it immediately." He looks troubled. "We need to hurry."

"I can't believe them," I growl, jamming my feet into my boots and practically tumbling out of the hatch. "They probably offered Alexi something to call off the duel. Behind my back! And it would have to be something *enormous*. I can't think of a single thing that Alexi wants more than to go back home and take back his crown."

"No one could have convinced him to call off the duel," says Max grimly. "There's nothing Amba or Rama could have said to persuade him."

I glance at him. "Then you think Alexi will still be waiting for me? And the worst that will happen is that I'll look like an idiot who couldn't turn up on time to her own duel?"

"I don't know. I honestly don't. Why would Amba feel the need to be so secretive about this—"

We clamber down the mountain path, over ice and rocks, finding the quickest way to the Basin—the amphitheater—deep in the valley. The sun is in my eyes, sharp and real and alien, dancing off the white of the snow.

The Basin is built exactly as its name suggests, a grassy stage at its heart with stone steps rising around it in a circle. The stage is much too small for a tournament or competition, but it's perfect for a duel. An audience would normally sit on the steps to watch, but today's audience is on its feet, packed onto the steps, transfixed by the duel.

The duel?

I freeze at the top of the steps and blink the sun out of my eyes. "Have I lost my mind?"

Max doesn't answer. His gaze is fixed on the stage. Disbelief and fury war across his features.

Because there I am. Unmistakably *me*, copper in my hair and a sword in my hands, locked in a duel with my twin brother. I am not at my best today and Alexi seems to be holding back, but I am there nonetheless. One step back, another forward, my teeth gritted, my brow beaded with sweat, my sword hand quivering a little. The swords flash in the sun, and I notice that there's no snow on the ground beneath the duelers' feet, just green, green grass.

"I'm going to kill Rama for helping Amba pull off this nonsense," I mutter. "Where is he? He must be here somewhere."

I'll have to go down there now and humiliate myself by announcing that there's been a mistake, a goddess has been up to all sorts of tricks, and can we just start the duel all over again? And then everyone will fuss and complain because Alexi will have exhausted himself fighting already while I'm completely rested, so it won't be fair. And then what? We delay the duel for a few hours? What did Amba hope to achieve with this nonsense?

There are gasps from the crowd as Alexi almost nicks the other me on the cheek. I wince like it was my own cheek. It's bizarre and unnatural to see myself from the outside.

I start pushing my way down to the stage. Cold bites into my exposed skin, and my breath blows white on the air. Between the glare of the sun and the cold and the stuffy closeness of the crowd, it's difficult to even shove my way past the top step. I persevere. No one notices me, until a hand grabs my elbow.

"What the *hell* are you doing up here when you're also down there?" demands Sybilla. "Why is Max so angry?"

"Don't ask," I say.

I elbow my way down farther, one eye always fixed on the stage. The other version of me has just fallen, but scrambles up again. Behind me, I hear Max saying something to Sybilla, and she makes a choked sound.

The clash of metal, the flash of the sun. Alexi isn't far from beating the other me. She's nowhere near as good as I am with a sword. She jumps back, grips the sword with both hands, cuts sideways. Alexi dodges the blow and catches her sword with his. The blades flash, the sun glitters off metal on Alexi's back. My clone looks tired.

What is she? An illusion? A robot? Some other kind of artificial construct?

No. An illusion can't hold a real sword and machines like this don't exist. There's something much too human about my other self's movements, about her shaky hand, about the tension and exhaustion in her face.

It's someone else. Amba's gone back to the gods' old tricks. *She's cloaked someone to look just like me.*

What's the point? Why would she cloak a human for the first time in a hundred years just for this? Does she really think I'll stand back and give *Titania* up just because a false version of me is about to lose this duel? Doesn't she realize I'll put a stop to this whole fiasco and insist on doing it properly?

I push my way closer. "Where's Rama?" I ask, glancing back at Max and Sybilla.

"I don't know," she says. "I don't think I've seen him today."

"Not at all? He didn't come to the Basin with you?"

"No. I knocked on his door at the inn, but there was no answer. I didn't think much of it because I couldn't find you or Max either. He wasn't with you?"

"No," says Max.

"Where is he then?"

The prickle on the back of my neck is faint at first, but it soon grows, solidifying into fear. I spin my head around again and look at the other me, at the clothes that don't quite fit her properly and the tired sword hand and the wide eyes, and I see the traces I missed before.

And that's when I understand. *There was a vision, and the vision was inevitable.* Amba had to keep the secret from everyone except the person she needed to take my place. And it was all my idea. She said so herself. She stood in my room, and watched Lord Selwyn stab a duplicate of me, and she saw a way to help me. A silent scream builds in my throat and now I'm frantic, desperate, pushing the crowd, stumbling forward, determined to make this stop before it's too late.

The swords clash. And while Rama's eyes are on the swords, Alexi reaches for the metal glittering on his back.

And just as the scream breaks free of my throat, he slides the broken arrow into the false Esmae's heart.

Into Rama's heart.

My scream shatters the sharp, sunny day, but it's not the only one. As soon as the blood spurts over the other Esmae's shirt, as soon as the blood trickles down Alexi's hand and the broken arrow he pulls free of her chest, the crowd's cries and screams join mine.

The other Esmae tumbles forward onto the grass. Blood spills out from under her. The crowd goes quiet. Alexi drops the broken arrow and stands very still, just looking down at her. His face is pale, the bronze blanched into a deathly white.

And there it is, the inevitable vision that the gods saw.

A duel. A broken arrow. Blood on the grass.

And me, dying.

They said Alexi would kill me. I swore I wouldn't die.

In the end, we were all right.

By the time I break free of the crowd and stumble to Rama's side, he's transformed back. The small, sturdy body on the grass has grown taller and lankier, the coppery-brown hair has shortened and turned back to black, the light bronze skin and gray eyes have darkened to his brown. He's Rama again, in and out now.

There are confused cries as I kneel down beside him; the onlookers can't understand what's happened.

"Rama," I whisper. "Rama, stay with me. *Please*."

He blinks at me slowly, confused. Once, twice. The sun turns his eyes to gold.

"Ez," he says, and then he's gone.

CHAPTER FORTY

My heart collapses in on itself. I put my hands on Rama's chest and feel the wound there. I touch his still, dearly loved face with bloody hands. A howl locks in my throat.

Around me, noise and chaos erupts. Vale guards, who were stationed to keep the crowds in line, now herd them away. Sybilla has her hands pressed over her mouth and tears flood her eyes. Max is on Rama's other side. He gently closes my friend's eyes and reaches for one of my bloody hands, holding it so tight it almost reminds me that I'm still anchored to the world. Almost.

Then Max lets go of my hand and stands. I hear his voice, cracked down the middle, genuinely and truly shocked: "I never really believed you'd go *this* far. How could you, Alex?"

"It had to be done," he says. His voice is unyielding, defiant.

The sound of it splinters the howl of grief stuck in my throat, stilling my hands' frantic attempts to wake Rama from a sleep there's no coming back from, punching a hole in the chaos and the rage and the unbearable guilt. This is my fault, all my fault. And not just because I planted the seed of the idea in Amba's mind, saving myself and sealing Rama's death instead, but because none of this would have ever happened if I hadn't fired an arrow at a fish.

Watch, Esmae. Watch the forest burn.

I rise and face Alexi. This is not the golden hero of the star system. This is not the brother I've come to know and love over the past few months. That brother was a lie; here is reality, this hard, stony boy who will do whatever it takes to get what he wants.

"You killed him," I say.

"I didn't mean to kill the prince. I'm sorry for that."

"No, you didn't mean to kill him." My voice breaks. "You just meant to kill me. I'm your *sister*. You tricked me into a duel just so you could break the rules and murder me."

"I'm sorry." It has a false, hollow ring to it.

"No, you're not. Not yet. But you will be."

"Esmae," Max says.

I step so close to Alexi that we're scarcely a foot apart. The air turns white between us.

"People will remember today," I say. "They'll remember it as the day Alexi Rey abandoned his honor and fell from glory." I touch his face, my thumb leaving a bloody streak across his cheek, saying good-bye to the brother I never really had. "You will have the war you wanted so badly, Alex. Elvar and Max have held back on Kali; they've watched and waited to see if you would ever rise against them, but that's over now."

"Don't," says Max. His voice is raw, as if he can see the future unfolding in front of us. As if he can see what fate I'm about to seal into stone for myself. "Esmae, *don't*."

I was such a fool. The girl who stood in front of a war council and pleaded for a truce. I cared about Kali, about peace, about saving everyone, and let my best friend die instead.

They say the gods' favorites can wreak havoc with their words. I am one of those favorites. *Beloved by gods.*

And so I wreak havoc.

"People will remember today, because today is the day we start a war. It will be fierce and bitter and I will repay every betrayal, every lie, and every drop of Rama's blood a thousand times over. I won't stop until the world is on fire. I will win. And I swear this, Alexi: I swear I will break you before the end."

CHAPTER FORTY-ONE

I wait for her to come to me.

It takes three days, but she does come. Her body smokes into existence beside me as I stand at the peak of a lonely, spiky tower. She folds her hands on top of the rail and looks out at the Scarlet Nebula.

"You have always had a blind spot," she says softly. "From the moment I first met you, I saw that your heart would be the ruin of you. You see so much. You plot whole wars out like a game of Warlords, but you have never been able to see the moves your love has blinded you to. You failed to see the move that would have destroyed you."

"Love," I repeat bitterly.

"Blinded by love for your family," she says, "you never saw. You overestimated Alexi and underestimated Rama. You put your faith in the brother you wanted, the one I always knew would betray you, and failed to notice the brother you already had, the one I always knew could save you."

Tears stab at my eyes. "Did he know he would die?"

Don't let me lose her, he said to *Titania*. And he didn't. I lost him. No one expected that.

"Of course he knew."

"I don't believe that," I say. "He couldn't have *known*. Rama loved me, but he also loved his family and Wychstar and those bloody cats at the palace that he always pretended to loathe. He wouldn't have given all of that up. He wouldn't have agreed to your trick if he had known he would die."

Amba nods. "Then let me rephrase my answer. He knew he would die in as much as he knew about the vision. I didn't lie to him, Esmae, if what's what you want to know. I repeated the details of my vision to him. He hoped I was mistaken, but he understood the risk. He was told one of you would die and he freely took the risk that he would be the one."

Take good care of her, Titania, he told her. *She's as much my family as my brother and sisters. She once saved my life and she's made me laugh every single day I've known her.*

I scrub at my eyes. "Why did you do it?"

"You must know the answer to that," Amba says, a little sternly. "I care a great deal for you and I wanted to keep you safe. This was the only way to do that. I didn't even arrive at the solution by myself, as I'm sure you've realized already. It was unlikely I would have been able to find another one in time."

"That's not what I meant. Why did you do it to *him*? He may not have been certain he would die, but you were. You knew. Why did you choose to send him into that duel?"

"I knew he would agree," she says. "He was also—"

She stops, wisely, but I already know what she was going to say. My fists clench and unclench by my sides as I twist around to face her. "He was also dispensable," I finish for her.

"You're upset."

"That's very astute of you."

There's a chill on the air, a gust of annoyance. Her face grows sterner. "Do not try my patience, Esmae. I am sorry you lost a friend and I will allow you some latitude because of it, but do not forget that I am a goddess and you owe me respect."

I stare at her in silence. She is a goddess and could call down a universe of destruction on my head, but I don't care. "My rage will outlast your storms, Amba."

The chill vanishes as quickly as it came and she sighs. "I know it sounds like I'm being unkind, but I don't mean to be. He just wasn't important."

"He was important to me!"

"But not," she says quite gently, "in the grand scheme of—"

"*Everyone* is important. Rama mattered. There are whole futures that can't exist now, infinite possibilities that are lost. There are children he could have had that won't be born now. Thousands of good days he won't get to have, and thousands of good days other people won't get to have because he would have been the one who made those days good."

You owe me exactly two hundred and twelve favors for this, he told me once. How do I repay those now?

"You are correct, of course," says Amba at last. "I consider you important because you are important to *me*. He did not deserve to be dismissed as irrelevant simply because I was not especially fond of him."

I let out a ragged breath. I can still feel fury in my bones, but maybe that's just how I am now. Perhaps I'll never be free of the fury again.

I close my eyes and see the broken arrow slide into my heart as surely as it slid into Rama's. It feels like it's always there when I close my eyes these days.

"He's dead," I say.

"And you will unleash a terrible war for it," Amba, ever the war goddess, replies. "I never expected you to become one of mine. I wanted more for you than that."

Esmae Rey, the winner of warships. In command of Kali's forces, you'll conquer the enemies who won't bow and set fire to the entire world.

I give her a rather bitter smile. "I guess there's quite a lot of Kali in me after all."

She looks at me the same way she did at King Darshan's competition, when I held the bow and arrow in my hands and she wanted to stop me. Her eyes are full of sorrow and catastrophe.

"And so the House of Rey will crumble into a house of rage," she says before she blinks out of existence.

There's a custom in our star system to preserve the dead for thirteen days after the date of death, partly so that mourners from all over the galaxy can come to pay their respects, and partly because there's a belief that it takes thirteen days for the soul to ascend to whatever heavens await mortals in the gods' realms.

On the thirteenth day, I get *Titania* ready. I don't tell anyone that I'm leaving.

Even so, I'm not exactly surprised when, poised to clamber onto *Titania's* wing, I glance back and see Max in the dock.

He doesn't tell me he wants to come with me. I don't expect him to. This is who we are. He is the crown prince of Kali, the commander of the Hundred and One, and he has a realm to keep safe from the war I've unleashed; I am the winner of warships, swallowed up by white fire, and I have promises to keep that will take me far, far away from where I once dreamed I'd be. This is who we are, and we won't choose otherwise just for the sake of each other.

Max smiles ruefully. "I always knew one day you'd be gone before the stars even went dim at dawn."

I kiss him. It's possibly the last time I'll ever kiss him. "I'm sorry," I whisper against his mouth.

"I refuse to give up on you," he whispers back.

And then he watches me go.

We fly to Wychstar, *Titania* and I, and I trace the path the way I always do: there's a sealed boat and a newborn baby and they drift across the vast expanse of stars and gas clouds and moon rocks.

I'm expected. King Darshan meets me in a tall, arched temple where a glass coffin rests on a dais. Rama looks like he's asleep, a pose so familiar it dashes my heart all over again.

"Why would you want to do that?" Darshan asks when I request his permission to do what I came for.

I blink away tears. "I promised him I would."

The king looks at the coffin for a moment. He looks like he's aged at least ten years since we last met, his face worn and gray with grief. Finally he says, "Yes, take him. That seems like the perfect place to let him sleep."

The king summons the temple servants and asks them to carry the coffin onto *Titania*. They place it carefully where she directs them, in a space normally reserved for exit pods. The door hisses shut behind them and I settle next to the coffin in its quiet alcove.

It's time to keep my promise to Rama; I'll take him up into the stars.

Titania hurtles us deep into space. I watch Rama's face and speak to him like I used to whenever he pretended to be asleep. For a little while, I almost forget that he'll never wake up.

When the ship slows down, and then goes still, I rise and move to the window to look out.

I've never seen so many stars. They're everywhere, all around us, some in clusters and some spread across the darkness, some aglow with the radiance they give off when they're born and when they die. Milky clouds of gas pass by, tinted gold at the edges.

This is an extraordinary place, miles and miles away from anywhere known, and yet it doesn't feel lonely. How could you be lonely, surrounded by all these stars? *This* is what the heavens must look like.

"It's perfect," I whisper.

There's a smile in her voice. "I hoped it would be."

"Thank you."

"Go say goodbye."

I kiss the glass of the coffin, right over Rama's brow, and whisper my farewell. Then *Titania* seals me back into the control room and jettisons the coffin into the dark.

For just one instant it's suspended, among the stars, and then the glass shatters, exploding into particles so tiny they immediately disappear from view. Glass like that wasn't meant for open space. I watch as Rama hovers, limbs slack, and then he starts to glow. As the cells in his body break down and are absorbed into the universe around us, he glows until he loses shape and becomes a burst of brilliance.

And then that, too, fades until it's gone. Except Rama's not gone. He'll always be here, a part of the stars.

I sit at *Titania*'s console and don't speak for what seems an eternity. When I do, I say, "You don't have to stay with me."

She's alarmed. "What do you mean?"

"I failed you. You chose me because you hoped I'd end the war, not make it worse."

"This isn't the life either of us wanted," she says.

"I don't want you to be part of this if you don't want to be. You deserve better than to be tied to my fate. So you don't have to stay with me. Just drop me off somewhere with starships, and I'll make my own way from there. You're free to go wherever you like. If you want to return to Darshan or just go somewhere else, that's okay. It's up to you."

"What if I *want* to stay with you?"

I smile a little. "That's okay, too."

"Then that is what I intend to do," she says.

So we stay there together. I sit and look out at the universe and let *Titania* tell me stories until she drifts into silence.

And I wonder how long this can last, this interlude of absolute nothingness, where time and guilt and sorrow have no meaning. The world is so sleepy, so peaceful. Old stars die and new stars form all around us.

"It's so quiet," I whisper, afraid to disturb the stillness.

It's easy then to remember that Rama wouldn't have wanted me to avenge his death. He wouldn't have wanted me to destroy the world for his sake. And it's tempting to be swallowed up by the quiet and turn my back on wars and families and ruins.

Titania hums under my feet. "Shall we go now, Esmae? Shall we fly deep into the stars and never look back?"

Yes. I want to go.

And yet.

And yet, I am what I am, and what I am is fury. I can't let it go. I can't forget. I hear it growling under my skin.

I think of the friends I've left behind. I think of justice. I think of the austere spikes and towers of the realm I yearned for all my life and grew to love when I found it. I think of Max and of the way he looked at me when he told me he always believed I would disappear one day.

"No," I say, and it feels like a wound and a relief to make that choice. "We have to go back to Kali."

She spins us slowly, a compass pointing to Kali and Max and war. "Home, then."

"Yes," I tell her. "Home."

End of Book 1

ACKNOWLEDGMENTS

Hey, Jem. Before I say anything else, I'm going to say this: thank you. You won't remember this because you weren't even three years old at the time, but you gave me the spark to bring this story to life. I'd wanted to write something inspired by the Mahabharata for a long time, but nothing ever felt *right* until you became obsessed with space. You rattled off the names of the planets and told me what a black hole was and had a solar system placemat at the table and I ate, slept, and dreamed galaxies for a few months because it was Your Thing. And from that obsession came an idea: what if I told a story about Indian mythology . . . in space?

So thank you, Jemmy. Thank you for this idea. Thank you for being brilliant and kind and funny. Thank you for reading this book and asking me if bedtime can be just a *little* later so you can read more of it. To quote you, I love you to the end of the universe and through Cygnus X-1 and around all the dwarf planets—and *back*.

I started writing *A Spark of White Fire* in October of 2014, so this has been a long, winding journey. And almost four years later, I know one thing beyond any doubt: it wouldn't have been possible for me to write this book, or any book, if it hadn't been for my husband, Steve. Thank you for giving me the time and space to work, for looking after the kids, for the beta reads, for the endless supply of cold drinks (and for always remembering the ice!). Most importantly, thank you for believing I'm awesome, even and especially when I don't. (Pssst, I think you're awesome too.)

To Eric Smith, agent, friend, and the ultimate cheerleader. Thank you for fighting for this book and for shouting from the rooftops about it. I know you'll never forgive me for what I did to [Spoiler], but I want you to know I live for your anguish.

To Alison Weiss, who believed in me before this book even existed and played such a huge part in making it what it is today. You're an extraordinary editor, a wonderful friend, and I can't thank you enough for how hard you fought for and worked on *Spark*.

To Nicole Frail, who jumped on board the *Spark* train unexpectedly and has done such a fabulous job since. Thank you. I'll always treasure your amazing reaction to reading this for the first time.

To Kate Gartner and Mélanie Delon, for the incredible cover art and design. To Johanna Dickson, Emily Wood, and the rest of the wonderful folk at Sky Pony for all the work you've put into making Esmae's story shine.

Mum and Dad, thank you for the books, the history, and an awesome childhood. Thank you for the love you've given this book (that goes double for you, Dad). I also want to say a thank-you to Gramps, who is long gone but without whom my love for the Mahabharata wouldn't be what it is. Thank you for the stories.

To Emma Pass, Natasha Ngan, Kendra Leighton, and Kristina Perez for all the incredibly helpful feedback you gave me on early drafts of this. To my sensitivity readers (you know who you are) for all your help and support. To Samira and Kati for all the laughs and love. To Team Rocks in all its waterfall glory. And an extra shoutout to Julia, Erica, Alan, Dave, Mike, Lizzie, and Anna for your notes (I owe the elevators to you, Alan!).

Social media can be a pretty difficult place to be sometimes, but I'll always be grateful for the friends I've made in the writing community. It's simply not true that authors are islands.

To all the wonderful readers who have loved and written to me about *The Lost Girl* over the years, to the readers who have want more brown girls in fantasy, to the readers who have been waiting—I'm so glad I can finally give you this book.

And finally, Henry and Juno. Like Jem, you both inspire me every single day. I love you more than you love Frozen.

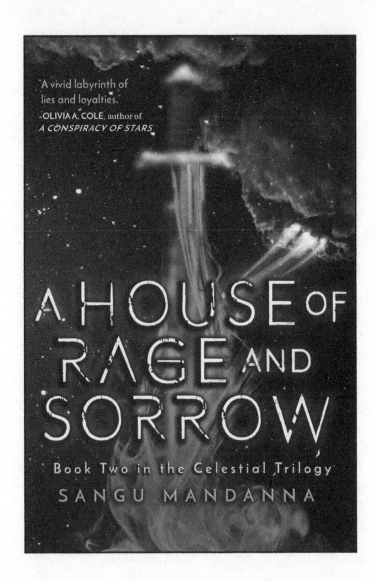

"A vivid labyrinth of
lies and loyalties."
—OLIVIA A. COLE, author of
A CONSPIRACY OF STARS

A HOUSE OF RAGE AND SORROW

Book Two in the Celestial Trilogy

SANGU MANDANNA

Coming 2019 from Sky Pony Press

CHAPTER ONE

My golden brother doesn't shine so brightly anymore. His armor is streaked with soot and the bow of light on his back has been doused in ash. He picks his way across the stony beach with a handful of his soldiers, checking the blazing ruins of his ships for survivors. Winter's sea roars beyond them, gray and foamy and cold.

The aftermath of battle is ugly. General Saka sent a small fleet toward Kali, presumably to test our defences or maybe just to test me, and *Titania* and I flew out to meet them. It didn't go well for them. We followed what was left of them back to Winter, where Alexi came to rescue them, but he was too late. They crashed onto this beach, somewhere in King Ralf's territory, and my perfect twin was powerless to stop it.

Almost as if he can tell he's being watched, Alexi turns away from the sea and looks at the cliffs beyond the beach. At me.

I'm on the cliff edge above him. *Titania* hovers close by. I can't see much of Alexi's expression from this far away, but I don't think it's friendly.

That's okay, Alex. Mine isn't either.

There's a ripple in the sky in the distance, a smear across the horizon. As it draws closer, the smear becomes more distinct. Ships. They're not Kali's, so they're either Alexi's or King Ralf's. I suspect the former. There's half a dozen of them, all powerful warships, and they cut across the silver sky until they stop behind my brother, noses pointed my way, black steel against the backdrop of clouds and water.

"Esmae." It's *Titania*, her voice in my earpiece. I feel her above me, engines humming, closer than before. "Come back inside."

She worries. These days, without my blueflower, I'm a whole lot easier to kill. They all worry.

The ships train their weapons on me. I can hear the sounds over the roar of the sea, the click of launchers shifting into place, the whir of machinery ready to fire. They're waiting for the order.

I don't move. *Titania* huffs in my ear, more exasperated than alarmed. "Have it your way."

I make sure the ships are in my line of vision, but I keep my attention on Alexi. He hasn't taken his eyes off me. One of his soldiers breaks away from the others and goes to him, speaks to him. It's my other brother, Bear.

The seconds tick by. The lash of the wind and sea salt, the roar of the waves, the whir of engines. Doused fires on the beach, ruined ships coiling smoke into the air. The battle smell of metal, ash, and smoke in my throat.

I wonder why I'm still here. What am I waiting for? To see what he'll do? To see if he'll give the order? Of course he'll give the order. He killed Rama because he believed Rama was me. Why in the world wouldn't he try again?

Except he hasn't. What's he waiting for?

That's when I realize he's waiting, too. He's waiting to see if I'll take that step, if *I'll* try to kill *him*.

After all, I swore I'd destroy him. A god even told me I would. I don't know what Kirrin meant when he said *destroy*, but one way or another, I will fulfill my vow and there will be justice for Rama. One way or another, somewhere down the line, I will destroy my brother. My twin. The one in the sun.

And maybe somewhere down the line is today. He's standing right there. As vulnerable as I am. I could kill him.

So why haven't I?

I reach for the Black Bow on my back, and slide an arrow out of my quiver. Alexi is out of most archers' reach, but I'm better than most archers. I nock the arrow. I slice the first two fingers of my right hand on the bowstring. It hurts, and it bleeds. Both familiar, except now neither one goes away. The wound doesn't heal. I ignore it.

I pull the arrow back. Aim for Alexi's bare throat. There's one small, lonely tremor in my hand.

Let go.

Let go, Esmae.

My hand trembles. My teeth chatter with cold, or maybe with fury. I don't let go. I lower the bow.

Bear leaves Alexi's side and approaches the cliff. He makes his way up to me. I haven't seen him since before the duel. His skin is paler than it was then, wan under its usual bronzey brown, and there's a dark bruise on his left cheek.

Bear stops in front of me. His eyes are sad, and soft. "Can I give you a hug?"

"Of course you can." I let him squeeze all the breath out of me. I hug him back and it feels so *good* that I want to cry. I feel like I haven't touched anyone like this in months. I let go reluctantly. "How are you?"

"Meh," he says, "You?"

"Meh," I reply.

He cracks a smile. He glances back at Alexi, then says, "He wants to talk to you."

I stiffen. "I have nothing to say to him."

"Please."

"No."

Bear sighs, then says, "I'm so sorry about Rama."

His name, out loud, is a cut. Is it possible to die by one thousand small cuts? I miss him so much. "Me too."

"But," he adds, with a wobble in his voice, "I can't believe this is what he would have wanted for you."

"You didn't know him, Bear."

"I didn't need to. No one who loves you would want this for you, Esmae." He points to the ruins of the ships on the beach. "Is this what *you* want for you? Really? You, who told me Wych folktales and ate honey cakes and read books under the yellow weeping trees in Arcadia? This war will break your heart. It'll ruin you."

I keep my eyes on the sea. "The folktales and the honey cakes are gone. Even if I were to look for them, I wouldn't be able to find them. There's only arrows and ash now."

"You can stop."

I step back, away from him. "Did *he* stop? When he pushed steel into Rama's heart, did he stop?"

"You're not him."

"No, I'm not," I agree. "I'm so much worse."

ABOUT THE AUTHOR

Sangu Mandanna was four years old when an elephant chased her down a forest road and she decided to write her first story about it. Seventeen years and many, many manuscripts later, she signed her first book deal. Sangu now lives in Norwich, a city in the east of England, with her husband and kids. She's the author of *The Lost Girl*, *A Spark of White Fire* and its sequels, and has contributed to several anthologies.